Love's Tempting

By
Maryann Jordan

Love's Tempting
Copyright © 2014 Maryann Jordan
Print Edition

This book is a work of fiction. Names, characters, places, and incidents either are products of the author's imagination or are used fictitiously. Any resemblance to actual persons, living or dead, events, or locales is entirely coincidental.

Cover Design by: Kari Ayasha, Cover to Cover Designs
covertocoverdesigns.com

Cover Photography: Mandy Hollis, MHPhotography
Cover Model: Julio Elving
Editor: Shannon Brandee Eversoll

ISBN: 0991652290

Dedication

I dedicate this book to women everywhere who through illness or injury, get up every day and face life knowing that it is not always perfect nor is it always fair. To the women who have endured pain, but have conquered. Have endured setbacks, but have continued. Have endured falling down, but have pulled themselves back up again. Have endured nightmares, but continue to hold fast to their dreams. Women are much stronger than we often realize and it is this strength that gives us the ability to continue through life, taking all from it that we can and giving back all that we have to give.

Acknowledgements

First and foremost, I have to thank my husband, Michael. Always believing in me and wanting me to pursue my dreams, this book would not be possible without his support. To my daughters, MaryBeth and Nicole, I taught you to follow your dreams and now it is time for me to take my own advice. You two are my inspiration. Also, special thanks goes to my daughter, Nicole, who is a software engineer and gave technical assistance to the story.

I met Lisa online when searching for information about women amputees. She runs the blog, Lisa on a Limb and has been a source of inspiration as well as a technical advisor. She patiently answered all of my questions (and I had many) and seemed genuinely interested in helping make Lily the best character that I could possible make. Please check out her blog: http://lisaonalimb.com/

My best friend, Tammie, who for eighteen years has been with me through thick and thin. You've filled the role of confidant, supporter, and sister.

My dear friend, Myckel Anne, who keeps me on track, keeps me grounded, and most of all – keeps my secrets. Thank you for not only being my proofreader, but my friend.

Going from blogger to author has allowed me to have the friendship and advice of several wonderful authors who always answered my questions, helped me over rough spots, and cheered me on. To Kristine Raymond, you gave me the green light when I wondered if I was crazy and you never let me give up. MJ Nightingale and Andrea Michelle – you two have made a huge impact on my life. Anna Mychals, EJ Shorthall, Victoria Brock, Jen Andrews, Andrea Long, A.d. Ellis, ML Steinbrunn, Sandee Love, thank you from the bottom of my heart.

My beta readers, on Jordan's Journey, kept me sane, cheered me on, found all my silly errors, and often helped me understand my characters through their eyes. A huge thank you to Denise VanPlew, Sandi Laubhan, Barbara Martoncik, Vanessa Spradling, Jennifer Alumbaugh, Anna Mychals, Danielle Petersen, Shannon Brandee, Leeann Wright, Lynn Smith, Kelly Williams and Tracey Markin for being my beta girls who love alphas!

Shannon Brandee Eversoll has been my editor for the past three books and what she brings to my writing has been amazing. She and Myckel Anne Phillips as my proofreader gave their time and talents to making Love's Tempting as well written as it can be.

My street team, Jordan Jewels, you all are amazing! You volunteer your time to promote my books and I cannot thank you enough! I hope you will stay with me, because I have lots more stories inside, just waiting to be written!

My Personal Assistant Barbara Martoncik is the woman that keeps me going when I feel overwhelmed and I am so grateful for not only her assistance, but her friendship. It has been wonderful to have someone, who is as passionate about my books as I am, help me stay organized, on task, and boosts my spirits when I need her words of encouragement.

This is the fifth book cover that Kari Ayasha from Cover to Cover Designs has created for me and her talent is evident in every detail. Thank you for working with me. This cover utilizes the amazing talents of Mandy Hollis (photographer from MHPhotography) and model Julio Elving. I thank all of them for capturing my idea and making it a reality.

As the owner of the blog, Lost in Romance Books, I know the selflessness of bloggers. We promote indie authors on our own time because we believe fully in the indie author community. I want to thank the many bloggers that I have served with, and who are assisting in promoting my series.

Most importantly, thank you readers. You allow me into your home for a few hours as you disappear into my characters and you support me as I follow my indie author dreams.

Author Information
Maryann Jordan

I am an avid reader of romance novels, often joking that I cut my teeth on the old bodice rippers. I have been reading and reviewing for years. In 2013, I created the blog, Lost in Romance Books to promote and showcase indie authors. In 2014, I finally gave in to the characters in my head, screaming for their story to be told. From these musings, my first novel, Emma's Home, The Fairfield Series Book 1 was born.

I am a high school counselor having worked in education for thirty years. I live in Virginia, having also lived in four states and two foreign countries. I have been married to a wonderfully patient man for thirty two years and am the mother to two adult daughters. When writing, my dog or one of my four cats can generally be found in the same room if not on my lap.

Please take time to leave a review of this book (on Goodreads). Reviews are the lifeline for indie authors.

Feel free to contact me, especially if you enjoyed my book. I love to hear from readers!

Facebook:

www.facebook.com/authormaryannjordan

Facebook blog:

www.facebook.com/lostinromancebooks

Booktropolous:

booktropoloussocial.com/index.php?do=/profile-1765/

Email:

authormaryannjordan@gmail.com

Author Blog:

www.maryannjordanauthor.com

Chapter 1

MATT MANEUVERED THE woman so he could unzip her pants just enough to work his hand down the front, feeling the soft flesh that was already slick and waiting for him. Hell, he hadn't done this in years – pick up a woman he just met and finger-fuck them in his truck. But he was tired of the looks he received when first meeting a woman. And this woman? She was perfect. Earlier as they talked in the bar, she looked past the scar on his face and never seemed to take her eyes off of his, peering straight into him. As though she understood everything about him. She was funny, smart, easy to talk to, beautiful. He couldn't remember the last time he'd laughed so much.

And now here he was with his hand down her pants. The dark of the night was penetrated only by the dim illumination from the street light in the parking lot, leaving the couple bathed in shadows.

Moving his finger in her pussy in rhythm with his tongue in her mouth, he heard her moan and felt his dick swell painfully in his jeans. She was so tight he could barely get his fingers in. Without breaking the kiss, he shifted her again so that she was partially laying back so he could get a better angle. *Damn, I wish I could take her home so I could really fuck her the way I want.* But he was meeting friends later and she said a friend was coming to give her a ride home, so here he was like teenager trying to get a girl off.

"Baby, can I slide your pants down some more?" he asked using his free hand to maneuver them down over her hips.

"No!" came the vehement reply. Her wide-eyes stared at him in distress and he hated that the suggestion had caused her fear.

"No problem, babe. It's all good," he reassured her as his fingers continued their ministration.

Her hips began to move in the age old rhythm of seeking relief and he could already feel her pussy grabbing his fingers. Using his other hand to slide up her shirt, he tweaked her nipple, hearing her scream out as her orgasm rocketed through her. She lay back panting as her body responded to the aftershocks.

Matt would bet his paycheck that she'd never done anything like this before. She was hot as hell, but it didn't seem as though she had a lot of experience. *I wanna see her again. Hell, I wanna be her only experience from now on.* Not knowing where that thought came from, he didn't care. All he knew was that for the first time in a year, he was tempted to spend more time with a woman.

As her breathing slowed, she sought out his eyes then quickly glanced away as a blush flamed her face.

Fuck. I wanted to see her again and she regrets this. Goddamnit.

Headlights flashed through the windshield blinding them for a second as another car came into the parking lot. She quickly looked over and began zipping her jeans.

"I'm sorry, that's my ride. I...um...I didn't get to...um," she glanced at his crotch as she tried to come up with the words. "Um, take care of...you. I'm sorry." He heard the catch in her voice that matched the shine of tears in her eyes.

Before he could think of what to say to make her feel better, she bolted from the truck, landing hard on the pavement, and made her way quickly to the waiting car, limping slightly.

Matt sat in the truck for a few minutes, partially in shock of the evening's events and partially to give his dick a chance to recover from a serious case of blue balls.

His mind went back to when he first saw her walk into the bar.

At the far end of the bar waiting on friends, he sat on a stool that accommodated his nervous habit of wanting his back to the wall so that he could see everything that was happening. *No surprises. Always prepared.* It had been a long time since he had been in a bar, battling daily the desire to drink until he was shit-faced. Staring at his beer he regretted agreeing to meet friends here. Out of the corner of his eye he saw two women approach. Pretty. Dressed to attract. Looking for action.

Yeah, let's see how far this goes.

"Hi handsome, looking for some fun?" the redhead said, sliding her boobs along his arm as she sat on the stool next to him.

"We're good and we don't mind sharing someone as big as you," the brunette said, moving next to her friend.

He kept his eyes on his beer sitting on the bar in front of him, a smirk on his face. He knew what they saw. Tall. Muscular. Brawny. *Let's see how many seconds this takes.*

Turning, he gave them a huge smile, "Whatcha got in mind ladies?"

Their eyes went to his face. And immediately he saw the flash of shock register in their faces. *Yeah, about two seconds. About average.*

"Oh sorry. We...um...thought you were...someone else," they claimed before hustling away.

Matt nodded to himself. Yep, the scar gets them every time. Glancing at his watch to see how much longer he needed to wait, his attention was caught by the movement at the other end of the bar.

There she was. Sitting alone looking lost, nursing her drink. Beautiful. Long, dark blonde curls down her back. A pixie face with dark brown eyes. And her clothes...in a room of scantily clad women she was dressed simply. Green blouse. Black slacks. Low heeled boots. And yet, the whole package together was gorgeous.

And he wasn't the only one noticing.

Glancing around, he saw the predatory eyes of a number of men scoping her out. *She's sitting there looking like a lost lamb in a room full of wolves and doesn't have a fuckin' clue.* Seeing two men start to walk over to the bar, he suddenly had the urge to intervene. To protect. To claim. *Claim? Where the hell did that come from?* Matt hadn't wanted to claim a woman since…*don't go there.*

Debating for only a second, he stood up and stalked over to the bar, sliding onto the stool as though it were his own. Turning to the beautiful woman, he smiled and said, "Sorry I'm late baby."

Her eyes grew wide as she peered into his, her brow lifted in question.

The two men stopped in their advance toward her and retreated, scowling. She turned her head slightly to see them leave, releasing a sigh of relief.

"Didn't mean to scare you but you looked like you could use a little help," he explained.

She turned her face back to his, beaming her smile his way. "Well, I thought it was a horrible pick-up line but now that I know it was just pretend, thank you."

Her smile pulled him in as he took the opportunity to gaze at her up close. *She's looking at my face but not focusing on the scar.*

"Well, if you want a bad pick-up line, how's this? I haven't seen you here before."

Ducking her head, she smiled. "I'm not big on the

social scene, but I had a tough day at work and I was supposed to meet a co-worker here tonight. But...she had to cancel and I've called a friend to come pick me up. So I'm just killing a little bit of time until she can get here."

He found himself wondering about her. Her bad day at work. Her friends. After going a year with little interest in forming any relationship, he felt drawn to her and wanted to keep her talking.

"So what do you do in this job that gives you bad days?"

She laughed. "Nothing very exciting for me to tell. I'm a software engineer." She halted as she watched his expression. "Your eyes haven't glazed over with boredom yet," she joked. "As soon as I tell guys what I do, they usually either fall asleep or find someone else more exiting to talk to."

"Then you haven't been talking to the right men."

Her eyes stared into his, seeing nothing but sincerity. "Maybe you're right," she said softly.

He heard longing in her voice and a flash of sadness in her eyes, finding himself wanting to take away both and yet strangely glad that no one had taken them away before him.

"So what do you as a software engineer?"

"I work as a contractor. I go in to different companies and design whatever software they need. Currently I work at medical facility. I'm designing some new software for them."

"Sounds interesting."

Laughing again, she responded, "Oh now you're exaggerating! No one thinks what I do is interesting." She smiled more gently and continued, "But it's interesting to me. And…it's…safe."

"Safe?"

"Yeah, I'm not much of a risk-taker, you know? I like using my mind and honestly – I like working in a quiet environment that doesn't have a lot of people around. I get to go in and do my thing and then leave and go to another place. I don't really like being around a lot of people."

Silence settled between the two of them for a moment as they let the loud noise from the rest of the bar fill in the quietness.

"What about you?" she asked. "What do you do?"

"Well," Matt started, looking discomfited. "I guess you could say I'm the ultimate risk-taker." Looking at her quizzical expression, he said, "I'm a detective."

Her eyebrows shot up in surprise, then shaking her head she admitted, "I wouldn't have guessed that, but now that you have said it, I think it fits."

"Fits?"

"Yeah. The desire to rescue, like you rescued me tonight. What kind of a detective are you?"

"Vice."

"Oh," she said, her brow furrowing. "Other than what I've seen with police shows on TV, I don't even know what vice detectives do."

Smiling along with her, he said, "Probably what you've watched on TV is right. Drugs, prostitution, gambling…things like that."

Leaning forward with her elbows on the bar, she placed her chin on her hands, staring at him with big, chocolate eyes. "You must be very brave. I can't image going into work every day not knowing what's going to happen," she admitted. "I go into work knowing exactly what needs to be worked on. What problem needs to be solved. I write codes to solve the problems. And when I'm done, I move on."

"I don't know that I would call my job brave. It's just what I do; it's who I am."

The silence once again settled between them, but this time neither heard the noise of the bar around. It was as though everyone else had drifted away, leaving only the two of them in the midst of their own little world.

Matt realized that for the first time in a long time he was having a conversation with a woman who wasn't staring at his scar. Or maybe more importantly, she wasn't trying to avoid it either. And because of that, he wasn't thinking of it either.

"So what favorite TV detective show do you watch?"

"Oh my, that's embarrassing to even admit. But I do have to say that I like the reality show Cops."

Leaning back on his stool smiling, he said, "Okay, I take back what I said earlier. That…is probably less realistic than some of the fictional shows on."

"Yeah, well, you won't find any shows, reality or not, about a software engineer. We're just too nerdy for cameras."

Deciding to find out more about her, he continued. "So if you don't go out partying a lot, what do you do for fun?"

Rolling her eyes to the ceiling as though deep in thought, she admitted, "I'm really boring. I read a lot, take care of my rescue puppy…and oh, recently I've been learning how to run."

"Learning how to run? Don't you just put one foot in front of the other?" he joked.

Something flashed through her eyes, but before he could question it, it was gone.

She smiled once again but it did not seem to reach her eyes this time. "Well, I guess I'm just clumsier than most."

Wanting to make her comfortable again, he moved the topic to something else and quickly her warm eyes were staring into his once again. The conversation continued to flow between them as he relaxed. They laughed and talked about books, movies, places they had been and would like to visit.

Looking down at his beer, he realized that it was only half finished. And that felt good. Not staring at the evening through the bottom of a beer bottle. Looking back up at her, he caught her staring. Not at his scar. But once again into his eyes.

Seemingly embarrassed to have been caught staring,

she looked at her watch, exclaiming that she needed to go catch her ride. Her eyes immediately went back to his, regret flashing through them.

"I'll walk you out," Matt said.

"You don't have to," she replied softly as she slid off of her bar stool, then leaned her head way back as she realized how tall he was.

Looking down, focusing on those chocolate brown eyes, he simply said, "Not havin' you wait by yourself in a dark parking lot, babe."

As soon as they were in the parking lot, her phone chimed with a message telling her that her ride was going to be a little late.

Turning her dark eyes back to his, she said, "You don't have to wait."

"Come on," he said, guiding her over to a large pick-up truck.

Before she knew what was happening, she was lifted as though she weighed nothing and placed in the passenger seat. About to protest, she was unable to speak before he pulled out a badge. **Matthew Dixon. Richland Police Department.** Looking at it carefully, she raised her eyes in question.

"I'm who I say I am. Not having you wait in the chilly night air. We'll wait on your friend here where it's warm."

Smiling hesitantly, she agreed.

He pulled himself up into the seat and turned to look at her as she twisted in her seat to face him. After finding so much to talk about, he suddenly couldn't think of anything other than her lips. Glancing back up to her eyes, he saw that she was staring at his lips as well. Leaning forward he came within inches of her delectable mouth and stopped.

"I'm tempted to kiss you babe. Are you good with that?"

Nodding shyly, she allowed him to lean in latching his mouth onto her luscious lips.

Matt immediately took charge of the kiss, angling his head for better access, licking the seam of her lips before plunging his tongue in. Capturing her moan in his mouth, he drank her in. The kiss continued as though neither of them could get enough. Before he knew it, she was leaning back and his hand was down her pants. And all he could think about was wanting more.

And now she was gone. *Damn, what the fuck happened? First woman I want in a year and I fuck it up. Jesus, I don't even know her name.*

A tap on the window startled him as he looked up to see his partner, Shane Douglas.

"You hangin' out in your truck all night or you gonna come in and have a drink?"

"Yeah, yeah. I'm coming," he answered as he got out, discreetly adjusting his crotch, hoping his hard-on was gone. The two friends walked in, nodded to the bartender and headed to a table.

"Tony's guys coming?" he asked Shane, referring to

a group of friends that worked for Tony Alverez Security Company. Having worked on several cases together, the group had become good friends over the years.

"Yeah, but Tony said most would be comin' later." Shane looked up as their beers were delivered, greeting the waitress.

"Detectives, how ya' doing?" the friendly waitress greeted. "So when's the big day?" she asked Shane.

Shane's smile beamed as he answered, "Annie and I haven't set a date yet. Still tryin' to work out the details with our parents. But, nothin' is keeping me from gettin' hitched as soon as I can."

"Well, you bring that pretty fiancé of yours in here soon and the drinks will be on me." Turning her gaze to Matt, she continued, "So what happened with that beauty you were just with a few minutes ago?"

Matt caught Shane's questioning look, but just shrugged, "She had to leave so I guess that means I'm stuck with ugly here," nodding to Shane.

"Well, the way you two were cuddled up talking forever, I thought for sure you'd be leaving here with her." She winked and headed back to the bar.

Matt said nothing, hoping Shane would let it go.

"So you gonna tell me about this beauty?"

"Not much to tell. Met her at the bar, we talked, and she had to leave."

The silence droned on between them until Matt couldn't take it anymore and glanced up at Shane's face. *That fucker is sitting there grinning at me. Goddamnit, it just isn't my night.*

"Fine. I met someone." Matt sucked in a deep breath then slowly let it out. "Been a long time since I've met any woman I felt like spending more than ten minutes with, much less wanting to spend a lot more time with her."

Shane knew Matt's past. Like most of their friends, he had been a bit of a womanizer in his twenties, but once he turned thirty Matt was ready to find the right woman to settle with. Unfortunately for him, he found the wrong woman.

"I came in here earlier tonight and saw the most gorgeous woman sitting at the bar. She looked lost, kind of sad. There was nothin' special about what she was wearing, but it didn't take long before I saw a couple of men scoping her out and knew it could be trouble, so I sat next to her to keep them away."

"Did she mind you doing that?" Shane asked.

Matt shook his head. "No, she said that she was grateful. Said work had been a bitch and so some friends were going to meet her here for drinks. Then they bailed on her and she didn't have a ride and had to call another friend to come pick her up. Hell, I even thought about asking her if I could see her home, but we ended up just sitting and talking. Know what's crazy, man?"

Shane sat silent, waiting for him to continue.

"She never once focused on my scar. Not once. It was like it wasn't even there for her. Damn, I haven't talked that long with a woman in a year."

"So where'd she go?"

Matt turned red and looked down at his hands.

"What? What the hell happened?" Shane demanded.

"I fucked up," Matt admitted.

Shane reared back in his seat. "Fucked up?"

"She was going outside to meet her friend and I walked her out to make sure she was safe. It was chilly so I suggested we sit in my truck to wait." Shaking his head, he continued, "Started making out like we were sixteen years old and the next thing I know…"

"Jesus, you fucked her in your truck?" Shane asked.

"No," Matt growled, then sighed heavily. "Just got her off, then it turned awkward when it was obvious that she had no experience with what had just happened. Then her friend showed up and before I could say anything she was out of my truck and into their car before I could even get her number."

Matt and Shane sat quietly for a few minutes, each to their own thoughts. Matt, miserable in the knowledge that he had taken advantage of a woman, and Shane, happy in the knowledge that Matt had found someone he could relate to.

Just then the bar became crowded and noisy as the men from Tony's company came in, and Matt and Shane joined their friends.

LILY'S FRIEND, SUZANNE, could tell something was wrong as soon as she picked her up. "You want to talk about it?" Suzanne asked.

Lily just shook her head, too embarrassed to tell anyone what had happened.

Suzanne didn't press Lily. That was one of the many things that made Suzanne such a good friend. She understood when Lily wanted to be by herself or didn't want to go out. She never pushed her and Lily was grateful for the respite.

"You know I'm always here if you need to talk," Suzanne said as she pulled into Lily's driveway.

Smiling at her friend, she nodded. "Yeah, I know. Sometimes I just have to work through things myself."

"Me too," Suzanne agreed, having her own secrets that she kept deep inside. "See you later," she called as Lily headed up to her door.

Locking the front door behind her she was immediately greeted by Pippi. Bending to pick up her wiggly puppy, she cuddled her for a few minutes, then walked passed the living room to the kitchen and put down her food. After Pippi ate, Lily let her into the tiny fenced back yard for just a few minutes, the whole time trying not to think of the evening's disaster.

Locking up again, she walked through the house, flipping off the lights. Her house was simple, but comfortable. Affording the one-level house in the quaint, old neighborhood in the city had been a triumph for her and one that she cherished. Making her way to the bedroom, she sat on the side of the bed. Leaning over with her hands on her head, thoughts of the evening swirled. *Oh my God, did I do that? What the hell was I thinking? I never do that! I go to a bar, literally pick up a man, let him finger-fuck me and then run out on him. Jesus, I'm such a loser.*

Sitting there for a few minutes, the only consolation was that she would never have to see him again. But then that thought made her sad. He was so handsome. Tall and muscular, dark hair with a sexy stubble of a beard. His black shirt stretched across his chest as his biceps bulged against the sleeves. Lips that made her wet just looking at them. And nice. She hadn't known what to do when she felt several men staring at her, but once he came over she felt comfortable. Safe. And he was easy to talk to.

It had been a long time since she had been kissed. A really long time. And she found that she wanted it more than her next breath.

Babe. He called me babe. Knowing that for him it was not a term of endearment but just a saying, it nonetheless sent a warm tingle through her as his hand rested on her back when they left the bar.

Stop dreaming. It would have never gone anywhere. He is so not for me. But for once, it was nice to pretend. To pretend that he knew and it didn't matter to him. That it wasn't a deal-breaker. To pretend that I was just like any woman out in a bar looking for a man. But...*give it up, girl. Not happening.*

She stood and walked into her bathroom, stopping at the mirror. Long, blonde curls framed her face before cascading down her back. Her face and figure weren't bad, but...the words of her mother came to mind. *"You'd better learn to use your intelligence because you won't catch a man with your body now."*

Sliding into bed a little later after she had taken care of everything she needed to do at night, she dreamed the same dream that had plagued her for eight years.

The cell phone vibrating on her nightstand jarred sixteen year old Lily Swanson awake. Sitting up in bed, she blinked several times as she picked the phone up to see who was calling. **Rose.** *Then glancing at the time, she blinked again.* **One thirty-six a.m.**

"Rose? Where are you?" she asked, thinking that her sister was in her room in bed.

"Lily? Can you come get me?" came her sister's slurry voice.

Now wide awake, Lily asked, "Where are you? Why aren't you home?" Even as the words came out of her mouth, she knew the answer. Rose had slipped out in the middle of the night to meet her friends. Mom and dad are going to have a cow!

"I went to a party LilyBelle," came the giggling response.

"Have you been drinking?" Lily's voice rose in desperation, knowing that their very strict parents would ground Rose for the rest of her senior year when they found out.

"Shhhh. Not so loud. I need you to come get me 'cause my friends left and I don't have a ride home."

"Rose, I just got my license. I can't drive without someone in the car with me."

"LilyBelle, I'll be with you."

"Not getting there, you won't. Look, I'll wake up mom and dad and let them come to you. I just can't," her voice pleaded.

"Noooo," he sister moaned. "It's my senior year and they won't let me do anything the rest of the year if they find out. You have to help me, you just have to," she pleaded. "I promise, I'm not far. I'm at Celia's house. Please, LilyBelle. I need you."

Lily flopped back on the pillows holding the phone to her ear. *I thought the oldest child was supposed to be the responsible one and the younger sibling be wild and crazy. Well, not in this family.* The two sisters had played together, fought together, and protected each other.

This is such a bad idea. "Okay Rose. I'll come," she whispered, hoping her parents were sleeping soundly.

"LilyBelle, you're the best! Celia's parents are gone so you don't have to try to sneak in here. And I promise we'll get home quickly and mom and dad will never know," her drunken sister promised.

Crawling out of bed after hanging up the phone, Lily pulled on her jeans, a t-shirt and her well-worn running shoes. A long distance runner for the cross-country team at their high school, she had running shoes scattered across her bedroom. Some newer than others, she tied on the ones she considered her lucky shoes. *Okay shoes, keep the luck going tonight. Only I don't need you to help me win a race – just keep mom and dad from hearing us tonight.*

After she pulled her long, curly blonde hair into a pony-tail she slid into a jacket. Grabbing the keys to the family van and her purse, she slipped out of the kitchen door running to the driveway. *Thank goodness mom hates to park in the garage. And that their bedroom is on the other side of the house!*

New at driving, Lily checked her mirrors, then backed slowly and carefully out of the driveway and onto the street. There was no traffic at two a.m., but she drove deliberately nonetheless. *Check rear view mirror. Check side view mirrors. Come to a complete stop at the stop sign. Look left and right.* It only took about ten minutes to get to Celia's house and as she pulled into the driveway she could hear the sound of music and see her sister weaving on the front porch.

"What took you so long?" her sister giggled again.

Lily got out of the van and hustled to the porch, hoping to assist Rose before she stumbled down the stairs. Helping her down, they made their way over to the passenger side.

"Do you want me to drive?" her sister asked. "I can get us there quicker."

"Oh no," came Lily's vehement answer. "You're drunk and I want to get home in one piece." *Of course, if mom and dad catch us then getting home in one piece won't matter. They'll never let us out again.*

Buckling her sister in, she rounded the van and climbed into the driver's seat. Once again, she carefully pulled out of Celia's driveway and began the slow trek home, while Rose babbled incessantly. Flipping on the radio, Rose began to sing loudly as she tried to get Lily to sing along.

Lily couldn't help but grin. Rose was a great sister. Even her wild side wasn't too wild. But her devoted side?

Lily knew that Rose would always be in her corner no matter what. The two sisters began to sing to the song on the radio and Lily could feel herself relax for the first time since getting the phone call, even as she drove as carefully as she could.

Check mirrors, look left and right. Drive defensively, she could hear the voice of her driving instructor in her head. Don't assume another driver will obey the rules of the road.

Approaching an intersection where she had the right-of-way, Lily's attention was diverted.

"I'm gonna be sick," Rose yelled as she unbuckled to bend forward to vomit.

Lily tried to grab her sister by the arm, but she was already getting sick.

She never saw the lights of the truck that ran the stop sign. She never had time to veer away. Or brake. She never saw it coming.

The sound of squealing tires, crunching metal, glass shattering was all that filled her ears. For an instant she saw Rose's body flying through the windshield as she felt the van crumple around her. Then nothing. Then black. Then her world changed. Forever.

Lily woke up in the familiar sweat, shaking. Sitting up she reached for the glass of water by the bed, letting coolness force the memories back to the deep recesses of her mind where she wanted them. Laying back down, she thought of the man with the blue eyes, wishing he would fill her dreams instead.

Chapter 2

MATT CAME IN from his morning run, sweat pouring off of his muscular frame. Having ditched his skin-tight running shirt half-way through his run, he pulled it from around his neck to wipe off his face. The Richland detective was used to physical exercise to stay in shape, but the humidity of the Virginia summers could really put a damper on his enjoyment of his morning.

Jogging through his apartment building's lobby, he nodded to the concierge. The security of the building was one of the reasons he chose this for his home. It was well-lit, clean, twenty-four hour security, plus had a laundry service and coffee shop. Punching the elevator to the sixth floor, he leaned heavily against the wall, watching the numbers change on the panel. Rubbing his hand across his face to wipe the still-dripping sweat, his fingers ran across the scar on his forehead. *Yeah, well the great security isn't the only reason I chose this place*, he remembered ruefully.

The elevator doors opened interrupting his musings, and he headed to his door. The living room of the one-bedroom apartment was large, filled with furniture that was not to his taste. The furniture remained, but he had taken down everything else that was a reminder of her. The ex-fiancé. Cassandra.

He walked to the spacious kitchen, snagging a bottled water from the refrigerator, drinking it in a few gulps. Tossing the empty bottle into the recycle container he headed through the master bedroom toward the bathroom. The master bedroom he had redone. It was his. All his. Unlike the living room, it was decorated minimally in grays and blues. Clean lines. No frills. Just the way he saw himself.

After a quick shower, he stood at the mirror shaving, wrapped in nothing but a towel slung low over his hips. Wide shoulders, muscular chest that tapered to a trim waist. He knew his body looked good, something that he could see in women's eyes as they appreciatively stared. Until they looked higher.

Looking down into the soapy water as he washed out his razor, he sighed. Lifting his eyes back to his face, he looked into the mirror. His dark hair was neatly trimmed, although currently wet and shaggy from his shower. His strong jaw was cleanly shaven. His eyes, as blue as his mother's eyes. Looking higher, his gaze rested on the long, thick scar that ran from his scalp across his forehead down toward his ear. Not nearly as visible as it had been a year ago. Not as red or angry looking. But still there. Right on his face for all to see. And for him…the daily reminder of why Cassandra left.

His eyes slid down to the bottle of prescription pain

pills sitting on the counter. He hadn't used them in a long time, but kept them there as a reminder. A reminder of how low he had sunk. The pain from the head wound had lasted for months. The pain from realizing what a loser he had almost permanently attached himself to was the same. The pills washed down nightly with some booze had made it all seem better.

It took his former partner coming in from being undercover and needing him clear-headed to help bring down a large drug ring that threatened Shane's girlfriend to finally get him to snap out of his funk. He tossed the pills down the toilet but kept the bottle as a daily reminder.

He realized that all morning he had been thinking of the beauty from last night instead of focusing on his miserable former relationship. *Why didn't I get her phone number? Or her name?* With a rude snort, he realized that he first assumed that she wouldn't be interested. Then, by the time he realized that she might be, he assumed they would have time for that after...*Well, assuming made an ass of myself and now I've got nothing!*

Shaking his head to clear his thoughts, he quickly dressed for work. As he strapped on his gun holster his cell phone rang. Looking to see who was calling, he recognized the name. **Suzanne**.

He had met Suzanne about six months ago when his partner Shane was involved in a case where he met a beautiful veterinarian, Annie, who was now his fiancé.

Suzanne worked for Annie as a vet tech and after a rocky start, they had bonded. Totally platonic. She was like a little sister, and even though she had an older brother, she rarely got to see him, so Matt was the stand-in.

"What's up Suzanne?" he said as he answered his phone.

"Well, good morning to you too!" she laughed. "I just wanted to make sure you hadn't forgotten about the party. I know it's not for another two weeks but I want to make sure you'll be there."

"You think I'm gonna forget Shane and Annie's engagement dinner? Hell, I work with the man sitting right across from me all day long," he joked.

"I know, but let's face it. You aren't the most sociable guy around."

"And you are, cupcake?"

"Okay fine, you win. Neither of us are going to win Miss Congeniality any time soon, but it'll be fun. We've got some of your friends from the force and Tony's group and some friends from the clinic."

"I'll be there, don't worry. And I'll be my usual charming self."

"Oh great, that'll make an impression on everyone," she laughed. "See you later."

Hanging up, he headed to the kitchen for a quick breakfast before going to the station.

He arrived about the same time as Shane, noticing how relaxed his friend looked. Shane had spent two years as an undercover cop in a drug organization that they managed to take down several months ago. The time undercover had been hard on Shane, and Matt was glad to see his partner looking healthier and less stressed. And he knew why. Shane's fiancé Annie, was a sweetheart of a woman. Beautiful, smart, and totally devoted to Shane. *Just what I thought I had. Just what I wish I had.*

Looking at Shane walking over to their desks, he couldn't help but be happy for him. *Of any man I know, Shane deserves the happy ending.*

The two men sat down at their desks, coffee mugs in hand, and began to look over the latest reports from their cases.

"So how's the wedding planning going?" he asked.

Shane's look spoke volumes. "Jesus, fuck. Between my mom and her mom, you'd think that they were plannin' something for the queen. The phone rings every night with one or the other of them talkin' caterers, flowers, venues. Hell, last night my mom called wanting to know what I thought about string quartets."

Matt laughed, already knowing what Shane's answer would be.

"I told her I didn't give a fuck about a string quartet!"

"What about Annie? How's she holding up against the moms?"

"She's trying to please 'em both, but we just want a simple ceremony with friends and family. I told her last night that if the moms don't lay off, I'm shutting this shit down and we're eloping."

Silence ensued as the two men focused on their cases. After Shane's ordeal with the drug underworld, he and Matt had put in a request for a change in assignments. For now, they were working on prescription drugs that hit the streets. No longer working cocaine or heroin, they were immersed in the fastest growing drug problem. The change in pace was good for both of them, but they were inundated with cases. It seemed that the recession had simply caused people to find new ways to make money off of drugs and sometimes the amounts were staggering.

Looking up from their desks as the chief called for a staff meeting, they grabbed their mugs and files and headed toward his office.

"What have you got for me?"

Matt opened the first file and reported, "The Oxycodone and Hydrocodone found at the bust last week indicated the possibility of prescription fraud, plus we're working two cases of Percocet and Vicodin. With those cases we're looking into a possible Medicare Fraud. The teens in last week's bust were mostly using the Oxycodone, but so far we're still tracing where it came from."

Shane spoke up, "We're investigating the possibility that there was a prescription drug theft, but not ruling out false prescriptions written by doctors."

Another detective added, "We're following up on tips from pharmacies and their shipments. There are some that have reported missing shipments."

The chief looked up from his notes. "Do we have any evidence supporting the false prescription? What's the motivation?"

Matt answered, "Oxycodone is six bucks retail but gets forty bucks on the street. Hell, they're all like that."

Shane continued, "At first we thought it was just a local problem, but we are starting to connect the dots and see that we may have a bigger drug ring than we originally thought. We are working the new task force, but so far we are still trying to connect the various tips we get."

"We're not convinced that we are dealing with one or two dirty doctors. The connections seem too wide-spread, but so far nothing concrete. Hell, in a capital city the size of Richland, there are doctor facilities all over the fuckin' city along with three major hospitals. It's like lookin' for a needle in a haystack."

As the chief dismissed the briefing, Matt and Shane headed back to their desks. Another long day head.

"COME ON LILY. It'll be fun, I promise," Suzanne said over lunch. They had met when Lily brought in her rescued puppy to the vet clinic where Suzanne worked. Annie, Suzanne, and their vet tech Leon had instantly bonded with Lily, whose love of animals rivaled their own.

"I've got running practice the following morning, but if you won't expect me to stay too long, I'm sure I can make it."

"Perfect. There will be a lot of people that you know, plus some handsome guys there as well. Shane's partner and Tony Alverez's crew will be around." Tony owned the security agency that had helped rescue Annie when Shane's drug case blew back on him. The men that worked for Tony were all handsome, and if Suzanne had been on the market, she was certain she could have found someone there.

"Are you trying to hook me up?" Lily questioned. "I'll have you know I can get my own men! What about you, dearie? Any interesting men for you?" She saw the flash of pain cross her friend's face before it was quickly hidden.

"Not really. You know me, I'm just not looking yet."

Lily heard the wistfulness in her friend's voice. Looking at her lunch partner, she saw a woman with long black hair and the most striking blue eyes Lily had ever seen. Her hair was pulled into a simple pony-tail and her figure was hidden by the scrubs she wore to work. *One day I hope Suzanne will tell me her past because that girl has got a story to tell.*

"Okay, I promise to be there," Lily agreed. "If nothing else, it will be great to see Annie, Leon, and Shirley again."

The friends parted after lunch and as Suzanne headed back to the clinic, Lily walked in the other direction to her job. The company she worked for contracted her out to other companies who needed software designed. She was currently working for the VanHeusen Medical Corporation and their headquarters was several blocks away.

The day was beautiful and the walk was invigorating. Always in slacks and sensible shoes, Lily felt frumpish next to the stylishly high-heeled women around. Smiling to herself, she couldn't help but think, *always practical – that's me.*

Once she entered the building, she quickly made her way to the fourth floor where her temporary office was located. Walking in, her assistant Andrea looked up and smiled. She was in her early forties, neatly dressed with her short hair styled to accentuate her long neck. Polished and professional, Andrea was the perfect assistant.

"Hey Lily," Andrea greeted. "Did you have a nice lunch?"

"Yeah. I met with a friend and we set up plans for the weekend. Anything going on while I was out?"

"Actually, Mr. VanHeusen himself came by and asked if you and Ellen would join him for a meeting in the Executive Board Room at two p.m."

"Hmm, wonder what he wants?" Lily mused. Walking to her computer station, she nodded at Ellen. They had been working on the computer programs for the medical company together for several months, and while they were not close friends, they were very friendly work partners. Andrea was a great assistant and Ellen was…just fun. She and Ellen were such opposites. Ellen was always up for drinks after work and Lily hated parties. Ellen loved creating riddles and Lily loved solving problems. Ellen loved talking to people and Lily loved her quiet. As her partner, Ellen assessed their needs of the company and then the designing was turned over to her. She liked it that way. Less interaction with people.

"Do you know what the meeting is about today?" she asked Ellen.

"Not really," came the reply, "But I know that Mr. VanHeusen mentioned that he was going to do some restructuring."

Lily looked over in confusion. "We're just here on contract. What does that have to do with us?"

Ellen shrugged. "I don't really know, but once we know who we will be reporting to, you and I need to talk about some things."

"What's up?"

Ellen looked disconcerted for a moment, then just said, "I just need to gather more data."

Ellen didn't seem to be in a hurry to share, so Lily began to work again, carefully designing the new programs until Andrea reminded them of the meeting.

Once in the conference room, Lily looked around at the familiar faces. Dr. Curtis Bennett, Dr. Allen Purser, and a new woman that Lily had seen around but did not know, were present along with a few of the other doctors that made up the administration. Curt's constant scowl was present and Allen looked over at Lily with a wink.

Just then Malcolm VanHeusen came into the room. As always, Lily noted that the atmosphere changed the instant that Malcolm entered a room. The air seem to crackle with electricity as he took charge of any meeting. Wearing an expensive suit, his hair groomed, he looked every bit the part of a successful businessman. She was awed by his intelligence and drive to succeed, knowing that he had the most successful corporate medical facilities in the area.

"Everyone, I'll make this brief. I want to introduce you to Dr. Penelope Alease. I have brought her on board to make some changes around here. She will be directly under me as Assistant Medical Director."

Lily's eyes cut over quickly to Curtis and Allen to gauge their reactions. It was no secret that Curtis wanted the job that was now being handed to an outsider. She saw anger flash quickly but he was smart enough to not let Malcolm see it. Allen's reaction surprised her. He seemed almost bored by the announcement. Moving her gaze back to Malcolm, she realized that he was staring at her.

"Ms. Swanson. Ms. Marsh. I have explained your contract position with us as you are developing the software to assist in our prescription drug programs. You will also be reporting directly to Dr. Alease."

"Thank you, Mr. VanHeusen," Dr. Alease said looking around the room. "You may call me Penelope."

Settling her gaze on Lily and Ellen she continued, "I know that you work independently. I would like to be brought up to date on any and all changes to our current computer program statuses as soon as you make them."

Lily thought her request to be reasonable and nodded, although she knew that Ellen would be the one to make the reports. As they all rose from the table she noticed the short greeting that Curtis gave his new boss before stalking out of the room. Walking out ahead of the other doctors, she glanced back to see Ellen already in discussion with Penelope.

Once back to her office area, Andrea looked up from her desk and asked, "How was it?"

"Strange," Lily replied. "VanHeusen Medical has a new Assistant Medical Director but he didn't hire from within."

"Ohhh, I'll bet that didn't go over very well with Dr. Purser or Dr. Bennett."

"That's what was interesting. Dr. Bennett seemed like he had swallowed razors, but Dr. Purser acted like he didn't care."

Finding the topic of office politics boring, Lily immersed herself in her computer programing once again.

Chapter 3

THE RAIN COMING down late at night gave the city streets an eerie glow from the neon lights and street lamps. Ducking out of the cab, trying not to fall on the slippery sidewalk, Lily made her way inside. The raindrops shook off of her long skirt and her wet sneakers made squeaky sounds as she walked. The medical building halls were well lit, although quiet as a cemetery except for the sound of her footsteps as she made her way toward her office. Glad that she had a pass-key to the building, she had made the late night run back from home to get her cell phone. *I can't believe I left it on my desk on a Friday night.*

The quietness of the building was unnerving and as her squeaks echoed in the noiseless hall she couldn't help but turn occasionally to look over her shoulder. *Nothing. Of course there's nothing, you nitwit. Who else would be in this building at almost midnight?*

Trying to shake the uneasy feeling, she was glad to have made it to the small office that she shared with Andrea and Ellen. She liked having their own simple work space. It wasn't that she didn't like people. She just felt awkward around them. It was different...a long time ago. She was full of pep, energy, excitement. But life changes and she changed too. Preferring to stay in the background where she and her computer could solve problems.

Pulling her office key out of her purse, she fit it into the lock. The door swung open without her turning the key or the knob. The office was dark except for the bluish glow coming from the computer screens. *I had the computers turned off when I left.* Glancing around, she saw nothing amiss. She walked around the computer stations to her desk, glad for the carpet that muffled the sounds of her shoes.

She did not have to search long, finding her cell phone right where she left it, partially hidden under a stack of papers. Yawning loudly, she was reminded how late it was and leaned over to turn off the computers so that she could get back home. Stretching her body across the table, she was reaching over when she caught a glimpse of something on the floor.

Pulling herself back up, she walked around the table to peer down. *Oh Jesus, Oh Jesus, oh shit!* Scrambling backwards, she ran into the desk, reaching out to keep from falling. Turning quickly she ran out of the room, dialing 911 on her cell.

"A body. I found a body. Oh my God. You've got to come," she screamed into the phone. The rational part of her brain knew that the dispatcher on the other end needed facts, but all she could think about was the blood.

"Yes, yes. I'm at the VanHeusen Medical Building on Fifth and Main," she cried as her hands began to shake uncontrollably. "What? Oh, fourth floor. Please send someone, there's so much blood."

Having made it to the hall, she felt her legs go out from under her as she slid down to the floor. "Name? Lily. I'm Lily Swanson. I work here."

MATT HATED PHONE calls in the middle of the night. No matter how long he had been a detective, late night calls were never good. Looking at the number, he was surprised to see his partner's number rather than the station.

"Yeah, bro. What's got you callin' after midnight?"

"Sorry to wake you. Got a call from homicide. There's been a possible suicide or murder in a medical building and they knew we had our eyes on any criminal activity in the medical community. I want to go check it out."

Rubbing the sleep from his eyes, Matt rolled out of bed. "Give me the address and I'll be there in about twenty minutes."

Getting dressed, he couldn't help but think about the difference between Annie and his former fiancé. Annie supported Shane in anything he needed to do. Cassandra...well, he knew that late night calls were just one of the reasons she left. But the mystery lady. *Why do I get the feeling that she would be supportive?* It had been a couple of days and he couldn't get her out of his mind. *If I ever see her again, I'm not letting her run away.*

Pulling up to the address, he looked up to see the sign on the side of the building. **VanHeusen Medical Corporation**. Meeting up with Shane outside of the building, they were briefed by the detective in charge as they walked inside and into the elevator.

"Time of death appears to be between eight o'clock and ten o'clock p.m. Victim was found in her office. Gunshot wound to the head. There was a suicide note left on her desk. The victim was Ellen Marsh. Thirty-eight years old. Single. Lives alone. She was under contract here as a software engineer doing needs-assessment."

"Where did you get that from? Needs-assessment?" Matt asked as they exited into a long hallway with offices on either side.

"From the woman down there," he said pointing to the far end of the hall. "We've got her in one of the conference rooms. She's the partner and office mate. And the woman who found her. Name's Lily Swanson."

"What was she doing here?" Matt asked.

"Says she forgot her phone and didn't want to be without it for the whole weekend. She has a pass-key to the building since she often works late or on weekends."

"Can anyone corroborate her story?"

"Yeah. She doesn't drive so she took a cab. The cabbie was waiting outside for her and vouched for her time entering the building. It was at eleven fifty one. The outside security cameras corroborate her times entering the building."

"You think we're needed? You think this has anything to do with the drugs we're finding?" Matt asked. By this time they had made their way to the conference room and he looked through the glass wall seeing a petite woman, head in her hands, long hair falling in a curtain around her. An eerie feeling that she was familiar slid over him.

"In questioning her, she seemed clueless as to why the victim would have committed suicide or been killed. She just said that they were working on software programs. I have no idea if it pertains to some of the cases you are looking at, but wanted you to have a shot at her." The homicide detective chuckled. "Sorry, bad pun."

Matt glared at him before moving through the door toward the woman sitting on the far side of the conference table. "Miss? Miss Swanson?" he called gently, knowing that the witnesses to violent crimes are often in shock. "I'm Detective Dixon and this is my partner Detective Douglas."

Her head came up and he was stunned. It was her. The woman from the bar. He couldn't take his eyes off of her face. *His woman. Her name is Lily. Beautiful.* Huge, dark brown eyes. Haunted. Full of fear. Shiny with tears. Her face was devoid of makeup, but he could see the trail left by tears and had to clench his hands by his side to keep from wiping them from her cheeks.

Dressed simply, in an old sweater over a t-shirt, she looked like a woman who ran out in the middle of the night to get her phone. And instead found a body.

Shane, recognizing that his partner seemed to be having an uncharacteristic reaction to a witness, sat on the other side, allowing Matt to sit at the end of the end of the table closest to her.

"You," Lily said softly. "You're here." Her eyes were staring at him, but shock had dulled their brightness.

He reached out to grasp her hand.

The simple gesture made her lips tremble once again.

She glanced between the two men and said, "I don't know what else I can tell you."

Matt continued to offer comfort, while Shane asked, "Ma'am, we know you've gone over the events of the night with the homicide detectives. But we'd like to know more about what you and the victim were working on."

Lily's face clouded over in confusion and Matt recognized the signs of shock. He glanced to the side at Shane. Their eyes met and after years of being partners, understanding passed between them. Matt continued.

"Lily. I just want you to tell me, in your own words, what you and the victim were working on for VanHeusen Medical."

Her eyes began to focus on his face and she licked her lips as she gathered her thoughts.

Matt's eyes dropped to her mouth and watched her

tongue glide over the bottom lip. Staring at her lips, he wanted to trail after her tongue with his own. Lick the seam, suck on her bottom lip, plunge his tongue deep into her...

"Detective Dixon?"

He was immediately jerked back to the moment, realizing that her wide, chocolate eyes were staring at him in question. *Jesus, what the fuck is wrong with me? She's a witness, not a conquest.*

Clearing his throat, he repeated, "In your own words, please. What were you and the victim working on?"

"Ellen. Her name was Ellen Marsh. Not *The Victim*," Lily spoke, her voice shaky, but with anger instead of shock.

Matt looked at her face, flushed instead of pale. *She's beautiful either way.* "Okay Lily. What were you and Ms. Marsh working on."

Licking her lips again, she said, "In the simplest terms, we were working on ways to integrate the medications that the doctors prescribe, which are already integrated with the patient files, so they will be linked to insurance companies, Medicare, and other billings."

Shane spoke up, "Was there anything that you or Ms. Marsh may have come across that could have been considered illegal? Or perhaps, just didn't seem right to you?"

Lily turned her gaze to Shane, a questioning look on her face. "Illegal? I...I don't know...what do you mean?"

"For example, why was she here so late at night? We're just trying to establish if there was a reason that Ms. Marsh felt as though she needed to take her own life. Perhaps something that she was doing here."

"She wouldn't have...she couldn't have done that."

"Done what, Ms. Swanson?" Shane prodded.

"She was happy. She...I don't know. Laughed a lot. She loved jokes and riddles...and people and..."

"Do you know of anything that she may have discovered that someone would have wanted her killed for?"

Lily began to shake her head, the memory of Ellen's body flashing through her mind and suddenly the tears slid down her cheeks once again. Her arms wrapped tightly against her body again as she rocked back and forth. "No, no. I don't know. We don't...there's nothing. I just write program codes. I don't..."

She leaned forward toward Matt, involuntarily seeking human contact.

He immediately reached his arms out, wrapping them around her body, pulling her close. One hand cupped the back of her head protectively and the other held her tight against his chest. For a moment no one said anything as her tears fell. Matt wanted to hold her all night. For the first time in a long time he wanted to hold and comfort a woman, knowing she asked nothing in return.

Shane spoke softly, "Ms. Swanson, I think we're finished here. You've had enough tonight, but if you think of anything else, you can call. The detective in charge of the case will be interviewing you more. Perhaps you will be able to think of more tomorrow."

Suddenly embarrassed, she jerked back away from Matt, afraid to look him in the eyes. "Yes, of course," she said while wiping her face. "I'm sorry I couldn't be of more help." Sucking in a huge breath, she let it out slowly.

She spared a glance into Matt's eyes, seeing no pity, but instead something that she could not identify. *I wish he could hold me all night long. If only…fool, I'd never be good enough for him. He probably has women throwing themselves at him. And me…I'd be an embarrassment.*

Lily stood up and as she started to walk, she faltered and stumbled. Matt and Shane both looked down to see if she twisted her ankle. It was then that they could see her legs for the first time. Her right shoe was on a perfectly normal foot. Her left shoe covered a prosthetic foot where the lower part of her leg had been amputated.

Chapter 4

MATT STARED. *JESUS, she's had an amputation. How could I not have noticed,* he thought, feeling immediately contrite for having tried to get her out of her pants that night in his truck. *What a dick she must think I am. Jesus fuck.* He leaned his head back and with his closed his eyes in agony, thinking how uncomfortable he must have made her feel.

Lily saw the look of shock on his face as he stared at her prosthesis. She'd seen that look so often in the past eight years. Sometimes it was followed by surprise. Or questions. Or disgust. Or eyes that were quickly diverted. Excuses made to make hasty exits. *I've seen it so many times before, so why does this time hurt so much?* Taking a shaky breath, she realized that this time she thought it might be different.

"Am I free to go?" she asked, her body rigid. "I'll need to call a cab."

"No," came the sharp retort from Matt. "I'll take you home."

"I assure you that I'm perfectly capable of seeing myself home."

"Matt," Shane's soft voice got his attention. "You

need to let her choose how to get home. She's a witness and you gotta be cool. And it's for her safety as well as yours."

Wrapping her sweater around her middle tightly in a protective manner Lily agreed, assuming Detective Douglas was saving his friend from the awkward situation of having to drive her somewhere. "Yes," she lied. "I would prefer to be driven home by a cab."

The desire to protect and comfort overwhelmed Matt as he looked at the beauty in front of him. Fragile and yet stronger than he could ever imagine. Clenching his fists at his sides, he watched as she turned and walked down the hall with the patrolwoman. Blonde hair hanging down her back, head held high, she walked straight and steady until out of sight. He glared at Shane and bit out, "What the fuck, man?"

"You cannot go after her right now. I figured out after a moment that she must the girl you met at the bar and have been hung up on for the past couple of days. But man, she's a witness, and you gotta keep your dick in your pants and not fuck the case up."

Matt stared at Shane incredulously. "You have got to be completely shittin' me. Seriously, Shane, is your head so far up your ass you can't even remember six months ago? When you met Annie, may I remind you, she was a witness you totally fucked."

Shane rounded on Matt and for a moment it looked as though the two friends would come to blows. Finally taking in shaky breath, Shane let it out slowly. "You're right, I did. I met her and nothin' was gonna stop me from having her. Not the case. Not my superiors. Nothin'."

Matt hung his head for a moment. "That woman has tempted something in me, Shane, that I thought was gone and I'll be damned if I let that go."

"I take it you didn't know about her leg?"

Letting out a breath he didn't realize he had been holding, Matt shook his head. "I had no fuckin' idea. Jesus, what has she been through?"

"You okay with it?"

Matt turned to look at his friend, his eyes narrowed dangerously. "What the fuck are you asking?"

Shane held his gaze. "I'm figuring she's had her share of men take one look at her and run in the opposite direction. Don't figure you're that kind of man, not the friend I know. But still, I don't guess that she'd appreciate being pursued if it isn't possibly going to go the distance."

"All I could think of was how I wish I could take away her pain. She leaned into me for comfort and I just wanted it to last. So no, man. The amputation doesn't take away one thing that I am feeling. I just can't fuckin' believe that I had to let her walk out of here, get in a cab in the rain, in the middle of the fuckin' night and not be able to do anything about it. You know, that cuts me deep. That's not the kind of man I am. And knowing she thinks it's her leg that is keeping me from her side right now? Fuck," he cursed as he drug his hand through his hair.

Nodding, Shane agreed. "But you've got a name now. An address. She's not gonna disappear. Give it a couple of days. Let homicide talk to her again and once she is cleared then you're free." With that he clapped Matt on the shoulder and they headed back out into the night.

MATT STOOD ON the other side of the two way mirror watching as Lily was being escorted into the interrogation room. She sat quietly, looking around in curiosity. Her face was still splotchy from crying last night. His hands fisted at his side as he watched her. Huge, dark brown eyes took in her surroundings and yet he could see nervousness in them as well. She was dressed simply, a pale green sweater over snug jeans. Pale green sneakers on her feet. *Does she prefer sneakers? Does she prefer pants?* He found himself wondering about her and surprising himself with how much he wanted to know more.

The detectives in charge walked into the room where she was sitting and introduced themselves. Shane entered the surveillance room where Matt was standing and watched for a moment before speaking.

"They rule homicide or suicide yet?"

"No. Medical examiner's report won't be in for a few days but they are treating it like a homicide."

"Does she know that?"

Before Matt could answer, the detectives began

questioning Lily. Matt listened as her clear, but soft voice responded to all of their questions.

At one point, she put her hand up to her forehead and rubbed as though in pain. Matt found himself wanting to charge into the room and tell the detectives to give her a break. He felt a hand on his shoulder as Shane spoke. "Steady man. She's doin' fine."

They listened as Lily grew more frustrated as the questions continued. Finally, she burst out, "She just wouldn't do it. But the alternative doesn't make any sense either. You want me to tell you something that would make sense of this, but I just can't!"

"What do you mean, Ms. Swanson?" the detective prodded.

Sighing, she leaned back in the chair. Taking a deep breath, she answered, "Don't you understand that none of this makes sense to me? Neither suicide. Nor mu...murder." Taking a moment to gather her thoughts, she continued. "She was not a suicidal person. I didn't know her before we were paired together for this job but I've seen her every day for the past three months. She was fun, people enjoyed being around her. She dated but never found a steady companion. She had a neat way of finding out what people liked and she did nice things for them."

"Can you give us an example?"

Staring off into the distance for a moment, she smiled as though recalling a pleasant memory. Looking back at the detective, she replied. "Our assistant,

Andrea, loves to knit. Ellen would give her gift cards to the expensive yarn stores, just because she knew that Andrea liked them." She looked down at the table before continuing in a soft voice, "I like riddles. You know, number problems. Sometimes to break the tedium of the programing we were doing, she would send me a coded riddle. Kind of like a number scavenger hunt." Looking into the blank faces of the detectives, she realized that she sounded like the nerd that she was. Blushing, she looked down, giving a little shrug. "I know it sounds dumb to you, but to me it…it was fun."

"So in your opinion, you saw nothing in Ms. Marsh's demeanor that would indicate a suicidal person?"

Shaking her head she looked up at the man sitting in front of her. "No detective. But the alternative is unthinkable."

"How do you mean?"

Her face paling, she whispered, "Murder."

Rubbing her hand over her forehead again she winced.

"Ma'am, are you all right?"

Lily nodded as she said, "Yes, thank you. I didn't sleep last night and well…I haven't eaten either."

One of the detectives left the room and immediately came back with some crackers and a soda. "Here you go, Ms. Swanson."

She smiled gratefully, then took a sip of the soda and nibbled on a cracker while the detectives sat quietly.

Pulling her lips in, she looked up. "I know. I can't stall. We have to talk about it."

"Can you come up with any reason as to why she would have been killed?"

"Detective, we weren't working on anything that was the least bit interesting to anyone other than VanHeusen Medical. We weren't creating anything new or innovative. We weren't involved in anything that hadn't been written for other companies before. In other words, there was no company espionage." At the quirk of the detective's eyebrow, she quickly said, "That sounded like something from one of the detective TV shows I watch." Leaning back again, she said, "I guess I'm just trying to explain how boring our job was. There was nothing that anyone would have wanted to kill her over. Nothing. It makes no sense!"

"Would there have been anything that she found out that someone wanted to silence her for?"

By this time, Lily was utterly exhausted. Her eyes filled with tears as she said, "Nothing. Nothing."

Matt growled as he watched her break down but Shane held him back.

"Let them clear her, man."

The detective finished with Lily and escorted her out. Walking down the steps of the police station, she entered a cab. She did not see Matt standing in the doorway of the police station, his blue eyes trained on her retreat.

Neither of them saw the car parked across the street,

their eyes trained on her as well.

THE NEXT WEDNESDAY afternoon Matt stood under a tree, separated from the mourners gathered for the burial of Ellen Marsh. Even from his distance he could see Lily standing with the others. Head bowed, blonde curls hanging down, once again hiding her face. As the short service ended he watched to see if she needed him. He prided himself on being a good cop. One who would never compromise a case. But the magnetic pull from her had him re-thinking his options.

Homicide had cleared her, but she was still active in the investigation. He and Shane had been looking into the work of the victim but had not questioned Lily again. That would come. But for now...he just wanted to make sure she was alright. From a distance.

The mourners all drifted away to their cars and for a moment he lost sight of her. A movement out of the corner of his eye had him leaning around the tree to watch her before silently following.

Lily walked away from Ellen's gravesite after the service, making the decision to visit with someone else. Coming to the grave she was seeking, she awkwardly kneeled down, placing her hand on the headstone.

Rose Ann Swanson Beloved daughter and sister

"You would have liked him so much, Rose. I would have never had a chance with him if you had been around," she said smiling. "You were always so beautiful." Her whisper floated on the air. "Beautiful Rose. That's what daddy always called you, remember?" Lily sighed as her fingers trailed across the words on her headstone. "I shouldn't have gone out that night." A single tear slid down her cheek and she brushed it absent-mindedly away. "Love you, Rosie. I miss you every day."

With that, she pushed herself up, brushing the leaves from her pants. Turning, she gasped as she saw a man standing right behind her. Her eyes flew open wide as she recognized him.

"Detective Dixon! What are you doing here?" Her eyes narrowed in suspicion. "Are you following me? Are you investigating me? Here?"

Matt quickly placed his hands on her shoulders, pulling her directly in front of him. "I'm not following you. I…just wanted to…" His eyes slid over her to the headstone.

"To what?" she accused.

He brought his eyes back to hers. "To make sure you were all right."

Drawing herself up, she lifted her chin. "I'm fine. I do not need you to keep an eye on me. I'm perfectly fine on my own." Pulling herself back away from his grip on her shoulders, she turned to walk away. After a few steps, she looked back at the headstone before turning her gaze back to him. "I've been fine on my own for a long time."

Matt watched her walk away, noticing a cab waiting at the entrance of the cemetery for her. Turning back around, he looked down at the gravesite of her sister. He touched his fingers on the stone as he walked by. "I'll look after her now Rose. She's not alone anymore."

FRIDAY AFTERNOON FINALLY came and the weekend was approaching. Matt thought about the engagement party that evening and while he was looking forward to spending some time with his friends, his mind was full of Lily. Closing the file on his desk, he looked over at Shane who was doing the same.

"It's been a helluva week," Shane stated. "I've got the preliminary report on Ellen Marsh. It's still being treated as a possible suicide, but the investigation is taking a careful look to see if it was homicide. No one knows why she was there that late on a Friday night. It appears she never went home. They questioned Lily and had her go back to the office to see if anything was missing or suspicious."

Matt growled at the thought of her back in the office where she had found the body.

"She says that nothing in the office was missing. They're having her check her computer files and data bases." Shane looked at him. "Have you seen her again?"

"Not officially."

Shane didn't reply but his silence created the question.

"I went to the cemetery to keep an eye on her." Matt paused, lost in thought, then continued. "She has a sister buried there as well."

"A sister?"

"Yeah. I looked up the obituary and then the report. Seems the girls were involved in a car accident when Lily was only sixteen years old. She was driving but it wasn't her fault. Her sister was killed and I'm assuming that's when she lost her foot. The report said that the firemen had to cut her out of the van."

Both men settled into silence, letting the idea of a young teen's tragedy fill their minds.

"So, what's up with you two?" Shane asked.

His mouth curving in a small smile, he said, "It's the damndest thing. I haven't been really attracted to anyone since Cassandra. Just figured it wasn't worth the trouble to start over in a new relationship after getting screwed over by that bitch.

"But from the moment I met Lily, there was something there. She's so fragile and strong all at the same time. I wanted to protect her. I wanted to know her. I just plain as hell wanted her."

In complete understanding, Shane nodded, having had the same reaction when he first met Annie. "So what are you gonna do about it?"

Smiling, Matt confessed. "I'm going to win her heart. I want her heart, soul, and body and she may not know it yet, but she's mine."

"And the case?"

"She's not a suspect, nor a person of interest. She wasn't a witness to the crime, just found the body. If it becomes a problem, then I will step aside from the case. Not the woman."

Shane nodded his agreement before closing the file on his desk.

"You ready to head out, man?" Matt asked.

"Absolutely," was Shane's reply. "I'm heading home to get Annie and we'll meet you at the Lakeside Bar & Grill."

The men walked out together and drove off in opposite directions. Matt watched his friend drive away, knowing that he was headed out to the suburbs to a house that now housed him, Annie, his dog Sarge and her three cats. Shaking his head as he climbed up into his truck, he thought back to his short engagement a year ago. *No home in the suburbs for Cassandra. Nope. If it wasn't a fancy-ass apartment with a view, then it wasn't good enough. And I'd been dumb enough to try to give her the moon. Look where that got me. A year's lease on an expensive apartment. But Lily? Maybe that house in the suburbs would be exactly what she wanted too.*

Driving home he began to dread the party. He didn't begrudge Shane and Annie's happiness, but watching them would be a slap-in-the-face reminder of what he did not have. Once home he took a quick shower then stared at himself once again in the mirror. *Snap out of it dickhead*, he said to his reflection. *Go out, enjoy their company, and stop feeling sorry for yourself.*

Arriving at the restaurant, he walked to the hostess stand to ask for the party. Her eyes quickly scanned his physique from his boots to his face. He saw the initial spark of interest that was common and then he waited until her eyes landed on his scar. *Yep, there it is*, he noted as her eyes dimmed. He had to give her kudos though…she continued to smile as she led him to the back room where the engagement party was being held.

As he walked around the bar he glanced over to the dance floor, recognizing Gabe, one of Tony's men, slow dancing with a woman whose dark blonde hair hung in curls down her back. The woman made him think of Lily and he wished that he could be here with her. *Soon. Just be a little more patient and then…* the woman turned in Gabe's arms and he saw her face. *Lily? What the fuck!*

Before he could make his way to the dance floor, Suzanne came over to give him a hug.

"Glad you came Grumpy," she joked.

"Why the hell is Gabe dancing with Lily?" he growled.

She strained to see over to the dance floor. "Lily? That's Lily Swanson, a friend of mine."

"I know who she is. What I want to know is why is she here with Gabe?"

"Jeez Matt. Chill out. She's here because she's a friend of mine and said she had a rough week. I wanted her to get out and meet some friends of mine."

"Yeah well, letting you know right now, I'd like her to be here with me," he proclaimed, stalking towards the dance floor, leaving a smiling Suzanne in his wake.

Immediately approaching Gabe and tapping him on the shoulder, he said, "Cuttin' in."

Gabe turned and saw the look on Matt's face. He couldn't help but grin, knowing that this girl must have gotten to Matt. Looking down at Lily, he drawled, "What do ya think darlin'? Do you want this guy cuttin' in on our dance?"

Blushing, Lily stared for a moment, unsure of what to do. The intensity pouring off of Matt made the room seem small. Looking up into his eyes, she felt his gaze burn right to her core. It had been easy to dance with Gabe. He saw her as just a friend. But Matt? She didn't know what he wanted and that unnerved her. Slowly she nodded, uncertainty clouding her face, and Gabe turned her toward Matt.

He took her in his arms and they began dancing slowly as he pulled her closer. *Finally, she's in my arms.*

Lily's heart began to pound as she was pressed tightly to his chest as they rocked slowly back and forth to the music. The warmth that she experienced the night they met in the bar returned. *Funny, I didn't feel this with Gabe.*

They slowly moved around in a circle, bodies pressed tightly until the song ended. She came to a stop and peered up into his face. He was so much taller than she but with their bodies together, it felt right. The music changed to a faster song and she tensed.

"I don't really dance," she said haltingly. "Slow

dancing is easy, but this…" her voice trailed off as she glanced around at the people starting to bump and grind near them. Feeling his hand on her cheek, pulling her face back toward his, she saw understanding in his eyes.

"You wanna sit, babe? We'll sit. Whatever you wanna do as long as you're doin' it with me," his husky voice melted over her.

She stood biting her lip, uncertain of his motives. "What do you want from me? If you're expecting…"

"No," he growled. "That's not what I'm after." He dropped his head for a moment, then sighed. Lifting his head to peer deeply into her eyes, he said, "Look, I know what happened was all kinds of fucked up and I'm so sorry. You didn't deserve to be treated that way. I just want to get to know you."

With a slight nod of her head, he took her hand guiding her back toward the party area. Seeing Shane and Annie, he headed in their direction. His long legs would have made it hard for Lily to keep up with his stride, but he matched his steps with hers.

Approaching the happy couple, they offered their greetings and congratulations.

"Lily, I am so glad Suzanne convinced you to come," Annie beamed, seeing Matt link his fingers with Lily's.

"Lily, it's nice to see you under different circumstances," Shane greeted, noting his partner's claim on the petite beauty.

Annie rounded on Shane. "How do you know Lily?"

"We met when a co-worker…um…died," Lily replied.

"Died? As in killed?" came Suzanne's voice from behind. "I know you said you had a bad week, but honey I had no idea it was that bad!"

Suzanne's loud proclamation had several heads in the party turning. Lily shrunk from the speculative glances coming their way.

Matt felt her body lean slightly in to his and he unlinked their hands so that he could wrap his arm around her shoulders pulling her in tightly to his side. "Enough," he said, his voice giving no room for argument. "If you'll excuse us," he said, leading her away to a private table.

She glanced up at him in gratitude, smiling at the way he seemed to know what she needed. First in the bar and then here. *Maybe having him for a friend would be a good thing.*

Neither of them noticed the huge smiles of the trio they left behind. Shane grabbed Annie, pulling her in for a kiss before giving a fist-bump to Suzanne.

Once settled at the table, Matt looked carefully at Lily. "You okay?"

Smiling, she just nodded before looking around nervously.

His protective instincts were on high alert as he noticed her eyes looking around. Reaching across the table the grasped her hand.

Lily's eyes went down to their hands on the table, then went back to his face. "Thank you for being so nice to me."

His eyebrows raised in question. "You don't have to thank me. I don't want anyone to make you uncomfortable."

"Why? You don't owe me anything just because we…um…did…um…you know," she said, the blush flaming across her face as she pulled her hand back.

"You think that's what this is about?" he bit out sharply.

Her dark eyes flashed in surprise at his tone. Inhaling, she replied, "I don't know. I don't know you at all. I've never done…that before. I'm not stupid. I mean I know it didn't mean anything to you."

"You don't know anything about me, so you don't know what it meant. But that's gonna change."

Pressing her lips together, her eyes filled with tears. "Pity? Is that what this is, because I don't need your pity. Believe me, I've been dealing with this on my own for a long time."

His voice softened, "This isn't pity. I've got no pity for someone that I consider to be so strong and independent. Admiration? Yes. Pity? No." Not wanting to sit across from her anymore, he slid over to the chair next to hers, pulling her in close.

"I felt something that night at the bar. Something I haven't felt in a long time. I never meant for what happened in the truck to happen, but I gotta say, it was amazing to see you fly apart like that."

Lily blushed even deeper, but before she could pro-test he continued.

"What happened next was fucked though. Before I could pull myself together to let you know that I wanted to see you again and explore the feelings I know we both had, you bolted."

Looking down at their joined hands again, she spoke softly, "I felt it too, but knew you would disappear in a puff of smoke if you knew about my foot. Every guy always has." Giving her shoulders a little shrug as she twisted to gaze into his eyes. "Don't get me wrong. I'm not ashamed. My foot was amputated and I finally was fitted with a prosthesis that works for me. I'm strong and I'm still a whole woman. But...sometimes I get tired of seeing the looks of either pity or horror from men. Or the creeps."

"Creeps?" he asked sharply, wondering who she was referring to.

"You know, the men who only want to have sex with women amputees."

"What the fuck?" he reared back, looking into her face to see if she were kidding.

Blushing again, she couldn't help but laugh at the look on his face. "It's true. There are websites just for men who want to meet women amputees."

"Jesus, fuck," he bit out.

"Well, I've never resorted to that," she said, still gig-gling. After a moment of silence, she looked back into his face.

"Matt? I don't know what to do with this," she said with such honesty that he felt the tightness in his chest ease a bit. "Us, I mean. I need you to be completely truthful to me, because I've never had a man stick around after finding out that I have an amputation. They see me as an amputee. And I'm not. I'm Lily. I just happen to have an amputation, but it isn't who I am or what defines me."

"I told you the truth earlier. I haven't had a reaction to someone in a long time and you have wrapped yourself around my heart. So you want honesty? Here goes. I'm a man who takes care of what is mine. That's not the same as taking over. I see a strong, smart, independent woman in front of me and I wanna get to know that woman a whole lot more." As he spoke, he leaned closer until his lips were just an inch from hers and he could feel her breath wash across his face. "I'm tempted to kiss you. You ready for that, LilyBelle?"

Her eyes widened, a gasp slipping out from her mouth as he looked at her questioningly.

"You called me LilyBelle." Pulling her lips in tightly, she remarked, "No one has called me LilyBelle since...well, since a very long time."

"Is it okay?" he asked gently, searching her eyes for signs of distress, but seeing none.

"Yeah," she said, a soft smile curing the edges of her lips. Leaning back in toward his mouth, she said, "It's beautiful." Then she moved in to continue the kiss he started before.

Her trust was overwhelming to him as he lost himself in her kiss. Sliding his arm around her shoulders, he pulled her closer to him, taking the kiss deeper.

Suddenly a loud greeting boomed out right next to them as Gabe and Vinny sat down in the two remaining chairs at their table.

Pulling away from her lips, Matt glared at his friends as he realized that Lily was once again blushing furiously.

She looked in confusion between the identical twins, knowing that Gabe had short hair but was now faced with a version with longer hair as well.

"So Lily. You've danced with my ugly brother and I wondered if you would give me the same chance to impress you," Vinny said as he tried to dazzle her with his perfect smile.

"You two wanna shove off?" Matt growled.

"Not particularly," Gabe shot back, grinning at his friend. "We just thought Lily shouldn't have to spend her whole evening with you."

Matt knew his friends were just giving him a hard time but he wasn't expecting Lily's reaction.

Jerking around, she glared at the two men. "What do you mean by that?" she exclaimed sharply. "How dare you imply that he isn't worthy of my time! I'll have you know that –"

Matt smiled at his two friends as he leaned in to calm her. "It's okay, LilyBelle. They're just kidding with you."

Her eyes narrowed on the twins as she leaned back into Matt's embrace.

Nodding, Gabe looked at his friend. "That's quite a tiger you've got there. I hope you appreciate what you've got." Then looking at her, he smiled at her as he stood. "Take care of this old cuss, Lily," he said nodding to Matt. Vinny followed suit, but before he left their table he leaned in to whisper in her ear, "Thanks, sweetheart."

"What was that about?" she asked, confusion in her voice. She was remembering why she liked her job more than socializing – numbers were easy to code, but people were confusing.

"I've got some fucked-up friends," he answered lightly. "But they mean well."

"Why are they so worried about you?"

His eyes hardened for a second before he answered. "Had a difficult time about a year ago and I think they were worried. Nothing too serious, but I let it change me and make me more of a loner."

"What happened?" she asked softly, watching his expression carefully.

Shaking his head, he said gently, "Another conversation for another evening. Tonight, LilyBelle, is about you and me."

She turned her beautiful smile toward him and another piece of his heart fell back into place.

Chapter 5

THE REST OF the evening continued as Lily met many more of Matt's friends and spent time with Annie and Suzanne. Matt continually kept a pulse on Lily, wanting to make sure she was having a good time.

"You okay, babe?" he asked.

She immediately looked concerned. "Do I not look like I am having a good time?"

"I just know you don't like crowds and I don't want you to stay on my account."

Smiling shyly she nodded. "That's usually true. It's hard sometimes, being an introvert. It's like people think they need to fix you as though there is something wrong." Giving a small shrug she continued. "I'm just not used to socializing much, but this has been a really nice party." Looking at her watch, she said ruefully, "But I really need to go. I have to get up early tomorrow."

"Tomorrow's Saturday, babe. Why do you need to get up early?"

"I have running practice." Seeing the question on his face, she said, "Learning to run with a prosthesis is different from walking. I'm getting coaching so that I can improve."

"I'd love to run with you sometime," he said, leaning down to capture her mouth once again in a soft kiss.

Licking her lips as she pondered his request, she said, "I don't know. I'd be self-conscious if you were there too."

"Will you think about it?"

"Yeah, I will. But for now, I really need to go home. I'm glad we met again," she said honestly.

"Do you have a ride home?" he asked.

Pulling out her cell phone, she laughed, "Of course. The cab company is used to me."

Taking the phone gently out of her hands, he said, "Oh no, LilyBelle. No more cabs for you. I'll drive you."

Narrowing her eyes, she asked, "Are you asking me or telling me?"

Sucking in a deep breath, Matt realized he needed to tread carefully. Letting the breath out slowly, he said, "Ms. Swanson, will you do me the honor of allowing me to escort you home this evening?"

Bursting out laughing, she said, "Why Mr. Dixon, I would be delighted."

Matt looked down in wonder at the beauty in front of him. It had been a long time since he had made a woman laugh and enjoyed the honest repartee. Standing, he offered his hand to assist her up. Walking over to Shane and Annie, they said their goodbyes and congratulations. Giving Suzanne a quick hug goodbye, she whispered in her ear, "Thanks for inviting me."

Suzanne winked as the women pulled apart. "Call me after you run tomorrow."

As Lily went to hug Annie, Matt cornered Suzanne. "Tell me where she runs."

Suzanne whispered, "You won't hurt her, will you? She's so strong but fragile at the same time."

Matt looked down at his friend, knowing she had her own demons. "No guarantees in life, Suzanne, but I'll never willingly hurt her."

Smiling, Suzanne whispered the name of the track into his ear.

Driving home, Lily couldn't help but remember the last time she was in his truck. *His hand down my pants. His fingers buried deep inside. Moving rhythmically. Until...* Glad for the cover of darkness, she assumed her blush would go unnoticed. But her change in breathing did not.

Matt glanced sideways, noticing how quiet she had become, with nervousness pouring off of her. Then her breathing changed. Knowing exactly what she was thinking, he found himself remembering the look on her face when she came. *Perfect. Fuckin' perfect.*

About fifteen minutes later Matt turned into an older neighborhood with neat little houses in a row. Hers was one-story with a small stoop in the front. He eyed her security quickly. One light on next to the front door. A faint light coming from inside.

"What are you looking at?"

"Babe, your home security is shit," he answered.

Her quizzical look would have amused him, had he not been so concerned. Getting out of his truck, he rounded the front to her side and opened her door. She swung her legs around and he placed his hands on her waist. Leaning in, he kissed her before lifting her out, making sure she was steady before swinging his arm around her shoulders to walk her to the door.

"Keys, babe," he said as they approached.

Pulling her keys out of her purse, she replied, "I have them right here." She moved to put them in the keyhole, when he pulled them gently out of her hands.

"What are you doing?" confusion in her voice.

"I'm checking your house," he answered simply.

"Why?"

"Babe, I told you. Your home security is shit with this poor lighting."

He opened the door, flipping on the light to the entry foyer. Immediately his ankles were attacked as some kind of animal jumped up and down on his shins.

"What the hell is that?" he asked.

Giggling, she bent over to pick up her dog. "This is Pippi. Isn't she adorable?"

He looked at the puppy wiggling in her arms, licking her face. A tiny golden-colored mutt, with long ears and fur that stuck straight up on her head. Eyeing it warily, he asked, "Where the hell did you get that thing?"

She turned an angry gaze to him as she admonished, "She's precious, Matt. Don't call her a thing! I rescued her when I found her wandering in the street. Dirty and thin. I tried to find owners but couldn't find anyone who claimed her."

He started to make a joke about why an owner wouldn't want to claim the puppy, but then saw the way Lily was being licked and he couldn't help but grin. *Anything that puts a smile on her beautiful face is okay by me.*

"Stay here with that…dog, while I check the house." He made a quick scan of the house before making his way back to the front.

"Matt, I've lived here for a couple of years and never had a problem."

"LilyBelle, you're a woman living alone. You can never be too sure. You need a security system. I'll call Tony tomorrow."

Putting her hands on her hips after setting Pippi down, she glared. "I can handle my own affairs, thank you very much."

Fighting the urge to kiss her senseless until she forgot her argument, he breathed deeply. "Just want you safe."

Pulling her lips in, she sighed. "I've thought about it, but never got around to it." Looking up at his blue eyes, she agreed. "Okay, you can get a quote."

Slipping his hands around her, he gently pulled her in so that their bodies were flush. "Sure babe", he said, knowing he would never let her pay. Tony was the best and what he had in mind would keep her very safe.

Kissing her goodnight, it was all he could do to keep from picking her up and carrying her back to her bedroom. Her breasts were pressed up against his chest. Her tongue was dancing with his. Her silky hair was wrapped around his hand. His dick swelled uncomfortably in his jeans, pressing against her stomach. Sliding his hand up her shirt, he cupped her breast feeling the pebbled nipple just waiting for him. Tweaking it between his finger and thumb he captured her moan in his mouth.

She pressed her aching core against his heavy, jean-clad thigh and began rubbing to ease the pressure building inside. With his hand at her breast and his mouth doing insane things to hers, she could feel the heat rising. *More, just a little bit more.* Suddenly, as he gently rolled her nipple, she felt the orgasm pulse through her as she grasped his shoulders, digging her fingernails in. Head thrown back, she could swear she saw stars with her eyes tightly closed.

The heat she felt from the kiss cooled as his body separated from hers. She looked up into his face, searching for understanding. His eyes were closed and his head leaned back as though in agony.

"Matt?" she asked softly.

Bringing his head back down, he peered into her questioning eyes. "Babe, I'm ready any time you are. You say the word and we'll be back in your bedroom before you can blink. But this isn't about me. It's gotta be about you. What you need and when you're ready."

He placed his hand along her cheek, rubbing his thumbs over her soft skin.

Slowly nodding her understanding, she pulled her lips in. "I…uh…think I…need…some more…time," she said, eyeing him carefully. *This could end so badly, with my heart being broken.* Glancing down at his bulging crotch, she blushed. Looking up into his face quickly, her distress shown in her eyes.

"Oh, I'm sorry," she exclaimed.

"What about, babe?"

"I left you…um…well…"

Sliding his hand from her cheek to the back of her head, he pulled her in and tucked her into his deep embrace. "You need more time babe, you got it. Whatever you need, that's what I wanna give you." Kissing the top of her head, he continued, "But LilyBelle, whatever fears you have, we're gonna work on them together."

She locked the door behind him and watched him drive away while standing at her living room window. Walking to the bedroom, she stared at her bed before sitting down on it, wondering what it would be like to have him here. Sliding her hand up toward her breast, she knew she wanted him. Here. With her. In this bed.

After slipping out of her jeans, she sat on the edge of the bed and removed her prosthesis. Looking down at her pedicured foot complete with pink toenails next to her residual limb, she wondered what he would think. *Can I risk it? Can I take the chance that we'll be hot and heavy on the bed and he'll look down and be grossed out?* Flinging herself back on the bed, her thoughts were a tangle as tears slowly slid down her cheeks.

The words of one of her first physical therapists came to mind. "Lily, I know you're afraid. But if you don't ever get up and try then you'll never take that first step. There's no shame in falling down, only in not trying."

Wiping the tears from her face, she crawled under the covers, thoughts of her handsome detective filling her mind and for the first time in many years her dreams were of a blue eyed man chasing her nightmares away.

THE NEXT MORNING dawned early and bright as Matt hustled out of his apartment in his running clothes. He had slept very little, thinking most of the night about the beautiful woman that had captured his attention. Remembering the jolt of electricity he felt when they kissed, he couldn't wait to hold her in his arms again. He remembered her gentle laughter as she would throw her head back, eyes dancing in delight.

He drove to the YMCA that was just on the north side of the city. Even in the early morning hours, there were quite a few cars in the parking lot. Knowing that many would be in the swimming pool or weight room, he wondered where to start looking for her. Parking near the track, he decided to take a look to see if she was outside before looking inside. The crispness of the fall air was perfect for running and he itched to begin himself.

Scanning the few runners that were pounding around the track, he latched onto the view of her toned body near the stadium seats, stretching. This morning, her long blonde hair was pulled into a high braid that swung down her back. The tank top showed off the curves that were only hinted at last night. Her ass, cupped in tight running shorts, was just as delectable as he remembered, but it was her toned legs that caught his attention. Her petite frame was lean and strong; the muscles in her legs had obviously been worked on.

Her left leg ended mid-calf with a prosthesis foot attached.

This morning, the cute hot-pink shoes were replaced with running shoes that looked as though they were specially made.

He stood to the side for a few minutes, suddenly filled with self-doubt. *What if she really doesn't want me here?*

His attention was diverted by a man who must have been her coach. He was young, definitely fit, and Matt knew that he would have been considered handsome by most women. He also had a prosthestic foot. And he just put his hands on Lily's hips, his fingers curving toward her ass. *Oh hell, no!*

Jolted out of his musings, he began to jog over.

"Come on, Lily, balance. Find your center of gravity

as you move to each foot. Walk, building up speed. Just keep increasing as comfortable."

Before Matt could reach them, he realized that the coach had been offering his hands as a way to steady her before she began. The jealousy still stung, but he was more determined than ever to be the one to help. Moving into the stands he sat, watching as the coach continued his instructions.

"Watch your breathing as you pick up speed. We use forty percent more oxygen and twice the energy just to walk compared to people with two normal legs. So you can imagine that you'll get out of breath when running."

Lily listened carefully, her face stoic in concentration.

Fuckin' amazing. Matt watched as she began jogging around the track, slow and steady, each step more confident.

"Take a longer stride with your good leg Lily then you can push off with more power with your prosthetic," the coach yelled as she came around a lap.

Matt watched in awe, wanting to have just a part of that strength with him always. After several laps he could tell she was slowing, limping slightly.

"Lily, don't limp. It throws off your gait," the coach yelled.

Matt watched her determined face as she moved by him, her concentration focused on evening out her pace. Red faced and sweaty as she ran, he thought he had never seen anything so beautiful. Suddenly, he wanted to be beside her more than anything he had wanted in a long time. He slipped out of the stands and jogged past the coach, picking up his pace to follow her. Admiring her from behind, he noticed that her gait was even and she appeared to have her balance.

She appeared to be concentrating as she pumped her arms in rhythm to her steps. Not wanting to startle her, he carefully jogged up next to her keeping the same pace that she had set.

"Hey, Lily," he spoke softly.

Her eyes quickly cut to him before widening in surprise. "Matt? What are you doing here?" she asked, surprise in her voice. *Oh Jesus, he can see my leg.* Her face flamed as she wondered what he must be thinking.

"I told you that I run every morning," he answered, not sure if he should tell her that he sought her out.

"Here? You run here?" she asked, keeping her concentration focused straight ahead.

"Well…" Matt hesitated. He'd always been honest and it suddenly didn't feel right lying to her. "To tell you the truth, no. I've never run here before."

Lily could feel her breath catching in her throat as she was trying to pace her footsteps, making her breathing more difficult. Not used to talking while running, she was beginning to tire quickly. Not sure what Matt was trying to tell her or exactly why he was here, she rounded the track again coming nearer to her coach. Looking at him, she could see a scowl on his face.

"Lily, concentrate. I can see you lose your concentration from here. Stop flirting and get to work!" came the shout from her coach.

"What the fuck?" Matt scowled as he started to round on the coach.

"Leave it alone," Lily warned. "He's just trying to help."

Continuing to set his pace with hers, Matt growled.

Trying not to giggle, Lily spared him a glance. "Look, I can't run and talk. And you are definitely distracting me."

"So I'm a distraction, am I?"

"Oh, please. Don't tell me that you aren't a distraction to most of the female population of Richland," she commented.

If she only knew that most women turn away when they see his scarred face. "Well, it hasn't been a problem in a long time," he answered back. "Look, agree to have breakfast with me and I'll leave you alone to finish your practice."

Glancing back over to see the sincerity on his face, she hesitated. *This could be such a bad idea, girl. He looks like he could steal my heart and then break it all at the same time.* The words she had remembered last night came back again...*there's no shame in falling, only in not trying.*

"Sure. I just need about another half-hour and then you can meet me inside after I shower."

"It's a date LilyBelle. I'll see you inside," and with

that he jogged away.

LilyBelle. With that one word, she was smiling again as she watched him disappear around the track.

MATT QUICKLY CHANGED into the clothes that he had brought with him and was pacing outside of the ladies' locker room. Every time the door opened, he turned quickly to see if it was Lily, each time being disappointed. Realizing he had scowled angrily at several elderly women exiting the locker room, he mumbled an apology. *Maybe she slipped out of the back. Maybe she really doesn't want to see me. Maybe...*

The door opened once more and this time she walked through, her gym bag in hand and her purse slung over her shoulder.

Scanning her from head to toe, he was struck again by her petite beauty. Her curls were again flowing around her shoulders. Her pink t-shirt was simple and yet draped tantalizing across her breasts. She was wearing jeans, the length just skimming the tops of her shoes. If he had not seen her prosthesis, he would not have known. *Is that what she prefers? For no one to know?* There was so much he wanted to learn about her.

Standing in front of her had him noticing how small she really was. Pressed into his embrace, the top of her head would tuck underneath his chin, and that was exactly where he wanted her.

Walking boldly up to her, he grasped the gym bag

from her hand and gently pulled her into his chest with his free hand wrapped around her body.

The gesture surprised Lily, finding herself rigid at first, then melting into the comfort of a simple hug. Her arms wrapped around his waist and she couldn't help but notice how right it felt. With her head pressed against his broad chest, it felt as though she belonged.

The embrace lasted a moment and then he slowly pulled away, a look of embarrassment on his face.

Lifting her eyes to see his expression she immediately jerked back, her face flaming. *What the hell is wrong with you, Lily? Jesus, a guy gives you a hug and you go all mushy.*

"I'm sorry," she stammered, stepping back.

Matt stepped forward, lifting her chin with his fingers. "On no you don't, LilyBelle. No more pulling away."

She looked up in confusion. "I don't know what you mean."

"This," he said pointing between them. "What's going on between us is happening. I feel something when we touch and I think you feel it too. I know I'm used to pulling back but I'm not running from this and I'm not going to let you run away either."

"You pulled away first," she said in gentle accusation.

"Holdin' you was more than my body could control and I didn't want to scare you away with my hard-on nudging you before breakfast."

She glanced down to see the bulge in his pants and quickly looked back up again, her face flaming even more.

He looked down as she ran her tongue over her pink lips and he couldn't take his eyes away. "Aw, fuck it," he said pulling her back into his embrace. Lowering his head as he lifted hers, he captured her lips in a kiss that sent a shock straight through him. Her lips were soft and tasted of strawberries. He licked them and as she opened, he plunged his tongue in.

The intensity of the kiss sent a jolt from her lips to her tingling breasts and down to her core. She raised her arms to capture his shoulders as she held on as though afraid of capsizing if she let go. Her breasts felt heavy as her nipples hardened. She felt sure that he could feel their points against his chest, but there was no pulling back with his arm tight around her holding her in place.

His tongue tangled with hers as he took her mouth in a long, wet kiss. His dick, already swollen painfully in his jeans, threatened to burst the zipper. He lost all sense of time and propriety as he continued to plunder her sweetness.

"Ahem," came a sound from behind them.

The interruption had them jumping apart as they turned to see who was standing nearby. Two older ladies in the hall just smiled indulgently as they indicated that the doorway was blocked.

"My apologies, ladies, but with a woman this beautiful, I just couldn't help myself," Matt explained as he hefted Lily's gym bag once again, tucking her under his arm and leading her out to the truck.

"Oh my God, that was embarrassing," she exclaimed. "I don't do that. I mean, I've never done…never made out like that."

He didn't care if it made him a caveman, he was secretly proud that she just admitted that making out in public wasn't something she normally did. Arriving at his truck, he tossed her bag behind the seats and before she could protest, lifted her into the passenger seat.

Hopping up in the driver's seat he was surprised to see an angry Lily staring at him.

"I'm not helpless, you know?" she said, glaring. "I've been getting along just fine on my own for years now, so don't think you'll step in and take over."

Sighing, he reached over to cup her face. "LilyBelle, I've got nothing but respect for your independence, but that doesn't mean that if I see a chance to make something easier for you that I won't do it. Hell, I would have helped you up no matter what just 'cause this truck is big. Why take a chance that it will cause you to fall when I can make sure that won't happen."

Lily sat thoughtfully while he drove to the diner. *I've always been so independent. Well, I kind of had to become independent.* She realized how difficult it was to maneuver through the murky waters of relationship building. *I wish there was some kind of support group for amputees who are thinking about dating!*

"We okay?" he asked smiling at her.

Smiling back, she understood that he had been giving her time to work through her thoughts privately. Reaching over to place her hand on his leg, she nodded. "Yeah, we're good."

When they parked at the diner, she allowed him to assist her from the truck, noticing that his strong grip on her waist did not release until she was steady on her feet. It felt comforting to be on a date with someone who wasn't trying to take over, but also wasn't ignoring her either.

Settling into the booth, they ordered their food and she was shocked when it came. A mountain of pancakes, eggs, bacon, and hash-browns were delivered.

"My God, how much do you eat?" she asked, surveying the mound.

Matt began to eat vigorously. "A lot," he said between bites. "I exercise quite a bit."

Giggling, she helped herself to a little of everything but was stuffed long before he was finished. Sitting there, she observed this man that had charged into her life in the past twenty-four hours. His dark hair was still wet from his shower, trimmed neatly but just shaggy enough to make her want to run her fingers through it. His biceps and pecs bulged and made her wonder how he ever found shirts that fit. She ran her eyes over his handsome face. Strong jaw, covered in stubble. Deep blue eyes. And yes, the scar that ran along his forehead. She was just about to ask how he got the scar when his cell phone rang.

Taking the call, Matt inwardly cursed. "Yeah, I'll be there. Give me fifteen minutes."

Looking across the table, he said, "Lily, I hate this but Shane just called. I've got to get into the station." He hated to leave their impromptu date, but he also remembered how angry Cassandra would get when he got a call.

"No problem, Matt. I hope everything is okay." Blushing, she said, "I guess that was a stupid thing to say, wasn't it? When a detective gets called in things are not okay. I should say that I hope you will be okay."

Standing, he took her hand and gently pulled her up with him as he threw some money down on the table. "Let me get you home, Lily."

"No, you need to hurry. I'll grab a cab." Glancing to his side, she said, "There's one now."

The cab pulled up and Matt leaned in to look at the driver. Checking his cab ID, he stated, "I'm a detective and you're going to treat this passenger as the precious cargo she is. You got me?"

The cabbie looked wide-eyes and nodded.

With that he pulled Lily in for a goodbye kiss that went on longer than he should have allowed. Looking down into her beautiful eyes, he said, "I'll call you later. Okay, baby?"

Feeling the kiss throughout her core, she managed to mumble, "Yeah."

He laughed as he saw her into the cab and watched them drive away.

Chapter 6

MONDAY MORNING FOUND Lily walking into the VanHuesen building for the first time since Ellen's murder the week before. Hesitating at the door, she stared at the handle for a moment before sucking in a deep breath and walking inside. Immediately the look of the receptionist was one of pity.

"Lily," she called over. "I'm to tell you to go straight to Mr. VanHuesen's office as soon as you arrive. You're not to go to your old office but to report directly to him."

Nodding her understanding, she moved to the elevator. *My old office. Oh Jesus, what did they do with the blood? Will I still work in there?* Heart pounding with unanswered questions as memories came flooding back, she nervously stepped off of the elevator onto the top floor.

Mr. VanHeusen's secretary looked up and immediately picked up the phone. "She is here now, sir. Yes."

"Ms. Swanson, you are to go straight into the boardroom now. You are expected."

Licking her lips, Lily had the strange sensation as though she were heading to the principal's office, but hadn't done anything wrong. The sound of her knocking on the door was simultaneous with the shaking of her legs.

"Come in."

Walking into the room, she was greeted by Malcolm VanHeusen himself as he rose from his seat and walked over to usher her to her chair. Déjà vu swept over her as she realized that the same people were in the room as the last time that she and Ellen were there. Curtis and Allen rose as she came in as well and Penelope was looking at her speculatively.

"How are you, my dear?" Malcolm asked.

Stunned by his conciliatory tone and endearment, she stammered, "F...fine. I'm fine." She sat in the chair indicated and clasped her hands in her lap.

"You can probably guess why we have called you in," he continued.

Her glance quickly flew around the room, but their faces gave her nothing. "Um...to be honest, I'm not quite sure."

"Well," Malcolm began smoothly. "We have had professional cleaners come to take care of your former space, but we felt as though you would be more comfortable in different offices."

Nodding slightly, she agreed. "That would be nice. I don't know that I could...well, work where...well..."

"It's fine," he interrupted. "The only thing is that we have not moved your computer stations or files. We didn't want to unhook anything until you were here in case there was information that would be lost. You will have to be in there this morning, but a member of our IT services will be with you to assist."

"Thank you, sir. That will be fine. I'll manage, I'm sure."

Silence descended upon the group and Lily nervously looked around the room to see the others staring at her. "Um, is there anything else?"

Malcolm's eyes cut over to Allen's before moving back to hers. "Well, Ms. Swanson. We were just wondering what you had been able to tell the police."

Eyes widening, she looked at him. "I don't know what you mean, sir. I just found her when I came back. I don't know what happened."

"No, no, of course not, my dear."

My dear? Why does he keep saying that? Sweat began trickling down her back as she felt the room closing in. *What does he want?*

"We were more curious as to why she was here so late and what she was working on. We wanted to know if there was anything suspicious that you know about."

Shaking her head, she replied, "I'm afraid I wasn't very helpful to the police. Most of her needs assessments were complete and she was just testing them against the programs I was developing so that I could tweak the codes if necessary."

His eyes bore into hers and she had the desire to look away. *He's just trying to protect his business, that's all.* Somehow that thought gave her no comfort under the intense gaze aimed her way.

"Well, we'll leave you to it. You will still report to Penelope and we will need to replace Ms. Marsh."

"My contracting company will be able to replace her with someone who has experience in this area. I hadn't worked with Ellen before this job, but there are several I have worked with before that would be excellent," she said.

"That won't be necessary. We will find a suitable replacement."

She looked at him in confusion, "But the parent company we work for would be responsible for a replacement."

Malcolm's eyes narrowed sharply before relaxing once again. "Yes well, we have discussed it and decided that we will take over the process now. Your contract job is secure. You will not be replaced, but we will be placing a new team member for you to work with."

Lily was confused but not willing to jeopardize her position by arguing with the boss. She merely nodded her acquiescence and tried to smile at the others around the table. Standing on shaky legs, she turned to walk out of the conference room when Malcolm's voice came back to her.

"Once you have determined what you need to have in the new office space, maintenance will move everything for you. With your disability, we don't want anything to happen."

"Disability?" she questioned.

"Your foot," he continued, looking down at her shoes.

"I do not have a disability, sir. I have a prosthesis if that is what you are referring to, but I am not disabled."

"Yes, whatever. We just don't want to be hit with another inconvenient loss during this process of our computer systems being re-written."

Inconvenient loss? She fought to keep her temper at his callous denunciation of Ellen's death. "I assure you I will be fine, sir. But I will definitely use the maintenance service." With that she turned and walked out of the room.

Shaking by the time she got to the elevator, she realized she had not asked where her new office would be. Running footsteps came up behind her as Allen hustled to her.

"Lily, don't let him get to you. He's an arrogant prick, you know that."

"No Allen, I really didn't. I just thought he was always a busy man who didn't have time for social niceties. And quite frankly, I prefer dealing with my codes and numbers anyway. But...he's...ugh."

By then, they had stepped into the elevator together.

"Yeah, but he is a brilliant medical director."

Lily snorted, but said nothing.

"Listen, you go do what you have to do in your old office and we'll grab lunch together. You'll need a friend to talk to by the time you deal with that."

Smiling she agreed. "Sure, just come get me when

you're ready."

Approaching the office door that she used to share with Ellen, she could see where the remnants of the police tape had been on the door. Taking a deep breath, she entered. The room looked similar to what had been left. The police had searched the room but had left it neat. *What was I expecting? That it would be trashed?*

Moving farther into the room, she could smell the antiseptic odor of the cleanser used. Her eyes involuntarily went to the carpet where Ellen's body had laid, but she saw no residual evidence other than a slight darkening of the carpet.

Go on. I can do this. Forcing herself to move forward she moved to the next smaller room and sat at her desk. Pulling up her computers and laptops, she booted everything up. Having missed a week of work, her email box was full. Sighing, she decided to tackle some of the emails before the IT person came in to help undo everything for the move.

Clicking through her emails, many could be deleted, several answered quickly, and there were several condolence emails as well. Saving the ones that would require responses, she came across several from Ellen, all work related. Tears stung the back of her eyes and she blinked rapidly trying to keep them at bay. *We'll never sit here and joke with one another again. We'll never gab over coffee as she tells me about her exciting weekends. I can't look at these emails now.* Then she noticed one with the subject line **8/8/88, A Riddle For You**. *That's odd. That was* *something that Ellen used to joke about was my birthday. My parents used to say that when I was born, the Chinese considered a birthday of all eights to be the luckiest day of the century. They used to tell me that until...* Shaking her head to stop her musings, she clicked on the email.

The content of the email was coded, but not a language that she recognized. Nervously glancing around as though she were guilty of something simply for looking at emails from someone who was deceased, she knew she didn't have time to deal with it before the IT person came. She quickly forwarded them to her personal email and then deleted and emptied the trash and recycle.

Right on cue, Chuck from IT walked in, pushing a cart. "Hey Ms. Swanson, are you ready to move? I hear they've got you a new office all set up in the basement."

"Basement?" she asked. "I didn't expect a suite of rooms with a corner office, but why the basement?"

"I wondered that myself. There's not much down there except some storage and well, that's where we're located."

"Fine. Whatever, as long as I'm out of here. Do you know if Andrea is already down there?"

"She was when I left there earlier." He grinned, saying, "She was complaining about the new accommodations."

Lily knew the building was filled with doctor offices and the administration offices as well, but was curious as to why there was no other place for her to be other than the basement. Soon she and Chuck were shutting down the equipment and he took a cart-full down to her new space. Maintenance came a few minutes later to get the office furniture. Following them down the elevator, she walked the long hall, hearing Andrea complaining already.

She couldn't help but smile as she entered, listening to Andrea fume.

"What the hell are we doing in the dungeon?" she ranted as she greeted Lily.

Shrugging, Lily said, "I don't know. I was called in-to a meeting this morning with Mr. VanHeusen, along with Curtis, Allen, and Penelope. I got the feeling I was somehow suspect. It felt weird."

The two women quickly worked to set up their space with the furniture and computer equipment. Chuck stayed to make sure everything was running correctly. Standing with her hands on her hips surveying the area, she was satisfied with the layout of her new office. Looking around, she lamented on the lack of windows when she noticed a small camera in the corner.

"What's that?" she asked.

Chuck looked up then replied, "Oh that's a security camera."

Her head whipped around. "Security camera? Do they think we're unsafe down here?"

He just shrugged. "Who knows? Maybe they just want to keep an eye on things."

Lily felt an odd sense of being watched already and hated the idea that someone was peering in on her. *I keep being asked if there was anything going on that Ellen knew about. We're just contracted and until about three months ago, neither Ellen nor I had ever stepped into this building.*

Nervously, she sat in her chair and began turning on her computers again. Remembering the email that she forwarded to her personal email, she was anxious to look at it again when she got off work. Getting an email from someone now deceased was eerie.

Several hours later, a knock on the door interrupted her thoughts. Looking up she saw Allen smiling at her.

"Oh my gosh, is it lunchtime already?"

"Nice digs you got here," he joked, looking around.

"Yeah. Nothing but the penthouse suite for little ol' me!"

They walked to a pizza restaurant nearby and quickly found outside tables to sit at. After ordering, Allen leaned back and asked, "So how are you really doing?"

Sighing, she replied, "Honestly? I'm still in shock. Ellen and I weren't good friends and we had only been working together for a few months on this project. But she was nice and pleasant to work with. We would occasionally have lunch and chat. It just still seems unreal.

"And you know what else is driving me crazy? First, I am questioned by the police about her death, which I knew nothing about. Then, I'm questioned by them again, to see if there was something we were working on. Which there wasn't. And this morning. I mean, what the hell was that? Malcolm calling me 'my dear' and wanting to know if there was something I could tell you all."

"I don't think he's implying anything. You know how he is about publicity. He doesn't want anything to affect the company's stock so he is probably just making sure. But I will tell you who I don't trust."

Lily looked up in curiosity. "Who's that?"

"Dr. Curtis Bennett. That prick thought he had Malcolm in his back pocket. He's been preening for years, trying to rise up in the company. Took over the pharmaceutical side of the medical company and has been angling to get the job that just got handed to Penelope."

"Lily," a deep voice rumbled behind her.

Twisting to see a very unhappy looking Matt standing nearby she smiled. "Matt! What are you doing here?"

"I got tied up in work yesterday and wanted to see how your first day back was. I was told you were out to lunch."

"This is Dr. Allen Purser. Allen this is Detective Matt Dixon."

"Detective? Lily, are they still after you?" Allen asked, glaring up at Matt.

Matt's growl was his answer and Lily quickly felt at a loss as to how to mediate between two males.

"No, he's not after me. I mean not that way." Blushing when Allen looked at her quizzically, she tried to explain again. "I mean he's not a detective after me. He's just a detective. But..."

Matt placed his hand on her shoulder, gently rubbing. "It's okay, babe." Sitting down in the seat next to her, he stared at Allen and continued. "What she means is that I am a detective. I am not investigating her. And I am interested in her. You got any more questions, doctor?"

Allen laughed saying, "No. I'd say that just about covers it. Tell you what. I'll get my pizza to go and you two can enjoy your lunch." Before Lily could protest, he hopped up and headed back into the restaurant.

"Matt. What was that all about?" she hissed.

He stared at her beauty for a moment before answering. Her long hair was pulled back from her face with a headband, leaving her curls to cascade down her back. Her usual slacks were paired with a pale blue blouse with blue sneakers on her feet.

Shaking his head to focus on her scowling face, he answered, "LilyBelle, that was a man letting another man know that the girl was claimed."

"Claimed?" she sputtered. "You just called me claimed?"

"Baby," he said leaning in closely. "That was not an insult. I don't mean that in a demeaning way. I simply mean that you're mine. For that matter, it means that I'm yours too."

Her face was still doubtful so he took another tactic. "Are you dating anyone else?"

Surprised, she exclaimed, "Of course not."

"Do you want me seeing anyone else?"

Squirming in her chair, she was uncomfortable with answering. "I…can't keep you from seeing someone else if you want to. I don't want to…make demands…"

"Baby. Just answer the question from your heart. Do you want me to see anyone else?"

Shyly looking down at her hands, she replied, "No." His silence had her looking back into his face, seeing the wide grin across his perfect face.

"Then there you have it. Until we decide differently, you're mine and I'm yours. I'm not saying you can't have a lunch with a friend but that darlin', was one man talking to another man in a way that clears the air."

The pizza came and they enjoyed lunch while catching up on the last couple of days. She explained her work situation and everything she told him alarmed him. *Two women, working alone in the basement of a large building. A security camera in the corner. What's VanHeusen's game?*

Vowing to do some checking, he kept his concerns from her other than to admonish her to be very careful. As their lunch time came to an end, he escorted her back to her building. Standing outside, hopefully in full view of any security cameras on the outside of the building, he pulled her into his arms.

"Matt, I shouldn't kiss you here in front of my workplace."

"We're not in your workplace. We're on the sidewalk." With that he tightened his embrace and bent down to take her mouth. The kiss was long, hard and wet. If he was honest with himself, he started it to show anyone who might be watching the cameras who she was with. But it quickly became a kiss between lovers, as though both of their souls were reaching out to each other.

Pulling back he stared into her eyes. "I want to see you tonight," he said, voice husky with need.

Lips swollen with kisses, she just muttered, "Yeah. I want that too."

"We won't ever do more than you're comfortable with babe, but you gotta know – you tempt me more than I have ever wanted another woman. I want you. But LilyBelle, it'll always be about you."

With a parting kiss, he sent her back inside, dreaming about what would come that evening.

He wasn't the only one watching her enter the building.

★ ★ ★

(Surveillance)

"DO YOU THINK she knows anything?"

"If she did, that detective would already be all over it."

"Do you think she can find out anything?"

"Jesus, stop asking me dumb-fuck questions. I don't know what she can and can't find out."

"Well, we didn't think that Ellen woman could find out anything either and look where that got us."

"It was never proven that she knew anything. She just kept asking questions and snooping around."

"No shit."

"Yeah, well, I don't think anyone thought her line of questions would lead her down the path she started going."

"And look where that got her. Dead."

"Keep an eye on peg-leg. If she starts snooping too, she'll find the ending of her contract the same way that Marsh woman did."

Chapter 7

THAT EVENING WHILE waiting on Matt to come over, Lily sat down on her sofa and pulled her personal email up on her laptop. There were the emails from Ellen. They all dealt with data that she was working on that she usually sent to Lily each evening. Nothing surprising. Nothing new. Just Ellen being her efficient self.

Lily began to think for the first time about what Ellen's evening must have been like. Working late. Shooting off emails. Cleaning off her desk. Lily smiled. *Ellen always wanted her desk clean when she left so that she could come in the next morning to start fresh. Me? I leave one disastrous mess from one day to the next. It was something we joked about.* The tears threatened again but Lily wiped them away quickly.

Moving to the next email, she opened it up again, looking at the body of the message.

8/8/88 Aren't birthdays fun? I remember the dinner we had a few months ago when we celebrated. Remember the bartender, Rick? Hope we can go again and see him. If you ever go without me, be sure to tell him hello from me.

The next part of the message was lines and lines of computer code but not in the language that they were using for the VanHeusen project. In fact, she didn't recognize it.

She thought back to her last birthday when she and Ellen got drinks after work. Nothing special had occurred and in fact the celebration only last about an hour. *Bartender? I don't even remember a bartender.*

She printed off the email and then downloaded it to a thumb drive before deleting and trashing. She closed her laptop and then grabbed the message off the printer. *Is this another one of her riddles?* Ellen had promised that she was going to create a programing code that would confuse even Lily. Not in the mood to try to look at it that evening, she folded it carefully and put it in her purse. *Later, when I can work on it and not cry.*

Pippi was jumping around her legs begging for attention. Lily leaned over and scooped the small dog up in her arms, receiving a round of licks in response.

"Oh, Pip. I used to love going to work, but now with everything being so crazy and creepy, I would like to just stay home with you." The idea of working from home began to take root and she wondered if Mr. VanHeusen would ever agree to it. *I could bring the files that Ellen worked on home and just write my code from home. In my pajamas. In my bed.*

Before she could ponder those thoughts any more, she checked on the time knowing that Matt would be over soon. She went to the bedroom to change clothes.

Looking down at her prosthesis, she wondered what his reaction would be if they continued their relationship. At least he's not a weirdo, she thought as she pushed away the memories of a few propositions that had come her way over the years.

Deciding to be bold, she dressed in a flowing ankle length skirt and peasant blouse. *He saw the prosthesis when I was running, so he shouldn't be shocked.* Breathing deeply to stave off her nerves, she nonetheless jumped when her doorbell rang.

Opening the door, she stared at the man on her porch. *How did I get so lucky?* Matt was wearing a navy t-shirt that was tight across his chest and biceps. His waist tapered deliciously into his jeans that fit snugly over his manhood. Tall, dark and...grinning right at her.

"Baby, you keep looking at me like that and we won't make it through dinner."

Blushing, she stepped back allowing him to enter. The smell of Chinese wafted through the hallway as he came into the kitchen. Pulling down the plates, she quickly set the table as he put the food out.

The conversation flowed and they laughed and talked throughout the meal. Cleaning up afterwards, they moved into the living room, sitting on the sofa. He twisted his body to face hers and she propped her left foot on the coffee table and tucked her right leg under her. She saw his eyes travel down the length of her, ending at her feet before moving back to her face.

"It's okay, you know. To look, I mean. It doesn't make me nervous. At least not with you. People are going to stare and that's okay. Kids even ask questions and that's okay too. But I don't mind. Not anymore. I guess I used to feel weird, but not now." Giggling, she admitted, "Okay, I'm babbling, aren't I?"

"A little," he agreed while grinning. Looking back down at her toes, he commented, "You paint your toenails?"

Untucking her right leg, she placed both feet on the coffee table. "Yep. When I paint my toenails, I go ahead and paint the toenail places on this foot," she said pointing to her prosthesis. "Sometimes I can even wear sandals, although I prefer sneakers. I'm more comfortable with shoes that have rubber on the bottom."

They were quiet for a moment, then he reached out and grasped her hand giving a gentle pull. "Come here, baby."

Sliding over, she allowed him to pull her into his lap as he captured her lips with his. The kiss started out soft. A slow moving of lips. Then his tongue slid into her open mouth and the kiss became hungry. Their tongues danced around each other and as he explored every crevice of her delicious mouth, she sucked on his tongue, eliciting the most delectable sounds.

Growling, he took over the kiss as he angled her mouth for deeper access. One hand slid down to her ass, kneading the soft globes, while the other hand slid the peasant blouse off of her shoulder. He kissed her exposed shoulder, sucking on the tender skin under her neck. His hand continued to pull the blouse down until it was under her breasts. Pulling her bra cups down as well, he latched onto a nipple, sucking it deeply into his mouth.

Lily gasped as the tug on her nipple had her throwing her head back in ecstasy. She felt him move between nipples and she moaned at the sensations that jolted from her breasts to her core. Feeling herself become wet, she began to move back and forth on his lap, trying to ease the need for friction.

While his mouth continued its ministrations on her breasts, he moved his hand up under her skirt until he found the prize. Her panties were soaked, just like he remembered from the first night they met and he slipped his finger underneath them. Plunging his finger inside her waiting pussy, he began a rhythm of nipple sucking in time with the movement of his fingers.

Lily felt the pressure building and she knew her release was near. But this was how it ended in the truck and she wanted to take care of him too. "Stop," she said.

Immediately Matt stopped everything he was doing and looked into her face. "Are you okay baby?" he asked with concern.

"I don't mean I want to stop," she moaned, pulling his face to hers. "I just want to make sure you're taken care of this time."

Smiling, he kissed her lips. "Oh, don't worry about me, darlin'. We're just gettin' started." He immediately continued where he left off and in just a moment she was crying out his name with her head thrown back and the beautiful flush making her glow.

"You ready to move this to the bedroom? I want you to be sure," he asked.

Smiling the lazy smile of one recently sated, she said, "I'm sure."

Standing with her in his arms, he walked to the back of the house and into the master bedroom. Laying her down on the bed, he stood and stared at the beauty in front of him. He had thought Cassandra was beautiful in her perfectly coiffed way. But Lily's simplistic, natural beauty took his breath away.

"I'd like to undress you. Is that all right?"

She nodded, hoping that this evening was going to go the way she wanted. *Please don't let him be grossed out. Please let this be okay.*

He leaned over the bed and pulled her blouse off then quickly removed her bra. Her breasts were full and rosy tipped and he couldn't help but give a quick suck to each one as they were exposed. The wetness from his mouth and the exposure to the cool air had them puckered and waiting. As he slid her skirt down her legs, his mouth latched over a nipple again, this time nipping it with his teeth then sucking to sooth the sting.

Lily moaned and writhed on the bed, pulling his head back to her lips.

He rose back up and slipped her panties down her legs as well, completely exposing her beautiful body to his perusal. Perfect. Her left leg ended half-way down her calf and the prosthesis completed her leg and foot. He hesitated, not sure of what she was comfortable with.

"What would you like me to do, LilyBelle?"

Her pink tongue darted out and ran nervously along her bottom lip as she replied, "I'd like to take it off, if you don't mind."

She sat up on the bed and leaned over her leg. Unlatching the pinlock on the prosthesis, she slipped it off and set it on the floor next to the bed. There were several socks over the prosthesis liner and she slid those off as well.

She spared a look up at Matt, terrified of what she would see. His eyes met hers, shining with encouragement not disgust. Sucking her lips in, she hesitated.

"It's okay, baby. We'll go at your pace. Always at your pace," he assured.

"Um…I think for now, I'd like to turn the lights off…and just maybe leave the light on in the bathroom."

Matt rose and flipped the switch on the wall turning off the bedroom lights before walking to the bathroom. Turning on that light and almost closing the door allowed a sliver of light to give a slight illumination to the bedroom.

By the time he had returned to the bed, she had slipped off the liner and had covered her residual limb with a soft sock-like covering.

Looking at him in concern, she admitted, "Um, maybe I can leave the covering on for now?"

"Baby, we're gonna do whatever makes you comfortable."

Nodding, she smiled. Leaning back on the bed, she opened her arms for him to come. Her blonde hair spread out on the pillow behind her, warm brown eyes shining.

Not wasting another minute, he quickly divested himself of his clothes. Grabbing a condom from his jeans pocket, he quickly rolled it on.

She looked at his cock protruding from his body and she wondered how it would fit. *What if it doesn't?* As she looked back up at his face, she saw the smile on his face.

"It'll fit, babe. I'll make sure of that," he said with pride.

Climbing on the bed, he knelt between her legs and used his hands to gently part her legs further. He licked her pussy lips before plunging his tongue inside.

Lily had never felt such a sensation and as he took her near the edge again and she threw her head back. Feeling him pull out, she started to protest until she felt him suck her clit into his mouth and with that she screamed his name as he pulled her over the edge and her orgasm roared through her. Laying there sated, she felt him move up her body and place his cock at her entrance.

Grabbing his shoulders, she pulled him to her as he

plunged his cock to the hilt. The pain was intense for a moment and she gasped, wide-eyed at the feeling of fullness.

Matt looked down suddenly, his face full of surprise. "Lily?" he questioned. "Are you a virgin?"

Swallowing nervously, she replied, "No."

He held her stare and she began to avert her eyes. "Lily?" he repeated.

"Well, I'm not. At least not anymore," she admitted.

"Jesus, you could have told me!"

Her eyes filled with tears at the thought of ruining things. "I just wanted...I just..."

"What babe?" he said softly.

She looked into his beautiful blue eyes. "I just wanted it to be normal. Not poor little Lily that no man would want."

"Oh baby. You're not poor little Lily to me and anyone who ever made you feel that way is a piece of shit." He gathered her in his arms, wrapping them around her body, willing his comfort to blanket her.

The pressure of having his dick inside her was beginning to build and she began moving her hips back and forth. "Please Matt. I need..."

"What do you need, baby?

"I need you. Now!"

Grinning, he said "Yes ma'am," before capturing her lips in a soul searing kiss again. Moving gently in and out, he allowed her pussy to acclimate to his girth before he began plunging harder and faster. Her walls grabbed at his cock and the tightness almost had him coming immediately.

Keeping a watch on her face to make sure she wasn't in pain, he saw her eyes closed with a look of ecstasy radiating from her. *Jesus, is this what love is like? I thought I was in love before but I never experienced this.*

"Come on, baby. I want you to come one more time to make it easier on you."

Not understanding what he meant, she nonetheless felt herself climbing once again to the precipice. The prize was just out of her reach and she began to move her hips in time with his to help her get there.

Leaning down he sucked her nipple deeply in his mouth once again and that was all it took for her to fly apart. Throwing her head back against the pillow she held him as he continued to power through his own release. A roar ripped through him as his orgasm was milked by her slick, tight pussy walls.

He crashed down on top, barely aware that he was crushing her. Their ragged breathing sounded loudly in the quiet of the room and as he became aware again he rolled to the side taking her with him. With his arms wrapped tightly around her, he pressed her head to his chest.

Lily smiled as she realized that she had experienced her first sexual encounter with someone that she loved. *Loved?* Her eyes flew open as she lay next to him, her body held flush against his. Smiling again, she realized that she did love him.

"You okay, baby?" his rough voice rumbled against her cheek.

She leaned back so that she could stare into his beautiful eyes. "I'm great, honey," she said honestly.

Grinning, he kissed her lips gently. "Oh, you're more than great, LilyBelle. You're perfect!"

"Are you upset with me, about...you know?" she said blushing.

Matt looked down at the woman in his arms. He knew it made him a caveman, but the fact that she had given her virginity to him made his chest swell with pride. He had something of hers that would always belong to him.

"Babe, there's no way any man in his right mind would be upset about the gift you just gave me. I'll cherish it forever just like I plan on cherishing you."

The smile on her face was worth a thousand kisses and it took his breath away. She lifted her hand and rubbed her fingers over his lips, around the tiny lines at his eyes and then smoothed his scar on his forehead.

He immediately stiffened.

"Don't honey," she pleaded. "Don't back away from me."

"Why doesn't this scar bother you?" he asked.

Her forehead crinkled in surprise. "Bother me? Matt, you must be kidding? I don't know how you got this scar, but knowing you it was probably something heroic. And good grief, look at me. I'm missing the bottom of my leg! You think a scar is going to bother me?"

When it was put to him that way, he suddenly felt a weight lifted. Never having been a vain man, it stunned him how he had let his ex-fiancé make him feel inadequate. As though the scar devalued the man.

Leaning down to snag the covers, he pulled them over their cooling bodies.

"Are you going to stay with me?" she asked, smiling.

"Is that okay, babe?"

Exhaling the breath that she had been holding, she said, "Absolutely."

And with that, they both slept peaceful in the knowledge that acceptance was one of the keys to falling in love.

THE NEXT MORNING, they left for work together and she couldn't help but think how she would love to experience this every day. *One step at a time. Things are new and men don't like to be crowded. Well, at least that's what the magazines say.*

As she walked into the office, Andrea looked up and gave her a pointed stare before cutting her eyes to the back work room where Lily's computer equipment was located. Before she could ask about Andrea's cryptic look, a woman walked back from the other office.

Tall, elegant looking with her hair pulled back in a French-twist, stylishly dressed with sky-high heels, Lily noted the air in the office immediately chilled. The lady's eyes swept over Lily from her head to her feet, holding for a moment at her feet. She walked over and offered her hand to Lily, "Hello. I am Carla Montrose. Malcolm has hired me to take charge here and continue the work that you've been doing."

"I'm Lily," she said simply, feeling suddenly uneasy. "Are you replacing Ellen for the needs assessment coordination?"

Carla smiled and explained, "I've been given the responsibility by Malcolm to look over all of Ms. Marsh's work before her untimely demise, and then you are to continue your work but it's to be passed through me before any implementation may occur."

Untimely demise? Who the hell speaks that way?

Pulling herself up to her full height, which was admittedly six inches shorter than Carla's, she decided to play hard-ball. "Do you code? Do you understand the language in which my codes are written?"

She noticed the flash of uncertainty in Carla's eyes before being replaced immediately with her air of superiority once again.

"No, I am not familiar with the code you are working in, but Malcolm has granted me access to be able to send samples of your work to other software engineers who will check your work."

"I'm not sure if you are familiar with the contract that I and my parent company have with VanHeusen Medical Corporation, but I would advise you to check into it. My company does not share its work with other companies, especially with engineers who may be working for software competitors."

At this, Carla's face settled into a look of distaste as her eyes cut back and forth between Lily and Andrea. "I see. Well, I will take this up with Malcolm and we will go from there."

With an insincere smile on Lily's face, she agreed, "You do that. Now if you will excuse me, I need to get to work." Turning, she walked into the workroom and fired up her computers. She heard the outer door close and Andrea came running in.

"Oh my God! What a piece of work that woman is!" Andrea exclaimed. "She was looking down her nose at me before you got here, but I thought she would tone it down with you."

Lily shook her head saying, "Did you see the look she gave me? As soon as she saw my leg she considered me to be inferior. It doesn't happen often but it does happen."

Andrea's face registered shock. "But...but...that's just...just dumb!"

Laughing, Lily agreed. "Some people make the assumption that if there is a physical limitation then I must be mentally challenged as well."

"But you are the smartest woman I know."

A sincere smile lit Lily's face. "Thank you. I'm certainly not the smartest, but I will not be treated as though I am below her or anyone for that matter."

"I think you surprised her," Andrea said, giggling.

"People assume that because I'm more introverted that I can't roar. I assure you I can roar with the best of them," Lily said defiantly.

Andrea went back to work and Lily pulled up her files on her computers. It was hard to concentrate with thoughts of Carla rolling through her mind. *Malcolm. She referred to him as Malcolm. What is their relationship? Why would he hire someone who didn't do software engineering? What is she after?* Her mind rolled over the past couple of weeks and the many times that she had been asked what Ellen was working on, assuming that her death had been tied into the job. *But there is nothing special we were doing.*

She worked through the morning and decided to take a quick lunch break on her own. "Andrea, I'm going to run down the street to the deli. Do you want anything?"

"Sure," and she quickly gave her the order.

The roads were crowded as usual, but Lily made her way across the road to the deli. A few minutes later, she was walking back across the street when she heard someone yell, "Watch it lady!" Turning quickly, she saw a black sedan with dark window barreling directly toward her. She barely managed to maneuver out of the way before throwing herself onto the edge of the road away from the speeding car.

People ran over to assist and someone dialed 911. "I'm fine, I'm fine," she kept saying as people crowded around. The police arrived quickly along with an ambulance. She recognized one of the policemen from Shane and Annie's party. Sitting in the back of the ambulance a few minutes later getting her scratches treated, she heard the squeal of tires and looked up to see Matt and Shane jumping out of their vehicle. Matt's face was dark with anger as he stalked over. Before she could reassure him that she was fine, he grabbed her up in his arms, swung around and sat down with her in his lap.

"Report," he ordered the policeman who was first on the scene. As the man began to speak, Lily twisted around to look into his face.

"Matt! I'm right here. You can ask me what happened."

He closed his eyes for a moment, gathering his wits before speaking. When the call came from his friend in the unit that had responded to a possible pedestrian hit and run and the victim had been his Lily, his heart stopped. Shane insisted on driving, knowing that Matt would have killed them getting them to the scene. He felt a small hand on his face and he opened his eyes to her beautiful chocolate eyes staring back.

"I'm okay honey."

Shane had moved in and knew what Matt was dealing with having had situations like this with Annie.

"What happened, Lily?"

"I was walking across the street and I heard someone scream for me to watch out. I twisted around to see a black car with all dark windows speeding and they were coming straight for me. I wasn't even in the middle of their lane and they were headed for me. I guess they must have lost control of their car," she added naively.

Matt and Shane shared a look over the top of her head, then Matt's face hardened into a grimace. He cut his eyes over to the EMT and asked him for his assessment.

"She's fine sir. She scraped her elbows and arms a little when she landed on the sidewalk. I know her legs were twisted a bit too, but they seem fine. She hasn't walked since the incident, so I can't report on her prosthesis." He looked at her and continued, "Ma'am. I would suggest that you walk on it for a bit, then if it feels uncomfortable at all then you take it to your prosthetist to have it checked."

Nodding, she agreed. Looking up at Matt's face, she said, "Honey you can let go of me. I need to see if I can walk."

He reluctantly set her down on her feet, but held on to her hips as she tested out walking a few yards.

"It seems fine. It doesn't feel different at all. I really need to get back to work."

Kissing him quickly goodbye, she hurried inside.

Shane turned to Matt. "What are you thinkin', bro?"

"This was no coincidence. I'm calling Tony right now. Goddamnit. I should have called him when I first saw her house." Rubbing his hand over his face, he swore again as he pulled out his cell, walking away.

Coming back a few minutes later, he looked at Shane. "Tony's heading out there now. He'll do a preliminary work up and then he can get his men to install it tomorrow."

Driving back to the station, they discussed the situation. "There's got to be something that Ellen was working on. Something that she found out. Something that Lily has no idea about."

"But if someone thinks Lily knows then they could be coming after her."

"Fuck that. I'm staying with her or she's moving in with me."

Shane looked over at his friend and grinned. "So it's goin' that way?"

"Hell yeah. This woman's everything."

"Annie called it, you know? Suzanne too."

"What are you talking about?"

"You and Lily. Suzanne and Annie decided a while back that if they could get the two of you together, you'd be great."

"Jesus fuck, bro. Can't you keep that woman of yours in line?" Matt joked.

"Sure, about as much as you can control your quiet little spitfire back there. Are you sure she's gonna agree to move in with you?"

Sighing, Matt said, "I have no idea."

Once into the station, they were called into the chief's office. He looked up from his desk and asked about Lily.

"She's fine sir, but it seems as though there was a hit and run."

The chief looked up sharply. "What do you think it means?"

Matt answered, "I don't know. We think it may have something to do with the death of Ellen Marsh. I'm gonna talk to the homicide guys this afternoon and see what they have found."

"Based on these new developments, I'm calling them in. I have no idea if Ms. Marsh's death is tied into the drug cases you're working on but considering that she was working for a medical company and the murder occurred there, it's worth looking at."

"Thank you, sir."

"Do you think Lily Swanson is in danger?"

"I don't know sir, but I intend to take action to make sure that she is safe."

The chief smiled as he looked between Shane and Matt. "So, first Shane falls and now it's your turn. Wondered when you'd get over that other woman you were hooked up with last year."

Ducking his head, he grinned. "Yes, sir. I've fallen all right. This time to a worthy woman. One that I plan on protecting…and keeping."

Chapter 8

SEVERAL DAYS LATER, the couples were out for a dinner date. Matt had Tony completely set up Lily's house with state of the art security and had it wired in to not only the police, but to Alvarez's Security Company. He hadn't shared the total cost with her, knowing that she would be upset with the arrangements. He had Tony send her a portion of the bill as though that was the final cost and he paid the rest. He didn't care as long as she was protected.

The dinner was fun, with both couples sharing stories and laughs. The men shared anecdotes of their stranger police adventures and Annie talked about her sillier moments with her animals and their owners at her veterinary practice. As Lily listened attentively, she realized that she was completely relaxed in the company of others. *Good friends make a difference.*

Matt's phone rang and he answered it, listening for just a moment.

"We gotta roll," Matt called to Shane as he hung up. "Some neighbors reported a loud party going on in the house next to them and when the patrolmen arrived, a large number of pharmaceutical drugs were found."

Annie and Lily looked up from dinner and expressed concern.

"Are you all going to be all right? You haven't hardly been able to touch your steak," Annie said.

"I'm sorry, baby, but we gotta go. Box it up for me and don't let Sarge have any," Shane said, referring to his dog.

Leaning over to kiss Lily, Matt said, "You ladies stay and enjoy dinner, but make sure to lock up when you get home." Turning to Annie, he asked, "Since we'll take my truck, can you take Lily home?"

"Oh honey, I can just take a cab."

He swung his irritated gaze to her but before he could speak, Annie piped up quickly, "Of course I'll take her home."

"Mind if I come over to your house when this is all finished? It may be in the wee hours." Seeing her smile in response, he kissed her soundly then turned to join Shane as they walked out.

Once inside the truck, Shane asked his friend, "So I take it you haven't shared your concerns with Lily about her safety."

"I don't know what the fuck to do. I don't want to worry her, but I just can't be with her all the time."

"Well just so you know, I told Annie so that she was aware."

Nodding, Matt thanked him.

Desperate for a break in the drug cases that were piling up, they were hopeful for some leads to tie them together. Arriving at the home, they noted the upscale neighborhood.

"The more money the kids have, the more designer drugs they can buy," Matt commented ruefully.

The house was well-lit and the number of police cars in the vicinity indicated how large the party had been. Going inside of the house, they bypassed the rooms filled with teens that were being arrested or having their parents called. Some were in tears, some stoned, and other cussing or threatening the police. "Wait until my dad's lawyer gets hold of this you fucking dick."

Shane and Matt looked at each other in disgust. "Jesus," Shane commented. "If I had spoken that way to an adult when I was that punk's age, my dad woulda…" He paused a moment remembering his wonderful father who had also been a detective. "Hell Matt, I can't even imagine that scenario."

Nodding, Matt agreed. "It's fucked, but some of those kids in there who have rich daddies will get off with nothing and the others will be doing some time."

They continued through the house until they arrived at the kitchen, which was the gathering point of the drugs that had been confiscated. Hundreds of pills of various shapes and sizes were piled on the table. Prescription bottles littered the area. Matt quickly recognized that most of the drugs were Oxycodone, although there was plenty of variety.

One of the vice detectives that was already on the scene reported, "According to what some of the kids were saying most of the Oxycodone came from Jeff Roberts. His parents live about three doors down and are out of town. He's eighteen so he could be looking at some time. We've got him in the dining room right now. I think they are separating the ones who were just here using from the suppliers."

Matt glanced in the room next to the kitchen, seeing some handcuffed teens sitting at the table. "Dumb-fuck kids. Don't have a goddamn clue they'll be charged for distributing as well as possession, using and on top of that, are now adults."

"You can't arrest me. I've done nothing wrong. My dad's lawyer will eat you for breakfast," came a voice from the dining room.

Matt and Shane walked in, scanning the area. Matt walked over to the young man, handcuffed and red faced, wearing designer jeans and a polo shirt, showing off his muscular build. "You Jeff Roberts?"

The young man defiantly looked up at him with a sneer. "Who the fuck wants to know?"

Matt's eyes glanced to the others around the table before pulling his gaze back to the young man. The teens next to him looked on, wide-eyed and tearful.

Matt leaned in closely, looking carefully. "Your eyes are clear. You're not high."

The young man reared back, his eyes narrowing in suspicion. "What the fuck is your problem, man?"

Matt smiled a slow smile, the corners of his mouth turning up a bit at a time. "Not my problem, dick-head.

But will be yours. You're not here using. That means your whole purpose for being here is to sell. With all that shit on the kitchen table that we won't have any trouble identifying who it belongs to, so you're looking at hard time."

Fear flashed through the young man's eyes before being replace by bravado. "My dad's lawyer gets this, I'll be out in no time."

"Hear you got a football scholarship waiting for you?"

The young man blinked a couple of time as though to bring the bravado back to the forefront.

"Don't know of a school that's gonna keep their money on a drug dealer who will have a jail sentence waitin' on them."

"My dad's lawy-"

"You still tryin' to hide behind your dad? Jesus, fuck. Pull yourself up like a man and stop acting like a wuss." Looking over at the cops in the room, Matt said, "Get him outta here. In fact, go ahead and take the others too. Book them and then let their parent's come to the jail to pick them up."

He and Shane headed back to the kitchen to note more of the evidence. "There's got to be half a million street value laying on this goddamn table."

One of the detectives looked up as they were leaving. "You gonna interrogate them now?"

It was late, but needed to happen. "Yeah, we're heading back to the station." He looked over at Shane, who agreed. "Guess we'll let our women know it'll be a late night."

Later, they were sitting in the interrogation room with Jeff Roberts and his lawyer. His lawyer had first advised him to keep quiet until the detectives realized who Jeff's father was. Dr. James Roberts. And more interestingly, he worked for the VanHeusen Medical Corporation. As soon as the lawyer understood the implications for Jeff's father, he immediately began to encourage him to cooperate.

Jeff turned angrily to the lawyer, "What the fuck man? You're supposed to be looking out for me."

The lawyer leaned in to whisper to his client, "Jeff, you're eighteen years old although you are still in high school. Your father has retained me and I cannot represent both of you in this case. Your actions are likely to harm your father's reputation."

"Fuck his reputation!" Jeff bit out, fear beginning to seep across his face for the first time.

The lawyer excused himself to talk to Jeff's father about retaining a different law firm for his son.

The men sat in the room for a few minutes letting the silence drag on. Jeff's eyes darted nervously between them.

"What happens now?" he finally asked.

"Well, a lot depends on you. You might as well know that your friends are rollin' on you left and right."

"I wasn't the only one bringing in shit," he defended.

"Gonna be honest. I want you taken down, but I'm more interested in where you got those drugs. You start talking about that and shut up about your damn dad's lawyer and the judge might be willing to reduce a sentence."

Jeff contemplated for a few minutes.

"So what's it gonna be?"

"I don't know," he bit out angrily.

"You don't know what?" Matt answered back sharply.

"I don't know where they come from."

Matt stood, motioning to Shane. "Let's go. This loser's got nothin' to tell us."

"No, I'm telling the truth. I don't know who gets them for me."

Matt stared at him a long time. Sitting down slowly, he continued, "Let me tell you how this is gonna go. Detective Douglas and myself were having an amazing steak dinner with our ladies. You interrupted our dinner and we hate having our dinners interrupted. Now we've spent half the night listenin' to your bullshit and we hate havin' to listen to your bullshit. So you're either gonna start talking or we're gonna go back to our ladies and you'll sit in jail, contemplating the length of your sentence. And since you're eighteen, you won't be in juvie like some of your friends. You'll be in jail. You got me?"

His words seemed to finally sink in to Jeff and he began to cooperate.

Looking down at his hands on the table, he said, "I don't know where they come from. I have a place where I go when I need them."

"Who do you meet with?"

"There's a strip joint down near the warehouses by the docks. I get them in the alley behind the club."

"Details, Jeff. We want to hear exactly how this works."

He looked fearfully into Matt's face. "I was at a party about six months ago and a bunch of us were getting high passing around shit and stuff. I was bragging about my dad being a doctor and how easy it would be to get my hands on stuff. I later got approached by some dude I'd never seen before and he told me to get some stuff for him from my dad and he'd make sure I made good money. I didn't really have a way to get anything from my dad, so I just took a bunch of pain pills from our house."

"Where'd you get it?"

"You know. Just stuff left over. I had pain pills from my last football injury. My sister had some left over from when she had her wisdom teeth out. My dad's back hurts, so he had some. I brought them to the next party and the guy gave me four hundred bucks for it all. Then I watched him turn around and sell it all for probably a total of about a thousand dollars. Jesus, what a profit."

"Keep going. How did you get more?"

"He told me that if I would sell them at parties and

get others to do the same, he would keep me supplied."

"And you, rich boy, just decided to jump at the chance to make that kind of money."

"No! It wasn't like that. I didn't want to get more involved, but he said he would let people know that my dad had supplied them. I couldn't let them do that to him. So I started." Shrugging his large shoulders, "Then I got deeper. The more I sold, the more I couldn't get out."

"So go back to the nightclub."

"I have a number I text when I need more. I'm texted back a date and time. I go the alley behind the club and there will be a package for me taped to the inside of the dumpster."

"And the money?"

"I take my cut and then put the rest in a bag and tape it to the dumpster where I got the pills."

"You ever seen anyone, other than the first guy at the party?"

"No, no one."

Matt and Shane rose from the table and turned to walk out.

"Hey. What about me?

Looking back over his shoulder, Matt shrugged and said, "Guess you wait for daddy's new lawyer to show up."

As the two detectives made their way back over to their desks, Matt looked at his watch. "Jesus, it's three a.m. Let's wrap up the initial report and get the hell outta here."

"You got no argument from me about that. I'd like to at least wake up in bed with Annie." Glancing over at Matt, he asked, "What about Lily and your late nights? Does she deal with them?"

"Yeah," he answered grinning. "I know she hates it for me, but she doesn't make me feel like an ass because my job has me going out at night."

An hour later, Matt had the chance to show Lily just how much he appreciated her allowing him to do his job. And after she came twice, he tucked her into his embrace and fell into a deep, peaceful sleep.

SEVERAL DAYS LATER, Lily worked late trying to finish a particularly difficult code. Standing to stretch her back, she walked around the room for a moment. She was more tired than she had been in a long time. Matt had a new security system installed in her home and insisted on staying nights when he could. Smiling to herself, she couldn't say she minded. *It certainly makes my nights more exciting* she thought, remembering their discovering of each other's bodies. She still hadn't taken off the residual leg covering. *Not yet. I'm not ready for that yet.* But he had been patient.

The relationship with Carla, while not strained, was certainly not what she shared with Ellen. Carla had reviewed Ellen's files and data, but seemed unsatisfied. She questioned Lily several times about what they worked on and Lily had repeatedly answered her questions, specifically and to the point. *What the hell do they think we were working on? State secrets? A new invention? Jesus, we just wrote computer programs for their new prescription base.*

Carla and Andrea had left, but Lily wanted to stay for just a little bit longer. She had finished with one part of her program and walked over to where Ellen kept her files on the needs of the company. This allowed Lily to see what was needed in the computer programs so that she could write them. Flipping through the files, they seemed...incomplete.

I know that Ellen was doing more research into the company's prescription history than they originally thought they would need to. Smiling to herself, she remembered a phrase that Ellen used to say. *You can't go forward without looking to see where you have been.* She would say this every time Lily would tell her that she was wasting her time looking back through old prescription and insurance claims.

I miss her. The sting of unshed tears hit the back of her eyes as she realized that she still grieved for the co-worker who had been so good to her. *She really took me under her wing and taught me a lot.* Lily's mind wandered to Carla. *Funny, but Ellen never seemed to pay any attention to my foot and Carla keeps staring and then trying not to stare.*

Uggggh, this is getting me nowhere. Shaking her head to clear out the cobwebs, she continued to look through

Ellen's files. *There is nothing new here.* The camera in the corner of the office had her constantly on edge and she knew that someone could easily tap into her work computers to see what she was working on. *Is it possible that someone went through Ellen's work during the week that I was out after her death? Why would someone want the data that anyone could find on their own? But then they replaced her with someone that was not from Ellen and Lily's company.* Narrowing her eyes, she looked up at the camera as though to glare at an unknown person there. *Someone must have gone through her files hoping they could figure out everything on their own, and then they could have released me from my contract.*

Slamming the desk drawer closed, she realized that Mr. VanHeusen played dirty. *Well, he wasn't able to get rid of me so easily!*

Walking back over to her desk she sat down heavily. With her elbows resting on the desk and her head in her hands, she sighed. Rubbing her temples, she tried to will the anger away. With her days busy at work and her evenings filled with Matt, she hadn't had much time to ponder the email that Ellen had sent. *Forget this, I want to work on something fun that Ellen had planned for me. I'll solve her puzzle.*

Her cell phone vibrated with an incoming message and she pulled it out of her pocket to see it. Matt's text said he was going to be late and reminded her to use the security system. *Like I could forget since he reminds me every day.*

Her mind began to think again of the message riddle she got from Ellen about her birthday. *Why did she mention that date? Or that restaurant? Or the bartender by name? Unless...she wanted me to go back there. But why? Is that the next piece of the puzzle?*

Looking at the clock, she decided to leave work and take a little detour on the way home. Walking down the long hall, she felt the hairs on the back of her neck prickle as though she were being watched. Glancing behind her, the hall was empty, with her footsteps being the only sounds heard. The realization that Ellen had been murdered in the building swept over her once again.

Sucking in a deep breath, she waited at the elevator anxious for it to arrive. Finally, the door opened and she entered, pressing the button for the first floor. By the time she arrived, her heart was pounding and she was grateful to step into the lobby, feeling less vulnerable there.

She caught a cab outside, giving him the address to the restaurant. Arriving at her destination, she paid the cab driver and walked inside. Glancing around, she made her way to the bar, pulling herself up onto a barstool. It was just as she remembered from months ago. Nothing spectacular. Just a bar in a restaurant like so many others in the city. *What were you trying to tell me, Ellen?* She rubbed her forehead, wondering if she were chasing ghosts.

"Hey hun, what can I get you?" the pretty bartender

asked.

Rarely a drinker, she was suddenly reminded of the bar she met Matt in. Smiling at the memory, it gave her the first peace she had had since leaving work. "Um…just a glass of white wine, please."

"Sure thing, hun."

Looking down the bar she saw two other bartenders, both male. Trying to remember if one of them looked familiar, she was drawing a blank. *Leave it to me to have seen a hot guy and not even pay attention to him.*

"There you go, hun," the friendly bartender said as she placed a wine glass in front of her.

Lily hated to draw attention to herself, but couldn't think of another way to find out what she wanted to know.

"Is there a bartender here whose name is Rick?" she asked, feeling the blush on her cheeks.

"Sure thing, hun. It's the handsome one down on the end. You want me to get him for you?" The bartender leaned in closely, "Got to tell you sweetie, he's married and totally unavailable."

"Oh no, I'm not interested. Not like that. It's just that a friend had met him and um…wanted me to ask him something."

Shrugging, the female bartender moved over to the man she identified as Rick and spoke to him. Lily saw his eyes cut over to her with a question on his face. Sucking in her lips, she was sure the blush on her cheeks had spread to her whole face. *Probably my whole body by this time. Jeez, get a grip.*

Forcing a smile on her face as he made his way over, the butterflies in her stomach threatened to overtake her.

"Hey, Miss. You looking for me?" Rick asked.

Leaning forward so that she could whisper, "Yes. Well, I think. I don't really know." *God, I'm babbling.* "The truth is that I had a friend that I think wanted me to look you up and I don't really know why."

Rick crossed his arms on his chest and stared at her in confusion. "Can't you just ask your friend?"

"No. I...well, you see. She...um...well...," Lily stammered.

Rick laughed and said, "Just spit it out darlin'."

Looking into his face, she blurted, "She's dead. Um...she died. And um...she left me a note that mentioned this restaurant and you."

Rick reared back as though slapped. "What the fuck?"

"It's no joke, I swear. You can look it up if you need to. It was in the papers."

His eyes narrowed speculatively. "What was your friend's name?"

"Ellen. Ellen Marsh."

Eyes widening in recognition, Rick stared. "What's your name?"

"Lily Swanson. We worked together."

Looking down at her drink, he said, "Sorry you didn't like the wine choice. I'll get you another glass," and he walked away.

Face flaming, she thought, *What the hell do I do now? He thinks I am a complete liar and loser. God, this was such a stupid idea.*

He moved back in front of her placing another glass of wine on the bar with a new napkin under it, removing the previous one. Leaning in, he said, "Your friend used to come in here a lot. She gave me something a few weeks ago and said for me to give to you if you ever came in. Don't know what it is and don't want to know. I figured it was just a joke, but here it is."

Standing back away from her, he announced, "Hope that glass is better, Miss," and he walked back down to his side of the bar.

Not wanting to draw any more attention to herself, she sipped wine and then put her hand on the napkin feeling a small lump underneath it. Scrunching up the napkin in her hand while grasping the object in it as well, she pretended to dab at her lips and then reached into her purse to pull out her cell phone while slipping the napkin inside. Fiddling with her cell phone, she couldn't believe what she was doing.

Heart pounding, she slid off the bar stool after tossing some money on the bar and tried to casually walk out of the door to hail a cab. Once inside the cab, she leaned her head back against the seat, breathing deeply. *This is like something out of a movie.* Placing her hand in her purse, she found the object and realized it was a thumb drive. *Jesus Ellen. What the hell were you doing?*

Ellen liked to play jokes and was always the first to set something up on the computer as a way to trick Lily. *Is this what you were doing when you died? Did you go back to set up another one of your practical jokes?*

After the cab dropped her off at home and she entered, alarming her house, she sat down on her sofa, grabbing her laptop. She inserted the thumb drive and found more pages of code. *I need to tell Matt.* Deciding to send a text instead, she typed **Have something to share with you when you get home.**

In just a minute, the reply came back. **Tonite sucks babe. Got something I have to deal with. Will see you tomorrow. Can't wait.**

Damn. Glancing at the code, she knew that it would take hours to decipher, so she placed it with the other thumb drive.

Shaking her head, she went through her bedroom and turned on the shower. Removing her prosthesis, she sat on the shower chair letting the water cascade over her body. Breathing deeply as she relaxed, she realized how tense she had been for hours. As the warm water carried away her tension, she longed to see Matt. Not just for the case, but for the way he made her body feel.

Sliding her hands over her breasts, she tweaked her nipples the way he did, feeling the familiar sensation down to her core. Lowering one hand to her pussy she began fingering in and out, circling her clit in between strokes. It didn't take long for her to orgasm, panting through the release as she leaned back in her shower chair.

The water began to cool as she slowly came down from her orgasmic high, smiling as she turned the shower off. Getting in her pajamas, she used her crutches to make her way to the bed, sliding under the covers.

Laying there, she thought of what all Matt had brought into her life. *I thought I was complete before. I was independent, but not really complete. He makes me feel whole again.* She turned to face the side of the bed that he slept in, reaching out her hand to touch his pillow. The words of her mother returned to her once again. *"You'd better learn to use your intelligence because you won't catch a man with your body now."* You were wrong mom. About a lot of things.*

WAKING THE NEXT morning, deciding she couldn't wait to see Matt, she dressed quickly and planned on surprising him at his house before she went to work. *I need to tell him I love him.* Thinking for a few minutes, she debated with herself. *Is it too soon? Will it send him running?* Strapping on her prosthesis then slipping on her light blue sneakers that matched the jewel blue shirt she was wearing, she stood and looked at her reflection in the mirror. The same blonde wavy hair. The same dark brown eyes. The same face stared back at her. But something was different. Her smile. For the first time in many years, the smile was genuine. Heartfelt. Totally real. Loved. *Yeah, I'm going to tell him.*

The cab let her out at Matt's apartment building.

Looking up at its height, she realized that it wasn't at all what she pictured him in. It looked…fancy. Walking through the door, she saw that the lobby was nicer than the VanHeusen Medical Building and she had thought it was very up-scale. Suddenly nervous, she debated what she was doing.

Taking a deep breath, she rode the elevator up to his floor and walked down the hall to his apartment, taking in the décor. *My house is so frumpy compared to this.* Filled with self-doubt, she hesitated at his door.

Before she could knock, she heard a female's voice from inside loudly declare, "Matt, I know you are still in the shower, but I've got to get to work. Thanks for last night. I'll let you know when I'm coming back."

The door opened and Lily stood numbly with her hand raised, still in the position of knocking. The woman she was staring at was exquisite. Straight, silky blonde hair pulled into a tight pony-tail at the back of a long neck. A face that belonged on the cover of a magazine. Tall and willowy, even without the four inch heels she was towering in. Clothed in an expensive suit of navy silk with a delicate pink blouse underneath that accentuated her flawless makeup. Large blue eyes peered back at her.

"Are you the new cleaning lady?" the woman asked.

Lily stammered that she must have the wrong apartment before turning and running to the elevator. Jumping in as soon as the doors opened, she sagged against the wall. Stomach revolting, she clapped her hand over her mouth to quell the feeling of nausea rising. *Oh, Jesus. I'm such an idiot. I should have known it wasn't what I thought. What would he want with me when he can have that?* The elevator doors opened and she hustled out of the building, turning to walk blindly down the sidewalk.

The tears slid down her cheeks faster than she could wipe them away. *Oh, God. I slept with him. He must have been so grossed out. Why? When he had that, why would he have slept with me?* She bumped into several people on the crowded sidewalk as she continued to walk to…anywhere. Her leg began to ache and she looked up not knowing where she was or how long she had been walking. A small park was off to her left, so she crossed the street and found a bench to sit on. Arms wrapped tightly around her middle as though to protect herself from any more pain, she finally allowed the tears to slide unrestrained down her face.

The pain was so intense she could hardly catch her breath. *I haven't hurt like this since…*

She realized that grief begets grief. The pain of her broken heart jerked her right back to the pain of losing her sister. And her foot. Bending over, she cried harder, the sobs racking her body. Glad that the park was virtually empty at this hour, she allowed the grief to overtake her. Consume her. Until she had no more tears left to cry and she just sat, not caring about anything.

Chapter 9

MATT WALKED OUT of the bathroom, the towel slung low on his hips. Angry at how his night had progressed, he was anxious to call Lily as soon as he was awake and set up a time to meet. He hated not being with her last night, especially since she had texted that she had something to talk to him about. Smiling as he slid into boxers and his pants, he was startled when Cassandra walked back into the bedroom.

"What the fuck are you still doin' here? I thought I made it clear last night that you needed to be gone." Looking at her, he couldn't believe he ever fell for her shallow beauty. It was cold. Calculating.

Putting her hand up, she rolled her eyes. "Don't worry, Matt. I'm leaving. I just thought I would tell you that some woman came by here a bit ago. I asked her if she was your cleaning lady, because I wanted to tell her that I thought your kitchen was a mess, but she just mumbled and ran to the elevator. Well, sort of limped away."

At this, Matt turned his attention back to Cassandra, his heart beginning to pound furiously as a sick feeling washed over him.

"What did she look like?" he growled.

"Look like? I don't know. Plain and boring."

"What. The. Fuck. Did. She. Look. Like?"

Huffing, she replied, "Short. Long, blonde hair. Kind of wavy. Definitely dressed in department store clothes. You know, basic pants and a blouse. I figured she must be the cleaning lady. Who else would wear sneakers to work?" Throwing her head back as she laughed she continued, "Little flat sneakers. Blue ones that matched her shirt!"

Turning to pick up her large designer bag off the sofa, she said, "Anyway, thanks for last night. I can't believe that jerk locked me out of the house," referring to her latest lover. "I had been wanting to talk to you about some of this furniture anyway since we bought it together. I'll arrange a moving van to get the pieces you said you didn't want."

"I don't give a shit what furniture you take, Cassandra. I never liked it anyway. So get out and let me know when the movers come."

With that she walked out as he charged back into his bedroom to grab his cell phone. *Come on baby, please pick up.* His heart sank as it rang continuously before going to voice mail. "Baby, whatever you are thinking, that is not what happened. You need to call me and let me talk to you. Please, baby."

Over and over he tried. *Fuck!* He quickly drove over to her house and banged on the door. Hearing Pippi barking inside, he used his key to let himself in, gently pushing the little dog out of the way. Once in, he quickly searched but she wasn't at home. Running back through the small house he locked the door then ran back to his truck. Heading to the VanHeusen Medical Building, he called her office phone, but when Andrea answered she told him that Lily had not shown up for work. In a panic and not knowing what to do, he called Shane.

"What's up?"

"Man, I've fucked up again."

"With Lily? What happened?"

"I got in late from our bust and went to my place instead of Lily's. In the middle of the night, Cassandra shows up."

"What the hell did that bitch want?" Shane asked.

"Seems she's screwed over her latest lover and he kicked her out. Anyway, she was upset and wanted to talk about the furniture. Jesus, I'm such a dickhead."

"If you let her in your apartment, then yeah you are a dickhead," Shane agreed.

"She wanted to talk to me about the furniture since we bought it together. I told her that in another month my lease was up and I was getting the hell out of that fancy-ass apartment. As far as I was concerned, she could have it all."

"Was that it?"

"I wish. She wanted to crash on the couch and I told her no, but then she reminded me that it was two in the morning and it wouldn't be safe for her to go out. So like a dumb-fuck, I agreed."

"Is she still there? You want me to come eject her ass?" Shane volunteered.

"She's gone. But before she left, Lily showed up."

"Oh fuck."

"Yeah, you can say that again. Cassandra said the woman ran, or rather limped, to the elevator before disappearing."

"Look, Lily's smart. And she trusts you, man. Just explain and she'll get it. Believe me, it was rough when Annie found out about Rochelle, but she understood that was someone from my past."

"Lily won't answer her phone. And she's not at home. And I've just left her work place. They told me she never showed up today. So where the fuck is she?" Matt pulled into the station parking lot, his hands shaking. "Shane, I've just gotta…"

"I'll call Tony. Where are you now?"

"Outside."

"Come on in and wait for Tony to call us back. I'll have him trace her cell."

Hanging up, Matt sat in the truck for a few minutes, his heart still pounding. *Babe, where are you?* The knowledge that she was somewhere hurting because of him tore him apart inside. *She's suffered so much, I never wanted to give her anything but joy.*

He had just made it inside when Shane came rushing up. "Tony called back. He got a trace on her phone. She's at a park about two miles from where you live.

He's already got Gabe watching her. It seems Gabe lives near there, so he went immediately."

"Thanks, man. I owe you."

Shane looked into the ravaged face of his partner and friend. "No you don't. You pieced me and Annie back together. No debt, man."

Matt drove to the park, pulling behind Gabe's vehicle. Gabe met him as he tore out of his truck.

"She's okay, Matt," Gabe assured. "She's still sitting on the bench and no one's botherin' her."

Matt looked over the distance to the small figure sitting alone on the park bench, head bowed. His hand rubbed his chest as he hurt for her hurt. Ached for her ache. Feeling a hand on his shoulder, he turned.

"It's okay, man. Whatever happened, I've seen the two of you together. You'll figure it out."

"I hurt her. Unintentionally, but hurt nonetheless."

"It happens. But that woman cares about you. We've all seen it. Whatever it is, she'll forgive."

Sucking in a deep breath, Matt looked into his friend's face, seeing only sincerity. Nodding he headed over toward the bench.

Approaching softly so as not to startle her, he walked around the front, his heart aching as he heard sniffles. Her hands in her lap, she was so pale and still. "Lily?" he asked gently.

Jumping at the sound, she looked up in surprise as she pressed her trembling hand to her mouth. Staring at him, she couldn't form words. At least not without sobbing, so she just stayed silent, chin quivering.

He took in her red-rimmed eyes and blotchy face and thought she never looked more beautiful. "Baby?" he asked again. Moving over to sit on the bench without crowding, he turned to face her.

She sat perfectly still. *Why is he here? What does he want?* She could feel the familiar emotion of embarrassment flow over her and it made her angry. *I don't want his guilt. I'm not some simpleton that can't handle things.*

He noticed when her demeanor shifted from desolation to anger. *Fuck, I've gotta make this right.*

"Lily, will you look at me?" He watched her eyes cut over to his. "Baby, what happened this morning is not what you think. It's not what it looked like."

"It's…" her voice barely whispered. "It's fine. You really don't have to explain. I…um…well, it…doesn't matter," she stammered so softly he had to strain to hear her.

"It does matter. It matters to me," he responded, his voice shaky with emotion.

She turned her head to look at his face. It looked sad. Hurt. His eyes were full of pain. She had seen that look in her own reflection too many times to not recognize it in others.

"Please," he begged, "Let me explain." When she didn't deny him, he took that as a positive.

"Two years ago, I met Cassandra. At the time, I was taken in by her looks, personality, everything. I didn't realize how much I let her influence me and for a man like me who likes to be in charge, I really let her call the shots. She dictated where we'd live, the furniture we bought, where we'd eat. Everything. But I thought we were in love, so I agreed. Looking back, there were no compromises. I made all the concessions." Rubbing his hand over his forehead, he continued, "A little over a year ago, we were out late at a bar and two men got into a fight. I saw that there wasn't any security so I jumped in. I subdued one man while telling the other man to halt or he would be arrested too. That's when I got this," he said rubbing his scar.

"What happened?" she asked in a whisper.

"The other man had broken a bottle on the bar and slashed out like some damn scene in a western. He caught me right on the forehead and slashed me open." Giving a rude snort, he said, "Cassandra was screaming about the blood getting on her clothes."

Sparing a glance her way he was relieved to see Lily's face frown ever so slightly at that last comment.

"Anyway, I ended up having a lot of stitches to sew my forehead together. They didn't have a plastic surgeon on call so I just had the ER doctor sew me up. He did a good job, but the broken bottle didn't cut me clean like a knife would have. It was jagged and pretty shitty looking.

"That's when things started falling all to hell. Well, maybe they were already there and that just made it clear." Sighing, he twisted around to look into Lily's eyes again. The anger in them was replaced with wariness.

"Cassandra couldn't stand the scar. She said it was horrible to look at. She stopped wanting sex saying that it was like screwing Frankenstein."

At that, Lily gasped, but stayed silent.

"I slowly realized that she was exactly what she seemed – the raving bitch that everyone else thought she was. She started working late, never coming back to the apartment. Then I found out that she was screwing two different guys from her law office. Lily, what I realized was that it didn't hurt to see her leave. It made me doubt myself. Doubt my ability to see someone's true self. And my self-esteem took a huge hit. So sex just became a physical release."

Lily winced. It was one thing to know that he was sexually active. Another thing to have it so bluntly talked about. As though it wasn't special when the very act to her had been monumental.

Matt saw her wince and panicked. *Babe, please keep listening. Please hear the whole story.*

"The cut was deep and there was some nerve damage. The pain was excruciating sometimes and the pain pills they prescribed became the only way I could get through the day. Then as they wore off, the pills and booze together worked to get me through the nights. I stayed in a fog for months.

"I was lucky that I had a scare that got me off both, cold turkey. I was on a stake-out with some other detectives and during a take-down of a drug ring, my

partner was almost shot and I was too slow to stop it."
Matt stopped at this point, staring off into the distance
as though lost in the memory.

"Really shook me up and I knew I had to make a
change. I dumped the pills in the toilet, but saved the
bottle. Stopped going to bars with the other officers at
night. Went to the gym or home."

"You saved the bottle?" Lily's barely there voice
asked haltingly.

"Yeah. It sits on my bathroom counter where I can
see it every morning. My reminder. Of what I lost."

Her eyes flashed pain once again and she said, "Cassandra. You lost her."

Matt's head jerked around, staring incredulously.
"Baby, no. Fuck no!" He slid off the bench and kneeled
in front of her, taking her cold hands in his large warm
ones. "I don't give a shit about her. What I lost was me.
For a long time, I'd lost me. First when I allowed myself
to change who I am for her. Then when I had to look in
the mirror every day and see my face. I felt like I lost a
part of me. Then when I lost myself in the pills and
booze. Baby, that bottle on the counter reminds me of
all of those things that I had lost and never want to
worry about again."

She looked down at her small hands nestled in his.
Raising her eyes, they bore into his searching…for
sincerity.

"Even as the scar began to heal, every woman I ever
met looked at the scar first, before looking into my eyes.

Except for you."

With that she looked into his eyes again, seeing them filled with pain mixed with hope. She continued to sit quietly, not trusting her voice to speak.

"LilyBelle, you are the only woman who ever seemed to look at me and see me. Not some scar. I knew then that you were special. You tempted me like no other. You were the one for me."

"What..." her voice broke. Clearing her throat, she tried again. "What about this morning?"

"I totally fucked up. But not in the way you are thinking," he quickly added as he saw the look on her face.

"What I mean is this. I got in late from a drug bust. About two in the morning, Cassandra shows up at my door. She was upset and said she needed to talk. I was pissed and ready to kick her ass out when she said she had nowhere to go. Found out she's been screwing around on her boyfriend with two other guys from her office and now all three of them dumped her. Since one is her boss she was afraid of losing her job. Personally, I didn't care, but she then said she wanted to get some of the furniture from the apartment since she may be out of a job as well as kicked out of her boyfriend's place.

"Lily, that was perfect to me. I'd already planned on dumping the apartment when the lease was up in a month anyway and living with you. That was why I never took you to my place – because it never felt like my place. It was just a place I slept in. Your house, babe, that's a home."

At that, Lily's eyes opened wide as she stared at him. "You never said anything."

"You're right. But I was gonna rectify that as soon as I saw you today. Baby, for the first time, I was happy with what Cassandra said. She was gonna take the dumbass furniture that I wanted to get rid of and that was gonna be the end of anything I had to do with her."

"Why was she still there this morning?" Lily asked, trying to hide the hurt that still resided inside.

"By this time it was almost three in the morning and when I told her to take a cab to a hotel, she begged to just crash on the couch for a couple of hours and then she'd leave. I didn't want her there, but it seemed harmless. That was such a huge mistake, baby. Not that I was trying to hide anything from you, because I was also going to tell you this whole story today anyway. I wanted everything to be out in the open. Done. Over with. Behind us. I swear my heart stopped when she came in to tell me that a woman had been at the door when she was leaving."

She sat quietly, not moving for a moment. "How did you know it was me?" she asked suspiciously. "I didn't give her my name. In fact, she thought I was the cleaning lady."

Matt dropped his head. "Baby, she's a fuckin', stuck-up bitch."

"How did you know?"

"She described you. Your hair, your size. I knew."

"What else?"

Matt looked up at her, pain on his face, saying nothing.

"What else did she say?" Lily whispered.

"She said you limped a little. And you had sneakers on."

Lily looked down at her shoes. Cute little blue sneakers. On little feet. On one little foot and one little fake foot. Not described as gorgeous. Not elegant. Not model-like stature. Not classy. Not even beautiful or cute. Cassandra may not have used the words "stumpy little lady with a stumpy little leg" but Lily felt the description nonetheless.

Suddenly exhausted, her breath hitched again. She saw Matt start to reach out to her, but she put her hand up quickly. She knew if he touched her she would fall apart. And for the first time in her life she knew that if she fell apart this time she might not ever put herself back together again. Pressing her hand to her mouth again she swallowed deeply several times to ward off the tears.

"Lily, please forgive me. I swear to you that nothing happened between me and Cassandra other than our last goodbye and in my opinion, good-riddance. I was so excited about seeing you today. I wanted to tell you that I'd like to move in with you. I wanted to tell you what I was feeling. About you. About us. Jesus, when I couldn't find you, I panicked. I never want to feel that again."

Her brow crinkled in thought. "How did you find

me?"

"Tony."

Seeing her questioning gaze, he said, "He had your phone location traced. Then Gabe was near here and he came and kept an eye on you until I could get here."

Lily jerked around looking at the road behind her. Face flaming, "Does everyone know what happened?"

"No, babe. Shane is the only one and he was ready to go kick her ass this morning. Tony and Gabe only know that you were upset. That's all."

Sucking in a huge breath, she sat on the bench letting all of his story float through her mind. He reached across and slowly placed his hand on top of hers, happy that she did not pull it back. They sat for several minutes in silence, letting the touch of their hands speak for themselves.

"It was my fault," her voice broke the stillness.

He looked at her in confusion. "What was, baby?"

"The accident."

The silence loomed between them. He so wanted her to talk to him but was afraid if he broke the silence he would break her. Sliding a little closer, he continued to hold her hand. Not too close. Not as close as he wanted. But close enough so that she wouldn't feel alone.

"I had the most beautiful sister. She was just two years older than me. Rose. Her name was Rose. Daddy used to call us his flower garden because my mom's name is Daisy." Shaking her head, she commented,

"Stupid, isn't it?"

Matt didn't respond but gave her hand a gentle squeeze.

"Rose was always so much fun and I wanted to be just like her. But she was pretty and a cheerleader and in the drama club. She was so popular. And I was just plain Lily. I was in the math club. I was the nerd, smart girl that all the guys wanted to study with so I could give them the answers, but no one wanted to date."

Looking out over the park, she said, "But I was never jealous. I loved Rose and she loved me and I just accepted that I would never be her."

Again the silence filled the air. Afraid to break the spell, Matt sat quietly, letting her weave the story in her own time.

Lily's eyes glazed over as though she were back in time. "I was sixteen, just learned to drive. Rose was close to graduating from high school and was at a party drinking. You have to understand. Our parents were very…. conservative. And her drinking would be a huge deal. So she called me to come get her. I didn't want to, but she convinced me that it would be okay. And that was my mistake. I should have woken up my parents and dealt with the consequences. You see, they would have grounded me forever just to keep me from doing something like Rose had done. But I snuck out and picked her up.

"She was drunk and silly but we were almost home when we were hit by another car that ran a stop sign.

Rose was killed and the firemen had to cut me out of the car." She rubbed her hands over her knees, "I made it out, but my foot didn't."

"Baby, how was that your fault?" he prodded gently.

"My parents blamed me. They said that if I had woken dad up to go get Rose then the accident wouldn't have happened. I was at the wrong place at the wrong time."

"You don't believe that do you? You were a teenager. You made a decision. An accident happened that wasn't your fault. No one can blame you." He gently pulled her in closer, tucking her into his side, willing for his body to give her strength. She didn't melt into him, instead sitting stiff, as though the cold had seeped into her very soul.

"I don't know. After that, I was pretty much on my own. My parent's insurance and the other driver's insurance paid for all of the operations, physical therapies, prosthetics. You name it, I got it. But I was alone. In my own house, I was alone. At school I was alone."

The silence stretched between them into the deep places that are usually kept hidden.

"No parents. No Rose. I finished high school and went to college. I majored in software engineering and found that l like computer science and numbers. I understand them. People? Not so much."

Matt thought about all that she had endured. *I want to take it all away. Her hurt. Her pain.*

"Momma told me that I needed to develop my

mind because I certainly wouldn't catch a man with my body."

"Jesus fuck, Lily," he said, sighing heavily.

"It's really okay, you know. I mean... I see women like Cassandra every day. At work. On the street. In bars. The kind of women that by their hair and clothes and make-up and sky-high heels...they're going to make men drool just by being in their presence. I'm never going to be that person."

Matt growled and gently pulled her closer, wrapping his arms around her. "Baby, that's fucked."

"Is it?" she asked, looking him directly in the eye. "Didn't you say yourself that you were taken in by Cassandra's looks?"

Matt opened his mouth to protest, but Lily continued. "Look, I'm not on some pity-party. Oh, poor little amputee. It is what it is. I've met other women amputees and we come in all shapes and sizes. And personalities. I've met women amputees who go to national conferences and speak in public. They have dynamic personalities and are so admired. I'm just shy. I'm never going to be that super-confident woman that says 'here I am' when walking into a room."

Matt gently rubbed circles on her back, willing some of the tension to leave. They were silent again for a few minutes as he continued to massage. Slowly her shoulders relaxed and he slid his hand up to massage her neck.

"I am strong, Matt. I'm just not the in-your-face

kind of wonder-woman. I get up every day, thankful to be alive, and go to work in a job I like. I have only a few friends, but they are awesome friends. I'm okay not being spectacular. But sometimes, it hurts when it all gets shoved in my face."

"Like this morning?" he asked in a pain-laced voice.

She nodded.

"Baby, look at me, please." He saw her hesitation. "Baby, please look at me."

This time she looked up, her chocolate eyes on his baby blues.

"The first time I saw you across the bar, I was struck by your beauty. Drop-dead gorgeous beauty." Seeing the doubt in her eyes, he continued. "No joke, babe. No lie. I couldn't believe someone so pretty was alone. And I saw the eyes of the other men around. They were hawkin' after you, but I could tell you were uncomfortable. All I wanted to do was be the one to sit next to you. Be the one you smiled at. You never looked at my scar. You just looked at me. I was so fuckin' stupid that night not getting your name or number. I never meant to take advantage of you like I did."

"Matt you hardly did anything I wasn't a willing participant in."

"Babe, a gentleman who's interested in a woman never treats her like that. It was wrong, but I didn't think the evening would end the way it did. I thought I'd get my chance."

"I shouldn't have run away. I just didn't know what

to do."

"Babe, when I saw you that night at the medical building, I vowed to see you again. I wanted you and was prepared to step off of the case if necessary. Then seeing you at the party was the clincher. As far as I was concerned, you were mine. You're beautiful, inside and out. You're the strongest woman I know. You make me ashamed to have squandered the last year of my life feeling sorry for myself. If I just had a part of your strength, I'd be a better man. And LilyBelle, you make me want to be a better man."

Sitting in silence once again, he slid his hand up from her neck to the back of her head, pulling her in so that he could place his lips on her forehead. The kiss was gentle. Patient. Loving.

"I need to know that you forgive me, baby."

Lily looked into the eyes of the man that she had planned on proclaiming her love to. Giving a small smile, she nodded. "Yeah." Her chin quivered a little and she joked, "I thought I was all cried out."

Smiling in response, he tucked her head under his chin and held her close to his chest. "Baby, you cry all you want."

She did. After a few minutes, she raised back up, wiping her tear stained cheeks.

"Baby, I need you to promise me something," he said.

"What is it?" she asked.

"Twice you've run away from me. This time I nearly

lost my mind. Please promise me, no more running away. I promise to never intentionally hurt you. So if you are unsure of something, let me know. We'll face it together."

The edges of her lips curved in a tiny smile as she nodded. "Okay, I promise," she whispered. Taking a shuddering breath, she looked at her watch.

"I've missed work and kept you from your job also. Are you going to be in trouble?"

"Nah. It's all good." He hated to ask any more questions, but felt as though he needed to know. "Lily, how are things with your parents now?"

Giving a little shrug, she said, "I see them occasionally. Nothing special. I still see recrimination in their eyes and I have come to peace with what happened so I just don't need their censure. To them, the accident will alway be my fault. And while they don't hate me, they don't show a lot of love either."

Matt sat quietly for a moment, the realization that she had emotionally supported herself since the accident along with dealing with her own grief had him in awe of her strength of character. Inwardly vowing to not ever let her feel alone again he kissed the top of her head feeling her silky hair against his lips.

"Let's go home, LilyBelle." With that, he helped her stand and with hands clasped, walked to his truck. Lifting her up gently, he set her inside then leaned across to buckle her in. Brushing her lips with his, their kiss felt like...hope.

Chapter 10

ARRIVING AT HOME, Matt tried to gently push Pippi away to keep her from jumping all over Lily, but the demanding pup would not be deterred. Lily bent over to scoop up the dog, snuggling her face into the soft fur.

"Are you hungry?" Matt asked, not knowing when she last ate.

Nodding, she headed into the kitchen. They fixed a quick breakfast, sitting at the table to eat. The exhaustion of the morning had taken its toll on her and Matt noticed her eyes closing as she finished her food.

Standing, he ushered her to the bedroom. She looked at him quizzically, but he just turned her and pushed her gently onto the bed.

"Arms up," he said. She complied and he lifted her shirt over her head. Pulling out one of his t-shirts that he had left there, he leaned around and unsnapped her bra. Trying not to be distracted by the beauty of her breasts, he slid the t-shirt down over her head and settled it over her chest.

Kneeling by her legs, he looked up at her face, seeing a mixture of fatigue and nervousness. "Do you trust me?" he asked.

"Yes," she answered, keeping her eyes on him. *No one has ever done this but me. Not my parents. No one.* But she realized that she trusted him completely.

Matt slid her pants off and lifted her prosthesis. Following the actions that he had seen her complete, he unhooked it and slid it off the end of her leg. His hand slid to the sock-like covering and he heard her gasp.

"Matt, my leg is hairy. Really hairy. I don't want you to see it." Seeing his questioning gaze, she sucked in a deep breath and continued. "I can't shave. Or wax. Or use Nair. Or anything that could possibly rub against the sock and cause an infection. A small infection could cause me to lose the rest of my leg." Giving her shoulders a defeated shrug, she admitted, "So, it's hairy."

"Baby, a hairy leg does not bother me. I swear."

"I trim it with scissors so it isn't too long, but it looks silly. The only thing I could do is electrolysis, but that is too expensive right now. I'm saving for it."

She saw his eyes. Gentle. Trusting. Accepting. Slowly she nodded. "It's okay if you want to take it off."

Encouraged, he rolled the sock off her leg, seeing the residual leg for the first time. He had braced himself, not know what he would see, but needn't have. Leaning down he placed a kiss on the end of her leg, then looked up to see tears in her eyes again.

Pulling down the covers, he lay her back and covered her up. "Baby, you're exhausted. I've called Andrea and told her you were sick. You stay in bed and rest today." Crawling in beside her, he wrapped her in his arms. "You sleep. When you wake up, I'll be here."

Lily fell asleep and for the first time, did not dream of her missing foot. Or car wrecks. Or her parents. Or even of Ellen's murder. She dreamed once again of a blue-eyed man holding her tight.

A FEW HOURS later when she woke, he was still there holding her. Smiling, she looked up and saw the time on the clock. "Oh my gosh, you need to get to work."

"Shane knew I was taking the morning off. I'll go in when you feel like getting up."

Lifting her hand to cup his face, she kissed him gently. "Maybe I don't want to get up."

Grinning, he agreed, "Well, I think a part of me that is already *up* is glad you want to stay in bed."

Pulling her t-shirt off of her head while he shucked his clothes, they fell back onto the bed. He leaned over to suck one nipple deeply into his mouth. Nipping with his teeth, she groaned as he licked it to ease the sting. Moving between breasts, he gave each one equal attention.

Lily was reeling from the electricity moving between her breasts and her pussy, rubbing herself on his engorged cock. Suddenly deciding to be adventurous, she pushed on his shoulders until he was on his back and she pulled herself on top.

Seeing his wide-eyed expression emboldened her and

she continued to rub herself along his dick. She held her breasts out to him as an offering, which he gladly took. She then centered herself on his tip and surrounded him to the hilt. Watching him throw his head back on the pillow continued to make her bold. Using her hands on his shoulders, she lifted herself up and down on his cock, feeling her juices start to flow, making the action easier.

He looked up at the goddess on top, riding him. Long, wavy hair hanging in a curtain around them. Her full breasts bouncing in rhythm to her movements. He reached up to hold them, fondling the mounds and tweaking the nipples. This time he watched as her head arched back, smile on her face as she flew over the edge.

She fell on top of him, boneless. He flipped them so that he was once again on top. Capturing her mouth in a kiss that she felt to her soul, he sucked her tongue into his mouth deeply and then began thrusting his tongue in the same action as his cock thrusting into her tight pussy. *Jesus, she feels amazing.* He alternated between sucking on her nipples and kissing her hard and wet. Both had the desired effect.

She began matching him thrust for thrust until she felt her orgasm close. "I'm there, honey. I'm right there."

He grabbed her hands in one of his and pulled them over her head ordering, "Grab the headboard, baby." Once he saw that she had obeyed, he began to pound harder.

Screaming his name, she felt the orgasm take her over the edge. Flying apart in a million pieces, she was barely aware when he reared back, powering through his release.

Over and over, until the last drop was out of him. He collapsed on top of her this time, before rolling over to the side. Consciousness slowly came back to him as he slid out of her wet pussy. Looking down at the semen on her thighs, realization washed over him and he flopped his head back on the pillow realizing as well, that for him, it wouldn't be a problem.

"Baby? I gotta tell you something."

"Ummmm," was the only response Lily could manage.

"I don't want you to be upset, but I forgot a condom. I promise you I'm clean. We get tested all the time at work, but baby, if you get pregnant, I won't be upset."

He looked over nervously seeing her glorious smile directed at him.

"It's all good, honey. I'm on the pill. We don't have to use condoms."

Matt felt a strange dichotomy. He was glad they no longer had to worry about condoms, but found himself wanting to have a child with Lily and wondered what her thoughts were.

She was still smiling as she responded, "But I wouldn't mind having a child with you some day."

Staring at her, Matt realized that he had never heard

more loving words from anyone ever in his life. Grinning back at her, he leaned in for another kiss. This one soft and sweet. And full of promise.

"Ah, LilyBelle, you sorely tempt me. Having a child with you would be my heart's dream. I love you, you know."

"I was coming over this morning to tell you that I realized that I love you too."

He shut his eyes in horror for a moment, realizing how close he came to losing everything. Rolling back on top, he held her face as he rained kisses all over. Her forehead. Her nose. Her cheeks. Her lips. Mostly her lips.

Giggling, she pushed him back. "I think I started to fall in love with you when you rescued me at the bar."

"You were the one who tempted me just by sitting there in all your innocence. I think maybe I started falling for you then too."

Looking at the clock, she began pushing him out of the bed. "You've got to get to work. It's only eleven-thirty. We can both get a half-day in."

Half an hour later, re-dressed and cleaned up, they headed out of her house. He dropped her off at work, promising to pick her up at the end of the day. Giving her a quick kiss, he watched her enter the building.

Once again he wasn't the only one watching.

(Surveillance)

"HAVE YOU BEEN keeping an eye on her?"

"Yeah, and I gotta tell you that her job is boring as shit."

"Doesn't matter. You just make sure you keep an eye on what she's doing. The boss wants to know the first time she starts acting weird."

"Don't you think that trying to run her down tipped her and that cop boyfriend off too soon?"

"Yeah. That was a dickhead move, but wasn't ordered from the top. The one responsible for that blunder has been taken care of. Permanently."

The shudders ran through the one whose eyes were glued to the camera in her office. The stakes were high in this game. He knew that. But then so were the payoffs. Really good payoffs. So he'd keep his mouth shut and his eyes on her. When she was at her desk, he could just focus on how beautiful she was. His dick recognized that too as he shifted in his seat.

The one in the room with him chuckled. "Keep your dick under control," he said before leaving and softly closing the door behind him.

LILY KEPT TRYING to reconcile the lack of records that Ellen had in her files to all of the work that she had seen

Ellen doing. Convinced that someone had gone through their work during the week she was out, she walked over to Ellen's old desk and began rifling through papers. Just then Carla came into the room, looking at Lily suspiciously.

"What are you looking for?"

"Ellen was working on the past patient prescription records when she was...killed." It was still hard to use the word *murdered.* "I need them to see how far back I'm going to write the program. She had more data than what I am seeing here. When I moved to this office, I am beginning to think that some of the information was...misplaced."

The air in the room crackled with intensity, causing Lily to look up from her searching.

"Are you telling me that Ellen had more files than what are here? Where are they?"

"I don't know. If I did I wouldn't be searching," she answered with frustration. *What is Carla's deal? Is she afraid of losing her job if she can't replicate Ellen?* Looking Carla in the eyes, she asked, "Can you think of someone who would have wanted to take our work?"

"Of course not. Why would anyone want that? Anyway, I wasn't even hired yet, so I wouldn't know about that," Carla said, her voice rising with irritation.

"Look, I'm sure they are around here somewhere," she said to placate Carla. "I'll keep looking."

Carla turned to stalk out of the door, flinging back over her shoulder, "You do that."

Watching the retreating back of her snarky co-worker, she shook her head. *Yep. That's why I like my programing. People are too damn hard to figure out!*

Calling out to Andrea, she looked up when her assistant walked in.

"What are you looking for?" Andrea asked.

"Were you in the office the whole week that I was out when Ellen was…died?"

"No, why?" Andrea replied, walking over to the desk.

"I know Ellen had more data for me to use, but I can't find it. My fear is that someone went through our stuff when we were out."

"Why would someone want to do that?"

"I have no idea. It would be useless to anyone else. But I am starting to get the feeling that I am always being watched."

Andrea looked around nervously. "Now you're giving me the creeps. But to answer your question, I took the same week off that you did. I know that they had professional cleaners come in and the office was closed for several days. I came back that next Monday that you came back. Didn't the police have you check everything?"

"Yeah, but I was so shaken that I just looked around to see if anything looked out of place. I didn't really look through things. That was probably a mistake, wasn't it?"

Andrea placed her arm around Lily, pulling her in

for a hug. "Oh sweetie, you can't blame yourself. We were all dealing with a shock, you most of all." Giving the office another glance, she continued, "Look, why don't I go out and get some lunch for us and I'll bring it back."

Nodding, Lily agreed. "That sounds good. Just get me whatever you are getting."

Lily continued to search the office area after Andrea left. Pulling out the top file drawer to search once again, her cell phone dropped out of her pocket. Stooping over to get it she knew she needed assistance to rise again. Reaching up to grasp the file drawer above her, she noticed a slip of paper taped to the bottom of the drawer. Re-squatting, she pulled the paper down and then hefted herself back up.

Unfolding it, she recognized Ellen's writing.

I'm all thumbs when it comes to my dates.

What the hell was Ellen doing? I swear her penchant for practical jokes was worse than I thought. Walking back over to her desk, she continued on her work until it was almost time to go home. Her cell phone chimed and looking down she recognized Suzanne's number.

"Hey girl, I haven't heard from you lately."

"I know, that's why I called. Annie and I wanted to get drinks after work. Will you come too?"

After such an emotional morning she just wanted to crawl into bed, but she also felt the pull to talk to them. "Sure. Actually I could really use some girl-time."

"Perfect, we'll grab a cab and pick you up when you get off work."

Hanging up, she felt lighter than she had all day. Even though things had ended well with Matt that morning, she still felt a little raw. *Maybe spilling it all out to some girlfriends will be just what I need.* She opened some files on her desk while absentmindedly shoving the note into her pocket.

SITTING IN THE bar with Annie and Suzanne had turned out to be the best decision she could have made. By the time they picked her up, the city lights were on and the neon signs created a colorful glow in the night skyline.

The friendly bartender kept their drinks coming as he made eyes at Suzanne.

"I think you've got a conquest there girl," Annie said as he sent another round their way.

Suzanne glanced over her shoulder at the handsome bartender winking at her. She giggled, but just turned back to her friends. "He's a cutie, but I'm just not interested."

Annie speared her friend with a pointed glare. "What is it with you and guys? I've known you for almost two years and you have yet to have a date."

Suzanne shrugged. "Just not interested. A broken heart several years ago that won't heal, is the best explanation that I can give." Then looking up at both women, she continued, "And the only explanation that I will give."

Annie looked over at Lily. "Well, I guess then it's up to you to spill about your romantic life. I hear your morning was eventful."

Lily wanted to be horrified realizing that Shane must have told Annie about the events of the day, but found that the concerned looks on Annie and Suzanne's faces had her wanting to talk.

Not used to chatting with girlfriends, she gave them a quick run-down. "I went to Matt's apartment this morning and ran into a gorgeous woman coming out saying 'thanks for last night.' Then she asked if I was the cleaning lady." Hearing the gasps from her friends, she continued. "So, I ran. Now that I say that, it sounds kind of dumb, but that's exactly what I did. I ran."

The girls were quiet for a moment before Annie asked, "Where did you run to?"

Looking into their understanding gazes, she said, "I really don't know. I just kept going until my leg was hurting and I realized a park was across from me. I found a bench and sat down. Then just cried." She hesitated for a moment before continuing. "I just kept crying. It was as though a lot of pent up grief came pouring out and I had no control."

Suzanne, with tears in her eyes, reached across the table and took Lily's hand. Voice shaking she said, "I know about grief, Lily. It can shake you to your very soul. And when you least expect it, it can pick you up and shake you again."

Annie and Lily looked into Suzanne's face, seeing tears making their way down her cheeks, both realizing that she had just shared more about her past than ever before.

Lily nodded saying, "Yeah. I thought about my sister's death – how my parents will always blame me for driving the car that she died in even though the accident wasn't my fault. I cried about giving my heart to a man that I thought had betrayed me." Shrugging her slight shoulders, she admitted, "I was just crying about everything."

"What happened then? How did he find you?"

"Good old Tony."

Both women nodded in understanding. Tony Alverez's men had helped Annie and knew that they would do anything for their friends.

"He had my cell phone traced and then Gabe, who was near, came to watch over me until Matt got there. Then Matt and I talked…about a lot of things." Smiling up at her friends she continued, "I forgave him although there was nothing to forgive. Well, maybe for letting that woman sleep on his couch. Then we went home and made up."

Annie grinned. "Make-up sex is the best, isn't it?"

At that, all three ladies begin to giggle again and Lily felt the weight of carrying her own burdens lift. *This is what Ellen was always trying to get me to do – go out for drinks to have a little fun.* Thinking back on her co-worker, she wished that she had not missed that chance.

After a couple more rounds, all three women were fairly drunk and were just about to call a cab when suddenly they were surrounded. Looking behind them, Matt, Shane, and Gabe were standing with a look of amusement on their faces.

"Looks like the women had a good time tonight, men," Matt announced, walking over to surround Lily with his embrace.

Shane captured Annie before she slid off of her chair announcing that he was taking home his drunken fiancé so he could have his wicked way with her. She slapped playfully at him before sinking into his arms.

Gabe looked down at Suzanne with brotherly affection saying, "Come on, doll-baby. Let's get you home before you decide to puke in my truck." Trying to glare at him only created a funny look on her face so she gave up and allowed him to pull her out of her seat.

Good-nights were said all around as the friends left the bar.

Arriving at home, Matt tucked Lily in bed before sliding in himself. Making sure to put her crutch next to the bed in case she needed to get up in the night, he watched her sleep for a few minutes before joining her. Pushing Pippi to the side, he curled his body protectively around her sleeping form. The fear from the morning slipped away as he slept soundly with her in his arms.

(Surveillance)

"ARE YOU SURE you saw her find a piece of paper?"

"Yeah, I'm sure. She found it on the bottom of a file drawer."

"Goddamn it, we have searched that office several times before. I've sent someone in to search it again, this time looking carefully for hidden items. What did she do with it?"

"I told you, I can't be sure. She was at her desk and then sat down. There were papers all over the fuckin' place so I have no idea. I don't know if she put it on her desk, in her purse, in a pocket."

"Fuck," came the expletive. "I want to know what it said."

"Well, she didn't act upset. She just kept on working all afternoon at her boring-ass job like she does every day."

"Keep an eye on her. I want to know the instant she does anything out of the ordinary. I will talk to the boss. It may be time to do something to get her away."

Chapter 11

THE DAY HAD been long and Matt was already looking forward to going home. Smiling to himself he realized how much of a difference Lily had made in his life. Before her, he hated going to his apartment and its reminders. Reminders of another life. Another time. Another person. All of which he was glad was over. But Lily? She tempted him out of his morose life and breathed fresh air into his very being.

"I would ask what the hell you're thinkin' about with that shit-eatin' grin on your face, but I have a feelin' I know," came the voice from the other side of the table.

Looking up into Shane's face, Matt just grinned even more. "Just counting down the hours till we can get out of here."

They were working on the categorization of the drugs from the latest bust. Several detectives, patrolmen, and even a couple of DEA agents were working with them. The labels on the prescription bottles had been partially removed but they were analyzing what was left. They were also cataloging the various types of drugs, taking pictures of the pills themselves, knowing that any identification to their origins would be vital.

The chief popped his head in the doorway calling out, "Gotta go. A call just came in from a pharmaceutical warehouse in the city. There's been a robbery and it looks bad."

Matt, Shane and the others jumped up to head out of the door. Driving to the scene, Matt rubbed his hand over his face. Sighing deeply he said, "Jesus, I am so fuckin' tired of being one step behind these guys all the time."

Shane agreed as they sped down the road. Coming to a warehouse, they noted the number of police vehicles in the area. Parking the truck, they flashed their badges as they walked into the facility.

They saw a woman holding a bloody bandage to her head as a policewoman sat with her. Three other employees were giving their statements. Walking up to the detective in charge, they asked for an update.

"At about four-thirty this afternoon, four armed men came into the front lobby with guns. According to the main lobby receptionist, they stormed up demanding that she open the door to the back. She refused at first, but then got clocked on the head. One of the men went around the counter and hit the door release and the other three went through. We've got that all on camera.

"The next camera picks them up as they run down the main hall, turning to the left at the first corner and proceeding to a storage room. That particular room held the anti-depressants and antipsychotic meds according to the men being questioned over there. Two of them are pharmacists and the other is a pharmaceutical tech. They filled their bags and then ran back out, picking up the man they left in the lobby. We haven't looked at the outside cameras yet."

Matt and Shane looked at each other. "You say they ran straight to the room holding these drugs? I wanna see those films."

"You thinkin' what I'm thinkin'? That this is an inside job?"

"Yeah, for them to know exactly where to go."

They walked to the security room where they were greeted by the security guard. Looking at him with suspicion, they asked to see the videos. While looking at them, it was obvious that the thieves knew what they were doing. The man who ran behind the lobby reception desk did not look around or hesitate. He ran straight for the door release. The others, once in the facility, ran straight to the room as though they were following a map. Or orders.

Turning to look at the security guard Matt asked, "You got any idea how those men knew what they were doing and how to do it?"

"No, sir I don't," he answered looking Matt directly in the eyes. "We've never had any problems here before at all. Mr. VanHeusen runs a tight ship."

At that Matt's head jerked up from the notes he was taking. "VanHeusen? As in Malcolm VanHeusen?"

"Yes, sir. This facility is owned by the VanHeusen Medical Corporation."

Matt and Shane shared a glance, a whole new set of questions on their minds. Finishing up with the guard's statement, they went back to the front where the others were still being interviewed.

"What are you thinkin'?" Shane asked, already knowing the way his partner's mind worked.

"I'm thinking it's not a coincidence that we are chasing our asses after a prescription drug ring and now a huge robbery has occurred in a warehouse owned by the same man who has a clinic where a woman was recently murdered."

Shane agreed. "It's time we paid Mr. Malcolm VanHeusen a visit."

Knowing it was too late to see him in his office, they drove to his house. Or rather, his estate. The man lived in a multimillionaire subdivision where each home seemed to rival the others in their chance to be the most opulent.

"Jesus fuck. How much money does it take to live in one of these mansions?" Matt wondered out loud.

"More than what you and I would ever realize," Shane answered. "I guess the medical corporation business must be very good."

"Or whatever he may have on the side," retorted Matt. He remembered Lily complaining about Mr. VanHeusen's high-handed way of handling her and he found himself wanting him to be their suspect.

After pulling into the long, curving driveway and parking, they were met at the front door by a butler. The man let them in and showed them to a library off to the right of an entrance foyer that rivaled some of the largest hotels in the city.

They did not have to cool their heels for very long before Mr. VanHeusen appeared. Matt remembered Lily's description of how the air in a room would change when he would appear. Dressed for dinner in a suit that Matt was sure cost more than his monthly salary, he noticed that Malcolm's eyes slid quickly over his and Shane's jeans and jackets. Matt had to agree that the man certainly walked into a room with an air of confidence that would easily overpower a weaker person. But for Matt and Shane, he was just another person of interest.

Malcolm eyed them quickly, assessment in his gaze. "Detectives, have a seat please." He directed them to the sofas in the room. The three men sat and stared at each other speculatively.

"I am assuming this has something to do with the theft at my pharmaceutical warehouse?"

"How did you hear about it, Mr. VanHeusen?"

"Detectives, a man in my position makes sure that I am constantly informed about *anything* that affects my company. I received the call as soon as the call was made to the police."

"What can you tell us? About the business? Your employees? What was housed there?"

Piercing them with a direct gaze, he began what they were sure was a practiced speech, as though he were being interviewed by a magazine.

"VanHeusen's Medical Corporation is a multi-million dollar medical company that now encompasses medical facilities as well as several pharmaceutical warehouses. We are based here in Richland, but have branches all over the country. Our medical facilities are staffed with the highest quality medical personnel, ranging from family practices to specialty medicine. Our patients' care comes first and we participate in most insurance plans as well as Medicare. We have found that our patients need assistance with the costs of pharma-ceutical needs and have branched out into pharmaceutical services as well. This allows us to buy wholesale and then pass on the savings to our clients."

His canned speech over, he sat back continuing to hold their gaze.

"If you offer discounted prices to your patients on their drugs, how do you make a profit?" Matt asked.

A flash of irritation flew through Malcolm's eyes, but was gone as quickly as it came. If Matt had not been staring at him, he was sure he would have missed it.

"I assure you the insurance companies are apprecia-tive of our prices and the pharmaceutical companies refund us for costs. We don't take a loss on the drugs, but we offer incentives for our clients to choose us."

"Do you have any idea who might have been inter-ested in stealing your drugs?"

At this question, the flash of anger across Malcolm's face grew larger and he leaned in. "Detective," he bit out. "I do not make it a habit to interact with the criminal element. I have no idea who may be behind these thefts, but I want them caught as much as you do. I won't be able to use the drugs even if you find them, so there will still be a loss, but I want the responsible parties to be brought to justice."

"You can't use the drugs?"

"Of course not. Any drug that has been out of the sanitized areas is no longer valid for us to use or sell."

"It would seem like you have lost a great deal in this robbery."

"Of course. I will tell you that they are insured so that my company will be reimbursed for the loss."

"So you will not be out any money, whether or not the thieves are caught?"

"Isn't that the way with most expensive items that are stolen, detectives?" he questioned with distain in his voice.

"You may be interested to know that the thieves had inside information."

With that statement, shock registered on Malcolm's face for the first time. For a man who prided himself on knowing all, it appeared that he was truly surprised. Or he was a very good actor.

"Inside information?"

"We have them on camera. They knew exactly where the door release button was in the lobby. And which room to run to once through that door."

Watching him, they saw as his mind began to click through scenarios. Matt continued, "So do you have anyone that you believe might have perpetrated this robbery?"

Snapping back to attention, Malcolm said, "No, I don't. But I assure you, detectives, that if I find out, I will turn them over." With that, he stood and said, "Now gentlemen, if you will excuse me I have guests to return to."

Driving away, Matt and Shane discussed the case. "I want that arrogant prick," Matt said.

"Why? Because he's insulting to Lily or because you really think he's guilty?"

Letting out a deep breath, Matt admitted, "Both."

"Yeah, well I think he's guilty too. Maybe not in any of this shit, but I just don't trust the man."

THE NEXT MORNING Malcolm was in his board room, surrounded by Curtis, Allen, Penelope, his head of security, as well as Carla.

"I want to know what the fuck is going on," he bit out in uncharacteristic anger. "The police show up to my residence when I am entertaining guests, and let me know that the robbery was an inside job."

The eyes around the table snapped to attention and began looking around at each other.

Malcolm's piercing gaze centered on his chief of security. "I want to know who was in and out of that building for the past three months. The police are going to be asking the same questions and I want to know everything before them."

Turning back to the other faces around the table, he looked at Curtis. "You, Dr. Bennett, have been very quiet since I brought Penelope on board. Do not think it has escaped my attention that you coveted the job, but I didn't think you were up to it." Turning to Penelope, he began his next assault, "You are my chief of staff. I want to know what is going on in this building at all times. I do not want any more surprises of any kind."

Allen was next on his tirade. "Dr. Purser, you have been traipsing along as though you don't have a care in the world. Well, that stops now.

"And lastly, Carla. You have been completely ineffective in continuing the job of the Marsh woman. The police haven't found her murderer and I want to know what is going on in that office.

"I run a multi-million dollar corporation and these kind of public incidents are making my stock-holders nervous. I do not want nervous stock-holders. We all have too much at stake. So either do your fucking jobs or you will find yourself on the street. Do I make myself clear?"

With that, he turned and stalked out of the room, leaving the top staff members in his wake.

(Surveillance)

"SOMETHING'S GOT TO happen."

"When?"

"Soon. As soon as you can arrange it."

"How big?"

"Big. But not permanent. But wait just a bit. They want to see if they can find out anymore information from her first."

"Just give me the word and it'll be done."

ANDREA GREETED HER the next morning. "Looks like troll lady is going to be late."

Lily couldn't help but giggle, but admonished Andrea all the same. "Look, I know she seems like a troll, and I honestly don't know why Mr. VanHeusen hired her since she cannot write software, but he must have had a good reason."

"Yeah, probably banging her," Andrea responded, her nose turned up at the thought. "By the way, Dr. Alease wants to have a meeting with you today."

Sitting down at her desk, she sighed. "Do you know what time?" *I need to get this job finished, but at this rate it will take forever.*

"She said she would come down to see you this morning."

Settling in to get to work, she was surprised to see Penelope coming through the door. Glancing at the clock, she realized that several hours had passed. Smiling at the doctor, she greeted her. "Nice to see you. What can I do for you, Dr. Alease?"

Penelope sat down in the other office chair and looked around. "They really squeezed you into a little room didn't they?"

Lily looked around the office that she had been loathed to move to, but was now so used to it that she didn't think about it much anymore. "It's okay. It serves its purpose." Looking back at the woman sitting across from her, she said, "What brings you down here today?"

"I just wanted to check on your progress. We haven't had a chance to talk recently and I needed an update."

"I'm sorry," Lily added. "The software for the physicians to use is basically complete. My company will be interfacing it with the software that your doctors already use. It was based on the needs that Ellen assessed before she...was...killed." Lily hesitated, looking into Penelope's eyes. "I still have a hard time saying that."

"Were you two close?" Penelope asked.

"Close co-workers," Lily admitted. "We enjoyed each other's company and were close here. But not close, personal friends. Anyway, with the new program the physicians will be able to prescribe medications for their patients and the software will analyze the patient's past medication history, any indications or exclusions necessary, and with it tied into VanHeusen's pharmaceutical warehouse they will know if the medications will be available through your corporation."

A look of surprise flashed through Penelope's eyes before she returned to a professionally interested, but bored expression. "Oh," she said casually. "I wasn't aware that you were using any information from the warehouse in your programing."

Shrugging, Lily replied, "I just took the information that Ellen gave me to work into the equations. Why? Is there a problem?"

Smiling, Penelope rose from her chair. "No, I'm sure it's fine," she said as she turned to leave the office.

Andrea walked back in after Penelope left. "What was that all about?"

Lily put her elbows on her desk and leaned her head into her hands. Sighing deeply, she answered, "I don't know. I get so tired, Andrea, trying to figure out people. And this job has been the worst."

Andrea sat down in the chair vacated by Penelope and looked kindly at Lily. "How so? Well, besides what happened to Ellen, which would make anyone want to run for the hills."

Looking up at Andrea's understanding face, she replied, "In most of my jobs Ellen, or whoever the team leader was, would do studies to see what the company needed and then we would go in and write the programs to make it happen. We used to do it all from our own parent company, but discovered that sometimes it was helpful to actually be in an office at the place where we were programing. We would work, get it done and then get out of there. Maybe meet a couple of employees. Usually we just kept to ourselves and did the job. But here? Jesus Andrea, this place is like some TV show. There are multiple people I have to interact with, all seemingly with their own agenda. I'm trying to do the job and now don't have the person who gathered the information. The top players in this corporation keep wanting to know what I am doing as though I am doing something wrong."

Taking a deep breath, she leaned back in her chair. "Oh, don't mind me. I'm just tired. And on top of everything else, I can't find some of the files that Ellen had completed, which makes my job harder and seems to have royally pissed off Carla."

A knock on the office door had both women looking up. Andrea jumped up from her chair, greeting, "Dr. Bennett. May I help you?"

Curtis looked around, scowling – which seemed to be his permanent expression. "Dr. Alease mentioned that you were using information from the pharmaceutical warehouse."

Beginning to lose her temper, she stated, "I used the information that was provided to Ellen. Is there a problem with the fact that we were and I still am trying to do my job?"

Taken aback, he looked at her speculatively. "One of my duties is to oversee the warehouse. I wasn't aware that she had any information. She didn't go through me."

"Well, that's not my problem. The information she collected has already been used in my programing. So there is nothing else left to wonder about. Now if you will excuse me, I need to get back to work."

Curtis stood, glancing around the room before stalking out.

Andrea shouted from the front, "I ordered take-out sushi and got some for you. I figured you would need to eat after the day you have had. They just called from reception and said it has been delivered."

Looking up gratefully, Lily agreed.

A few minutes later, Andrea and she took their boxes and began to eat. "I love their sushi," Andrea said. "It's always so fresh."

Lily thought hers tasted a little strange, but then after such a draining morning where she had been so stressed, probably everything would taste strange. After eating, she went back into her work area and began coding again. Her head felt heavy and the words began to blur on the page. Nausea crept over her as sweat broke out on her face.

Andrea walked back a few minutes later and gasped when she saw Lily.

Lily immediately pitched forward and threw up in the trash can. Andrea ran over pulling her hair back out of her way.

"Call...9...1..." was all she managed to get out before throwing up again. Leaning back weakly, she gasped. "I…,"

Andrea screamed as Lily fell to the side of the floor unconscious.

MATT RAN INTO the ER, flashing his badge at the security desk with Shane at his heels. "Lily Swanson?"

"ER Bay Four," came the quick answer.

Heading back, Matt recognized the doctor from VanHeusen's that had been at lunch with Lily. He was standing outside of the emergency room that Lily was in.

"Dr. Purser?" he called out.

Allen looked up in recognition. "Matt, right?"

"What happened?" Matt growled.

Allen's face looked grim. "She became ill after eating take-out that Andrea ordered. They're running toxicology right now, but it looks like food poisoning or a severe food allergy. I came along as a medical personnel from VanHeusen's."

Matt's heart pounded as he took a step back, then felt Shane's hand on his shoulder. "Food poisoning? What the fuck?"

Just then an ER doctor came out into the hall. He looked at the badges of Matt and Shane and asked, "Are you here for Ms. Swanson?"

Before Matt could answer, Shane spoke up, "Yes, he's her fiancé."

The doctor nodded and began speaking as Matt hung on every word. "We don't know exactly what caused her illness, but it appears that something was in her food. Something that caused either food poisoning or a severe food allergy and she almost stopped breathing. Luckily, she recognized that she was becoming ill and forced herself to vomit. That allowed to her to eject most of what she had eaten. She has a breathing tube in at the moment, but we will take it out shortly as she is completely breathing on her own. We are running the routine toxicology now and have obtained samples from her lunch as well as others from the restaurant. The Health Department has been called and will be investigating to see what type of food poisoning it was. Right now though, it seems as though Ms. Swanson was the only person who had food from that restaurant today that has gotten sick. Or at least sick enough to come into a hospital."

Matt slumped against the wall. "Jesus fuck. Can I see her?" Matt begged. The doctor acquiesced and Shane began talking to Allen to see what information he could give them.

Matt walked in and the sight nearly took him to his knees. Lily lay pale against the sheets, a breathing tube in her mouth and an IV in her arm. Eyes closed, thick lashes lay against her white cheeks. Her lips had no color as he touched them gently with his.

The attending nurse took pity on him and assisted him to a chair next to her bed. "She's just resting now, sir. Did the doctor talk to you yet?" At his nod, she continued, "Her signs are stable and the breathing tube will be coming out soon. He just wanted to leave it in until the danger had passed. You can talk to her and hold her hand. I'll be right back."

Matt scooted his chair closer and took her cold hand in his much larger one. "LilyBelle, what the hell happened, woman? I woke up with you earlier after we had such a rough morning and thought the fates had finally shined on me. They gave me the perfect woman. Perfect in every way. And you make me want to be the best man I can be. I couldn't believe it when Andrea called. I was so scared, baby."

He rubbed her hand gently, trying to infuse some warmth into her flesh. Suddenly, he felt her fingers move. Squeezing he hand again, he watched her eyes try to blink open. Slowly at first, and then they stayed opened. Monitors began sounding as her heart rate skyrocketed.

The nurse and attending doctor came running back in, followed by Shane and Allen.

"What's goin' on?" Matt asked, not letting go of her hand.

"She's waking up and most patients are frightened when they can't speak because of the breathing tube," the nurse explained, as the doctor leaned over Lily.

"Ms. Swanson, I am Dr. Yasari. You're in the hospital, but you are all right. You ate some food that wasn't good and you became ill. If you understand me I want you to squeeze my hand. Good, good. There is nothing to be afraid of. You can't speak right now because of a breathing tube, but we are going to remove it shortly. Do you understand that? Good. I am going to let this gentleman here stay with you if you would like?"

Lily's frightened eyes cut over to Matt and she squeezed the doctor's hand again. Once the tube was out, the nurse assisted her in drinking after they raised the head of her bed. Matt smoothed his hand over her forehead, pushing her hair back away from her face. She tried to speak, but could only croak.

Shane began asking some simple questions that she could easily answer, establishing that she had her own food, separate from Andrea's, and had not eaten anything other than what was in the take-out carton.

The doctor came back in and she asked, "When can I leave?"

"Well, Ms. Swanson, we want to continue to do blood tests to monitor your levels."

She looked at Matt beckoning him with her eyes. "Matt, I can't stay here. I hate hospitals. I feel like I'm going to suffocate here."

Matt and Shane shared a look. Turning to the doctor, he asked, "How much of a risk would she be if she went home and had someone monitor her?"

The doctor looked at the detective filling the room and he said, "Well, if she had a nurse for several days and would come in to the lab twice a day for a couple of days for lab work, I could agree to discharge."

Allen spoke up, "There are nurses on staff at VanHeusen's that could be used."

"That won't be necessary. I've got someone in mind who is completely trustworthy."

Allen bristled, "I assure you the nurses at our medical facility are top quality."

Matt rounded on him, "We'll take care of her nurse." He turned to Shane and winked. "And I've got the perfect person."

"LILY, HOW NICE to meet you," exclaimed the nurse that was waiting in her living room when Matt drove her home. "I'm Charlotte."

Lily looked at the attractive woman in her early fifties, wearing a nursing scrub top over comfortable jeans. She was taller than Lily, but then almost everyone was.

"I hope you don't mind me already being here. Matt called and explained the entire situation and I knew immediately that I wanted to be here."

"Thank you," Lily said, feeling a vibe traveling between Matt and the nurse.

"Mom, glad you could come," Matt said walking over and kissing his mother.

Lily gasped, "Your mom?"

"Matt, you didn't tell her who I was?" Charlotte scolded.

"She's had enough to worry about with worrying about meeting my mom," he explained. He scooped Lily up and headed back to the bedroom. "I'm putting her to bed and then I want to fix her something light to eat so that she will have some nourishment."

"Matt, you head to the kitchen since you know what she likes and I'll help her in the bedroom."

Lily felt as though she were totally out of control, but somehow she trusted Charlotte as much as she trusted Matt. Charlotte assisted her out of her clothes and into some pajamas. She also assisted her with her prosthesis before tucking her in.

Charlotte looked down at her with a twinkle in her eyes. "I wondered who would capture my son's heart. He was never really in love before." Seeing Lily begin to speak, she held up her hand. "Oh, I know all about that other one. She never held his heart. Only his interest for a little while. But you, my dear. You have tempted his heart out of hiding and for that, I am so thankful."

Pippi hopped up in the bed and curled up next to Lily. That was how Matt found her several minutes later when he went in to check on her – sound asleep with her tiny guardian dog. Leaning over to pet Pippi's head, he whispered, "Okay mutt. When I'm not here, you can be her guard dog."

Chapter 12

THE NEXT MORNING Lily woke hearing voices coming from the kitchen. Too tired to put on her prosthesis, she used her crutch to make her way to see who was there. Annie and Shane had joined Matt and Charlotte. They all looked up as she hobbled into the room and Matt assisted her to her chair.

She assured everyone that she felt much better, but agreed that Charlotte would drive her to the lab later that morning for more bloodwork. The discussion stalled out and she looked around at the anxious faces.

"I feel as though I've brought your conversation to a halt. What were you all talking about?"

It did not escape her notice that everyone seemed to avoid her eyes. "Honey, what's wrong? You all are scaring me."

Matt walked over and wrapped his arms around her and tucked her into his embrace. "Baby, we're just discussing how you got food poisoning and no one else from the restaurant did."

"Maybe I just had something that no one else ordered. Or bad fish. I know it couldn't have been intentional. I've thought about this non-stop. I couldn't be more boring. I know Ellen was much more outgoing than I was and I honestly don't know anything about her personal life, but there was nothing we were working on together that would have gotten her killed or have someone after me."

Charlotte entered the conversation. "Do you think Ellen could have been involved in something outside of work that was suspicious?"

Shane spoke up, "It doesn't appear that she was involved in anything. At least not that we have found. No boyfriend. No priors. No large debts. No major changes in her bank account. Had a group of friends, but no one suspicious."

The group continued to talk for several minutes before Shane and Annie left. Lily took a phone call while Matt and Charlotte coordinated when they would be available for Lily.

As she got off the phone, she said that Suzanne was bringing by some food later so that Charlotte didn't have to do all the cooking. Looking at Matt's worried face, Lily reached up to cup his cheek with her small hand. "Honey, it'll be all right. Suzanne won't kill us with her cooking."

Laughing, he kissed her before leaving for work, leaving Charlotte and Lily alone.

"Well, my dear. I think you should get back into bed and rest today. We will make a trip out for your labwork around noon."

Lily agreed, noticing that she was exhausted just

from having been up a little while. Before walking back into the bedroom, she grabbed her laptop and the two thumb drives with her info from Ellen. *Might as well get a little work done.*

It did not take long for the tedious work to put her to sleep. Charlotte found her later, asleep in bed, Pippi curled up next to her and her laptop still open on the covers next to her. Smiling as she looked down at the woman who had tempted her son into falling in love, she tucked the covers around Lily's shoulders.

THAT AFTERNOON, LILY heard a truck pulling into her driveway and looked out to see Tony and Gabe moving toward the front door. She opened it with a smile and invited them in.

"What brings you all here?" she asked.

Tony just raised his eyebrow at her and said, "Seriously? You even have to ask?"

Rolling her eyes, she smiled and said, "Matt? He must have called, but I don't need someone babysitting me. His mother is doing a great job of that."

Charlotte walked in and greeted Tony, whom she had met before. Introduced to Gabe, she offered the men some tea. They declined as they told Lily that they were there to check out her system. Tony said he was a little rushed the day it was installed and he wanted it checked out carefully by Gabe.

As Gabe went outside to check the connections and

camera, Tony looked down at the coffee table where Lily had her laptop and various papers strewn around.

"Getting some work done?" he asked.

"I'm totally stuck on a code that I cannot figure out and it is driving me crazy."

"I've got a new guy that's working for me. He does security also, but he's a computer whiz. New grad from college, but had done programing for a security company before coming on board with me. Matt wants someone out here anyway for a while when he's gone, so how about I send BJ your way?"

She shrugged and agreed, "Sure, why not? It'd be nice to talk nerd shop-talk with someone."

Tony pulled out his phone. "BJ? Got a new assignment for you. Matt's woman needs someone with programing experience who can also keep an eye on her for now. Yeah. Now."

Clicking his phone off, he then made another call. "Matt? Tony. Got a man with programing skills coming to Lily's house. Gonna keep an eye on things and help her while she is working from home." Smiling he said, "I'll tell her."

Looking down at Lily, he grinned. "Seems like I'm supposed to tell you that your boyfriend loves you. Hell, I feel like I'm in seventh grade," he joked.

Lily threw her head back and laughed, her eyes twinkling. Shaking her head, she turned to the kitchen to get some tea for everyone.

Tony watched her walk away, admiration in his

eyes.

An hour later, Tony and Gabe were finished with their security check. Satisfied that everything was in perfect working order they were ready to leave. Another truck pulled up to the street and a young man swung down from the seat. As he walked to the door, Lily was struck with how many handsome men Tony had working for him. This one was tall, bulky like all the rest, but with blonde hair. Tan face with blue eyes, he had a beautiful smile. Walking straight up to the group, he reached out his hand to her.

"Hello," he said politely. "You must be Lily. I'm BJ."

Taking his much larger hand in hers, she smiled. *Maybe computer nerd wasn't the right word for him after all.*

Lily and Charlotte went back into the house, while Tony talked to BJ for a few minutes. Hearing a truck leave, Lily looked up as BJ entered the front door. She had set up her laptop and papers all around the dining room table and he moved over there as well.

"What are you working on?" he asked, setting his laptop on the table next to hers.

Blushing slightly, she admitted, "Well, it's not work related. I'm trying to solve a puzzle that probably doesn't mean anything."

Seeing his interested look, she continued, "My co-worker was notorious for loving puzzles and creating almost scavenger hunts with computer codes. I had heard from others in our company that they used to compete to see who could solve her riddles the fastest. We hadn't worked together long, but she did enjoy doing that on her weekends and then on Monday mornings would tell me about them."

Sucking in a huge breath, she plunged ahead. "She was murdered-"

"What the fuck?" BJ interrupted, looking angry.

"I thought maybe Tony told you," she said softly, looking discomfited.

Rubbing his hand over his face, he sighed. "Sorry. You just took me by surprise. Tony didn't tell me any of that. Go ahead."

"Well, Ellen sent me an email before she was killed, but it was in a programing language that I was not familiar with. She wasn't really a programmer, but knew enough to do her job. I haven't had a lot of time to spend trying to decipher it. But I did find another clue where I found a thumb drive of hers. Anyway, I just want to solve it. Kind of a last tribute to her amazing talent for puzzles."

Nodding his understanding, BJ answered, "Well, let's have a look."

Several hours later Matt came home, finding his mother asleep on the couch and Lily sitting at the table deep in thought next to BJ who was typing away on his computer. Lily jumped up at his entrance, walking stiffly over to him.

"Baby, what's wrong with your leg?" he asked full of

concern.

"I'm just stiff. We've been sitting here for hours try-ing to work on some programing. I had no idea it was so late," she exclaimed.

Matt eyed BJ as he was packing up his laptop. BJ walked over and shook Matt's hand, introducing himself.

"Matt? Haven't had a chance to meet you. I'm BJ, from Tony's. He asked me to come over to keep an eye on Lily and since I have computer programing experi-ence, Lily asked for my help. I hope that's all right with you."

Matt eyed him carefully for a moment, liking what he saw in the young man's clear steady gaze. "If you work for Tony, then you have my trust. And if you can help my girl, then you have my gratitude."

Leaning over to kiss Lily's head, he said, "Be right back babe." He then walked BJ out of the house and she watched from the front window as the two men were in discussion walking to BJ's truck.

Charlotte had woken and came to stand next to Lily.

"What do you think they are talking about?" Lily asked.

Smiling, Charlotte wrapped her arm around Lily's shoulders. "If I know my son, he's both thanking BJ for helping, but also making sure he knows you're off limits."

Lily twisted around to look at Charlotte's face. "Off

limits? What kind of macho-man act is that?"

"Sweetie, my husband is the kindest man in the world. He lets me know every day that I am the center of his world. But he also made it very plain to anyone that was ever interested that I was his." Before Lily could question, she continued. "Not in a bad way, honey. But I was his. His to protect. His to cherish. His to love. And you know what?" She turned her understanding gaze to Lily, "I have known where that man laid his head every night that we have been married. I'm as devoted to him as he is to me."

Lily couldn't help but feel a pang of envy that Matt had grown up with two parents that so obviously loved each other and showered that love on their son. Taking a deep breath, she asked, "So he is claiming me?"

Charlotte threw her head back and laughed. Turning to hug Lily, she replied, "Oh sweetie. From the moment you tempted his heart, he's claimed you." Then turning serious, she continued, "But Lily, if you can't be that person for him then let him know. I don't want him hurt again."

Looking into the concerned gaze of his mother, she smiled and nodded shyly.

Eyes twinkling once again, Charlotte hugged Lily. "I knew it, sweetie, from the first moment I saw you two together. You're it for him. And I know my son. He's it for you."

Just then, Matt came back inside and was warmed by the sight of his mom embracing Lily. "Mom, you ready to head out? I'll walk you to your car."

"Charlotte, thank you so much for coming over the past two days to take care of me."

"My dear, it has been my pleasure. And…" she said, looking at her son. "Your father has already demanded that you two come over for dinner soon. He wants to meet Lily for himself."

Matt wrapped his arm around his mom, promising they would come as soon as they could. Winking at Lily over his mom's head, he walked her to her car.

Coming back into the house again, he immediately walked over to Lily and placed his hands on either side of her face. Pulling her forward he swooped in for a kiss, plundering her mouth. She clung to his shirt, feeling the kiss all the way through her core and she no longer trusted her legs to hold her up.

His kiss started out passionately, but soon felt as though he needed the kiss to survive. Tongues tangling, breaths mingling, his dick began to swell painfully in his jeans.

Lily let one of her hands slide down to palm his crotch, feeling it swell even more in her hands. She heard him groan, but was unable to think of anything other than what she wanted him to do to her.

The kiss had taken on a life-force of its own and she no longer knew where she began and he ended.

Matt lifted her up on the kitchen counter, pushing her long skirt up above her hips. Pulling her to the edge of the counter, his lips left hers and made a trail down towards the prize he was seeking. Slipping his fingers underneath the thin strips of her panties, he ripped them off, tossing them to the floor. Not able to wait any longer, he gently pulled her thighs apart and dove in with his tongue to her warm center. Lapping her juices, he knew she was it for him. No woman ever made him feel like she did, opening herself so honestly to him as she did. Using one hand he pressed on her stomach just enough to have her lean back on the counter and then he lifted her thighs over his shoulders.

Lily was in ecstasy but wished she could forget about her leg. It was always there in the back of her mind, even in the throes of passion. But as he moved his tongue around her nether lips and then pulled gently on her clit, she lifted her head to watch him between her thighs. Smiling, she suddenly realized that it didn't look so bad. The prosthetic leg below her left knee was so much a part of her. *If it doesn't bother him, why let it bother me?*

Giving over to the heat pounding through her, she grabbed his shoulders as she cried out, the shock waves radiating out over her entire body. Falling back onto the counter, the sated feeling washed over her.

He lifted his head from her drenched pussy and smiled at the beauty in front of him. Open. Trusting. Her blonde hair spilled over the counter and her chest moved up and down rapidly as she tried to catch her breath. And her face. Soft and glowing with a smile that melted his heart. *Goddamn. I want her in every way.*

Standing, he carefully lowered her legs and moved forward to put his hands under her armpits. "Come on LilyBelle, let's get to bed."

Allowing herself to be scooped up, she wrapped her arms around his neck as he carried her to the bedroom and gently set her on the edge of the bed.

"You're a little overdressed," she said smiling coyly, pulling her shirt up over her head, then tossing her bra onto the floor.

"Well, little lady, I reckon I need to take care of that," he replied, pulling his t-shirt off and adding it to the ever growing pile of clothes on the floor as she quickly began to take off the prosthesis. "Leave it on, babe," he ordered. Shucking his pants, freeing his swollen cock, he stalked over to the bed fisting it.

"You want this babe?" he growled.

Eyes wide, she grinned her response.

He pulled her to stand in front of him, dipping his head to slam his lips onto hers, palming her breasts. His tongue plundered her mouth once again and his hands tweaked her nipples. Capturing her moans in his mouth, he could feel her moving against him.

Turning her gently, he said, "Bend over. Hands on the bed baby."

As turned on by his order as the feel of his hands still on her breasts, she obeyed eagerly. She knew she was ready for him, but heard it confirmed when he growled, "Jesus fuck, you're soaked for me." Smiling she readied herself for the new experience. And was not disappointed.

Matt slowly entered her from behind, his dick screaming to take her hard, but he was determined to make sure she was ready. *Goddamn tight. Fuckin' amazing.*

He was touching a part of her that had never been touched before and the sensations had her spinning out of control. It did not take many thrusts to have her throw her head back and cry out his name as her orgasm milked his dick. Falling forward on her elbows on the bed she wasn't sure her legs could support her, then felt his large hands on her hips, moving her body against his.

He began pounding harder, each thrust shifting her body forward. One hand on her hips, helping her move against him and the other hand on her breast, he felt himself lose control. Her tight pussy walls grabbed his dick and he knew he was rougher than ever before.

"Are you okay, babe?" he checked. Her smile was his answer.

Feeling his balls tighten, he slapped her ass hard a time or two before rubbing the sting away. Just as his dick was about to explode he fingered her clit once again, sending them both over the edge at the same time. Throwing his head back, he powered through his orgasm, filling her waiting body. *Fuckin' hell, fuckin' hell. Never felt that before.*

Lily slid face forward onto the bed, her legs no longer able to support her as he fell forward as well and slid to the side. They lay there panting, their hearts pounding in unison, sweat mingling until slowly consciousness returned.

She lay with her back to his chest, a smile on her face realizing that he was treating her no different than if both legs were whole. *I can do this,* she thought. *I can be adventurous with sex. He's given this to me.* Suddenly empowered, she twisted in his arms to look into his face.

Wanting to tell him how she felt, she was halted by the concerned expression.

"What's wrong, baby?" he asked, still breathless.

Smiling her response, she assured him, "Nothing, honey. I'm great. That was…um…good." Feeling foolish, she began to giggle.

Sliding his hand up to cup her beautiful face, he growled jokingly, "Woman, you shouldn't laugh after sex. And never describe it as 'good' if you wanna stroke my ego."

"Somehow, I don't think your ego needs any stroking," she replied. "But I confess, it was…amazing." Her expression turning serious, she blushed and said, "Thank you, Matt."

He lifted his eyebrow in question. "LilyBelle, don't know what you're thanking me for, but you never have to thank me for what we just did."

Ducking her head, she said softly, "You accept me."

Lifting her chin with his fingers, gently forcing her eyes back to his, "Babe, I want your eyes when we're talking. I love you, Lily. All of you. I'm no hero for falling in love with you. That's what love is, babe. Acceptance. Understanding. We'll fight and we'll make up. We'll learn what works and what doesn't. In bed, I like control and I like to play. We start to do something you're not cool with, all you gotta do is let me know. This is all about you, but not in the fucked up way I tried before with Cassandra." Seeing doubt flash through her eyes, he continued, "And this is the last time I will ever mention any other woman's name in our bed. I'm only doing it now to get you to see that what we've got, is not my giving in. It's me finding a woman that makes life worth living. A woman that makes my life better just by havin' your smile on me."

Tears flowed down Lily's cheeks as the warmth of his love flowed over her. Her breath hitched as she planted her face in his chest, giving way to the emotions. Trying to speak, she choked out, "Never. I've never had that."

He let her cry, his massive arms wrapped around her body as it bucked with sobs. Sliding one hand to the back of her head, he held her as close as he could, making shushing sounds.

Slowly the tears subsided, leaving sniffles. He reached across her body to snag some tissues from the nightstand. She grabbed them, wiping her nose and eyes before looking back up at him.

"You wanna tell me what that was all about, LilyBelle?"

"I told you…my parents never…well, after."

He let her pull her thoughts together, still holding her tight.

Rolling on her back, she stared at the ceiling before he leaned up on one arm to peer down into her face.

Red nose and eyes, she was still the most beautiful woman he had ever seen. Strong. Fragile. Accepting. "What is it, babe?"

Sucking in a shaky breath, she continued. "After the accident, mom and dad just never...I don't know. They just never could forgive me. And with that, they never could accept me."

"Baby, you gotta know, that is totally fucked," he said vehemently.

"In my adult mind, I know it is. But when you're sixteen years old and your friends are worried about their looks when all they have to think about is their hair, makeup and how their ass looks in their jeans...well, it was real lonely worrying about using crutches, physical therapy, getting a prosthesis. No one to talk to. No one to understand. And my parents...every time they looked at me, they were reminded that Rose was gone."

Matt gave her a squeeze, knowing that she had endured what no one should have to endure.

"Baby, know this. I mean, really know this. Take it in and take it deep." He hesitated until her eyes met his and he was sure she was with him in the moment before he continued. "I'm in love with you. All of you. With everything that makes you *you*. With me so far?" At her wide-eyed nod, he said, "That being said, you gotta know that this goes both ways. My fucked up face is nothin' compared to what you went through, but I let it pull me down and I let it pull me under. But this," he said motioning between their bodies, "Is real. Pure acceptance and pure love, LilyBelle."

The smile she gave speared his heart and warmed his soul. Pulling her back into his chest, he kissed the top of her head. "Yeah, my baby gets me."

Lily grinned as she agreed.

Chapter 13

MATT AND SHANE got a call from the jail that Jeff Roberts wanted to talk. They headed over to meet with him, hoping that the possibility of time in prison had loosened his lips. Going through the check-in procedures, they moved down the hall to the interview room. Within a few minutes, he came in glancing warily around.

"Have a seat," Matt ordered, nodding to the gray metal chair at the table. Jeff continued to look around uncomfortably as he slouched into the chair.

"Gonna lay it out Jeff," Shane said. "You called this meeting. We're takin' time outta our day to get over here to give you that play. You dick us around, you won't get a second chance. You got that?"

Jeff's eyes settled on Shane's before sliding over to Matt. Licking his lips while nodding, he agreed. "Yeah, I get it."

"Good. So what's this about?"

Jeff sucked in a huge breath and let it out slowly. "My old man's not bailing me out. I've got no money on my own, so he said the only way he'll get a lawyer is if I come clean." Sighing again he continued, "So here I am."

"That such a hard decision for you to make? You that loyal?"

"No, man." Looking up quickly, he corrected himself, "No, sir."

"So there is a young man in there who was taught something."

The silence stretched out between them, Shane and Matt letting it settle, not rushing Jeff.

"It just seemed so easy. Easy money. Just…easy."

"You got somethin' against hard work? Your parents may be rich, but bet your dad works for it."

Jeff nodded. "I know you think I'm some rich kid punk, but I know my dad worked hard. He put himself through medical school and most of my life I just remember being in awe of him. Then I got older and I was in awe of how cool is was to tell people that my dad was a doctor. Almost like I had some kind of charm." Leaning back in his seat, he exclaimed, "Fuckin' stupid."

The silence settled once again.

"The second time I went to the alley behind the warehouse, I was scared shitless. I wasn't sure that I had taped the stuff the way I should have so I turned around to go back. Once there, I heard noises and hid. I peeked and saw a man get out of a car. A woman was with him. She got out, but stood kind of in the door of the car and didn't go anywhere else."

"You recognize them?"

"No. But I wasn't real close and didn't get a good

look at their faces. I was hiding behind them, slightly to the side."

"Anything you can tell us."

"They were driving a silver Mercedes. I know because it looked a lot like the kind of car my mom drives." Looking up he continued, "And before you ask – no, I didn't get the license. I wasn't even thinking about that." Licking his lips nervously, he said, "But what struck me was that they looked…normal. Not like hoods or dealers or anything. They looked just like they could have been anyone that we would see. You know, like someone's mom or dad."

"We're gonna get a police illustrator in here and you're gonna describe everything you can, right down to the most insignificant detail."

Standing up, Matt looked down at Jeff, still sitting in his chair, looking dejected. "What made you change your mind to help us?"

Jeff raised his eyes to Matt's and said, "You ever been in jail? It's scary as shit."

Matt and Shane shared a look and as they walked out, Matt mumbled, "Whatever works, man. Whatever works."

SITTING IN THE conference room at the station, Matt and Shane looked at the board they had created. As they were trying to tie the pieces together with the new information, the chief walked in with a couple other detectives.

"What have we got so far? Anything from that Roberts kid?"

Going over the evidence that was new, they began working the problem out loud.

Shane began the evidence. "From what we can tell, some dealers go to parties the teens are havin' and watch the ones who are bringin' something from mom and dad's medicine cabinet. Looks like they weed out the scared ones, the ones not serious, and pick up on the ones who are smart and driven. Especially the ones who may have something that can be held over their heads."

"MO is essentially the same then," Matt adds. "Kid is asked to get some drugs from home and is then given money. Sees their drugs being sold at huge profit and gets the idea that this is an easy way to get some money. The kid gets hooked in by stealing from mom, dad, grandma's medicine cabinet to sell them at the next party. Then the recruiter has the kid by threatening their future if they stop or tell."

Another detective reported, "I've interviewed most of the kids we arrested at that last bust. Seems that a hierarchy is used. Most of the kids stay low on the totem pole. They never see anyone but the guy at the party. We have sketches of him, but no positive identification yet. It seems like they report to the next kid who has made it higher up. In this case, it was Jeff Roberts."

"Why Jeff?" the chief asked. "What made him different?"

Matt answered, "Don't know. He's cocky. Smart. Had a lot to lose with his football scholarship. Also his dad's a doctor, so we don't know if that's the hook or not. Jeff was never asked to steal from his dad or try to get his dad involved in any way. So either his dad being a doctor was just a coincidence or it hadn't come up yet."

"Got anything on his dad?"

"Doesn't appear to be a tie-in. Dad's a straight up surgeon at the hospital. Good reputation. And gotta say, he cut his son no slack when Jeff ended up arrested. Said he would supply a lawyer only if Jeff cooperated."

"Anything from the warehouse?"

"So far nothing. We've had it searched and found nothing so far. If someone was watching it, then they know we know about it and are going to start using another drop-off point."

The detectives continued to discuss the case for a few more minutes before breaking up. Walking to their desks, Shane asked Matt about Lily.

"She's fine. Mom went home last night and she was going back to work today."

"You still think it was intentional?"

"I don't know. Maybe it was food poisoning. But I don't believe in coincidences, so I'm keeping an eye on her."

(Surveillance)

"IS SHE COMING back today?"

"That's what I heard. I'm keeping my eyes on her if she comes in."

"Hopefully she will be finishing up here soon. Boss wants her gone before she finds anything."

"She need another nudging? I thought poisoning her would have gotten her outta here quicker."

"No, not now. That cop boyfriend could become a problem if we move too quickly or often. Just keep looking at what she does and who she talks to."

"That's not hard."

"You keeping an eye on her is keeping you hard."

Laughing at their joke the door closed quietly behind the retreating figure.

LILY WALKED BACK into the building once again and was filled with the thought that she needed to finish this project and say goodbye to VanHeusen Medical. *Never have I felt this way about one of my work sites. I just want to get the hell out of here.*

Stepping off of the elevator into the basement hall, she was greeted by Andrea holding a cup of coffee.

Laughing she said, "How did you know this is just what I need?"

Andrea smiled and said, "I told the receptionist upstairs to buzz me as soon as you got here. I just knew you needed something to face the day." Her face softening she asked, "How are you?"

Lily looked over at her assistant as they walked to the offices. "My stomach is still a little queasy, but other than that I'm fine."

"Well, I'll warn you that the troll is already in there today."

"Great. Then thanks again for the coffee. I'll need all the help I can get to face her today."

Walking into the office, she was stunned to see Carla get out of her chair and approach her with a smile and what appeared to be concern on her face. *What the hell?*

"Oh Lily, I was so worried. How do you feel?"

"Um, fine. I'm…um, fine," she said awkwardly, not knowing what else to say.

"Well, I don't want you too overtaxed today, so you just let me know what you need and I'll take care of it."

"I'm finished with most of the programing but without Ellen's newer assessments, I need to get some information from the doctors so that I can test the programs."

"You let me know what you need and I'll be sure to get it," Carla assured her. Just then Andrea stuck her head in the doorway and said, "Carla, you're wanted in the board room."

Preening, she stood, smoothing her hands down her pencil skirt as she left the room.

Andrea rolled her eyes and winked at Lily behind Carla's back before going back to her desk.

Lily worked for an hour, until the frustration of unanswered questions began to take its toll. *I don't have Ellen's information and Carla is incompetent. I need to get it myself.* Hating to interrupt doctors, she knew she had no choice. Pulling out the medical release she had from Malcolm VanHeusen himself, she grabbed the forms she needed and walked out of the office. Andrea wasn't at her desk so she just left a note telling her she would be back soon.

Starting on the first floor, she began nervously approaching several of the doctor offices, giving her releases and forms to the doctor's receptionists. She was pleased to note that as soon as they saw the VanHeusen release, they immediately smiled and assured her that they would get the information to her right away. Giving them the download access, she was able to tell them that the data required would be downloaded to her computers.

Feeling empowered, she made her way to the second floor and was halfway through the third floor before being accosted by Dr. Bennett. *Great. Mr. Personality, himself.*

"What are you doing?" he asked in an accusing voice.

"My job. The one I was hired to do," she answered him just as forcefully.

"Your job is to get the programs written, not to go

door to door like some saleswoman."

Eyes flashing, she snapped. "Saleswoman? Let me tell you, Dr. Bennett. I have been patiently waiting ever since Ellen was killed for someone around here to help me. My parent company was not allowed to send someone in to take her place. The high and mighty Mr. VanHeusen hired an incompetent replacement who neither knows coding, programing, or basic assessment skills."

Warming to her speech she continued, advancing on him as her long held-back tirade spilled over. "Furthermore, I have been banished to the basement, have a camera on my office as though I was somehow responsible for Ellen's murder, and all I want is to finish this job so I can get the hell out of here."

Pulling herself up to her fullest height, which unfortunately was not very tall, she finished, "And that, Dr. Bennett, is what I was doing. Do you have any more questions?"

Turning on his heels he stalked down the hall, leaving her quaking with anger. By the time she got back to her office it was time to go home. Still angry, she decided a run would be a great way to get out some of her frustration. Calling her coach, she agreed to meet him at the track, then texted Matt to let him know where she was.

"GIRL, YOU ARE doing great," her coach called out. "You ready to do a couple of laps with me?"

Smiling at the encouragement, Lily agreed and he fell into step along side of her. Careful not to push her too hard, he asked, "So what would you think if I told you I was running in a five K race this weekend?"

Looking at him, admiring his gait and running form, she replied, "I would think that would be awesome."

"Okay, now what would you say if I told you that I registered you for the race also?"

At that, she stumbled and he reached out to steady her. Twisting her head to look at him she said, "No way. I'm not ready. I'm not good enough. Or fast enough. No way," she said adamantly.

"Look Lily. You don't have to be good or fast. Just determined to make it to the end. Time doesn't matter. There will be people of all ages and running abilities in the race."

"But it's a race," she said, her voice rasping as the pace had picked up a bit.

"Don't think of it as a race. Just think of it as a run. That's how lots of people view it. Sure there will be some there who are actually racing, but tons of others will just be there to run and meet other runners."

"But I've never run that far. I can't do it."

"You'll never know what you can do until you try."

Biting her lip in concentration as they began to slow down, she never noticed that Matt was standing on the side of the track. She walked to cool down with William staying by her side.

He gently shoulder bumped her. "So what do you think?"

They stopped and faced each other as she searched his eyes for courage. Taking a deep breath, she smiled a tenuous smile. "Okay, but don't tell anyone. If I fall flat on my face, I don't want anyone to know."

Rolling his eyes, he agreed. "You got it. It'll be this Saturday. You need to be there by eight a.m. and I already have you registered. Just come to Riverview Park and meet me at the registration booth and I'll give you everything you will need."

"Why do I think this will be a terrible idea?" she moaned.

William threw his arm around her shoulders as they walked back to the YMCA building. "Because anything new seems frightening. But you'll see. I'll make a runner out of you yet."

"Babe," came the deep voice from the side.

Turning to see Matt standing by the side, her smile beamed at him. She noticed several women in tight running clothes run past him, trying to catch his attention. But he had eyes only for her. Jogging over, she threw her arms up allowing him to scoop her into his embrace. Lifting her off the ground with one hand on her ass and one hand cupping the back of her head, he hugged her tightly.

"You looked amazing out there, LilyBelle. Just

amazing."

Nodding to William over Lily's head, he turned and began to walk away.

"Put me down. I'm all sweaty," she said.

"Not doin' it babe. Seeing you out there made me want to get all hot and sweaty with you."

Grinning, she tucked her face into his neck and purred as she licked him. "You got something special in mind?"

"Oh hell yeah, babe. And you keep playing like that and you'll find out just how special before we even make it home."

Giggling, she smiled at the incredulous looks of the other women around. "Then I guess you'd better get me home. But I really do need a shower first."

Matt grinned and she felt her heart melt as her core tingled. "Baby, you got a shower chair. We're gonna get creative while we get clean."

And he took her home and showed her just how creative he could get. In the shower. In the bed. In her heart.

Chapter 14

BY THURSDAY NIGHT, Lily was a bundle of nerves. She couldn't eat and paced the house. Matt tried to entice her to sit down to watch TV but she insisted on pacing. Stalking over to her, he grabbed her shoulders gently and pulled her around to face him.

"Babe, what the hell is going on? I'm not letting you get away with any more bullshit answers. Is it work? 'Cause if it is, I'm stepping in and getting you out of there."

"You can't order me not to go to work."

"I'm telling you that if you are this upset about something then it's not good for you and I will step in. I told you I like control and that includes controlling things about your life that are not good for you."

Placing her hands on his chest, she stared down at her feet for a moment before lifting her eyes back to his. "It's not about work. Although if it was, I would handle it, not you." She felt a slight squeeze on her shoulders. "Or at least we would talk about it first."

Sighing, she said, "You know, you're kind of dominant, aren't you?"

"Babe, for real? You're just figuring that out?"

"Matt, need I remind you that I've been on my own for a really long time. Not only is it weird for me to be in a relationship with someone, but for that person to be a controlling person is really bizarre."

Lowering his lips to her forehead, he said gently, "Don't you see? I'm dominant when it comes to taking care of you. And that's why you ended up with me. Deep down, as strong as you are, as independent as you are, there was a little piece of you that wanted to be taken care of."

She pondered his words as they flowed over her, spilling into all of the cracks and crevices of her soul. She couldn't argue. Couldn't deny. He was right. Part of her wanted to be cared for. Loved.

"So are you gonna tell me what is going on or does your ass need a little reddening to convince you?"

Her head popped up, eyes wide at his comment. "You wouldn't."

"How does that make you feel, babe?"

She hated to admit it but his words made her womb clench. And her breasts heavy. And her nipples tingle.

Laughing, he threw his head back. "Yeah, my baby likes to play a little too. I can see it in your eyes." Settling his look back on her face, he probed gently, "Okay, Lily, spill."

"I'm doing something this weekend with William and I'm unsure about it."

His body got still. "William? Your coach?"

"Um hmm," was her distracted answer.

"Baby, you want to elaborate? Let me put that another way. You need to elaborate."

She looked up at the tone of his voice and saw…vulnerability. Whatever it was, she realized that she had left the door open for misinterpretation.

"Oh, honey," she said, cupping his face in her small hand. "Nothing like that. I'm running."

"And…" he prompted.

"In a race," her voice said sounding small and unsure.

Instinctively pulling her into his embrace, he questioned, "A race?"

"William thinks that I'm ready and that I need more confidence. He said there is a five K fun-run race this weekend at Riverview Park and he signed me up. But if you don't want me to do it, I won't," she quickly added suddenly seeing a way out.

"Baby, I think it's a great idea. You've improved so much and it won't matter how you do, just give it a try."

"I guess," she agreed sighing heavily. *I hate this. I hate being such a wuss about something so silly.*

"Would it make you feel better if I ran in it too?"

Looking up she asked, "You'd do that for me?"

Smiling into her eyes, he said, "LilyBelle, haven't you figured out I'd do anything for you?"

"William said the race was full. But maybe you could be at the finish line? I wasn't going to tell you because I didn't want you to know, but now I think I'd like you to be there at the end."

"Baby, you want me there, then that's where I'll be. Nowhere else I'd rather be."

SATURDAY DAWNED BRIGHT and clear. A perfect running day. *Well, maybe for most runners. I want to throw up.*

Meeting with William near the registration table, she kissed Matt goodbye as he assured her he would meet her at the finish line. Pulling her lips in, trying not to cry, she just nodded.

After Matt walked away, William pinned her runner's number to her shirt. "Come on, let's go stretch." They walked a little away from the others and began to stretch and limber.

"Mommy, look at their funny legs," a small child said.

Looking over she saw the embarrassed look of a young mother trying to shush her child. She couldn't help but smile. "It's okay. It is a funny looking leg, isn't it?"

"Does it hurt?"

"No, not any more. But it helps me to walk and we can run as well," she said, indicating William's leg as well.

The child, curiosity satisfied, ran off as his mother mouthed 'thank you' to Lily before running after him.

William looked at her smiling. "You're good with

kids."

She looked over in surprise. "Me? I've never been around kids very much, but I'm totally used to the questions." She thought for a moment before continuing, "Kids are so much more accepting than adults can be. They look at it as an oddity and then when you explain it, they get it and move on. Adults act as though there is something wrong with my mind or other parts just because of the amputation."

William assisted her as they warmed their muscles in preparation for the race. "Do you want me to stay with you?"

Smiling at his friendship, she declined. "No, you run at your pace. I'm going to be fine."

"Yeah, you are."

As the runners were lining up, she gave him a quick hug. "See you at the finish line."

The runners began, her time starting when she passed the starting line. Taking a slow steady pace she quickly realized that the even surface of the track was completely different from the road they were traveling on, which included some gentle inclines. It took her full concentration to keep her pace and keep running. People passed her on either side, but she tried to focus just on her. *One step, one step. Steady, even.* She began to chant in rhythm to keep her gait steady.

Finally finding her pace, she began to look up more and realized that there were still many people around her and in back of her. *I'm not alone at the end,* she realized with glee. Smiling for the first time since William had suggested the race, she began to relax a bit. *Steady breathing, just like he taught me. In. Step, step. Out. Step. Step.*

At the one mile marker, she was winded but continuing. *I can do this. I can do this.* Her breathing began to labor a bit and her leg muscles were tiring. Suddenly she heard her name and looking to the side, she saw BJ holding a sign proclaiming 'Team Lily'. Smiling, she heard him yell, "Run to Gabe." Throwing a questioning gaze over her shoulder, she continued to run.

As the two mile marker came into sight, she was sure that she was going to have to quit. Battling back the tears, she continued to jog. Suddenly the air was filled with the sound of "Lily, Lily". Glancing to the side carefully she saw Gabe and Vinny holding a similar sign proclaiming they were on Team Lily and calling out encouragement. *Oh my God!* Smiling, she powered on, uplifted by their cheering. Gabe ran toward her, putting a cup of water in her hand before jogging away. She took a gulp and then tossed the cup like the other runners around her.

As she continued she realized that she wasn't bothered by them seeing her in shorts with her prosthesis showing. Used to covering her leg up in long pants except when she was at the track, it seemed strange to have others see her this way. Smiling as she plowed ahead, she was almost to the three mile marker when the terrain became a little rougher and the pain in her leg was making her limp. *I can't quit now. I'm so close.* Slowing down, she rounded the last turn and could see the finish line. The pain was almost blinding as she continued to put one foot in front of the other. For the last part of the run, the sideline was filled with William, Leon, Suzanne, Tony, Shane, and Annie yelling for Team Lily. Tears streamed down her face, making it harder to breathe.

The finish line was just ahead and as she crossed it she was swept up in Matt's strong arms before she could collapse onto the pavement. Wrapping her arms tightly around his neck, legs dangling, she sobbed into his throat. "I did it," she gasped.

One arm wrapped around her waist and a hand cradling the back of her head, he held on tight, not knowng which of them needed the other the most at that moment. But it didn't matter. Right then, they needed each other.

"I got you, baby. I got you."

His gravelly voice soothed over her, easing her tremors, as she slowly caught her breath. Pulling her face from his neck, she saw that they were surrounded by their friends.

Matt slowly lowered her so that her feet were once again touching the ground, but he kept his hand on her waist for support. Smiling down, he cupped her face and acknowledged, "You did it, LilyBelle. You did it."

William made his way to her side, congratulations flowing all around. "Lily, you've gotta stretch and cool your muscles down."

Nodding, she walked a few feet away and they sat on the ground as William worked her legs and stretched her muscles. Shane clapped Matt on the back saying, "Fuckin' amazin', man. She's just fuckin' amazin'."

Matt tore his gaze from his beautiful woman over to the friends surrounding him, a grin splitting his face. "She's something, isn't she?"

Just then a commotion off to the side captured their attention. A reporter with a microphone in her hand was dragging a cameraman along with her as she made a determined effort to push runners out of the way to get to Lily. "Come on. I want to get some videos of the crippled couple running."

Lily heard the woman, and hating attention, instantly panicked as William rose, his face angry. Before he could shield Lily a wall of masculinity developed, completely blocking the reporter's path. The reporter halted in her steps looking at the furious visages of Shane, Leon, Tony, Gabe, and Vinny. And the man right in front of her. A mountainous man with a look of pure rage. The deep scar across his forehead stood out as the veins in his neck pulsed.

Before she could begin to bluster, he growled, "Turn around and get the fuck outta here. You call my woman a cripple once more and I'll shove that mic down your fuckin' throat."

Her mouth opened and closed like a fish for a moment as her eyes darted back and forth between the men. Slowly backing up, tripping over the cameraman, she made her escape.

Matt's fury had not abated when he felt small, gentle hands first on his hips and then sliding around his waist until they were embracing him from behind. Dropping his head to his chest he took a shuddering breath to calm down before turning around.

"Honey, it's okay. I've been called lots of things."

"Not any fuckin' more," he growled as he turned, careful to wrap his arms around her as his body twisted into hers.

Looking around, she realized that once again their friends had encircled her in their protective stance. She smiled as she tucked her face into Matt's broad chest, and simply said, "Thanks guys."

She felt Matt's voice rumbling, "You stretched enough to go, babe?" She nodded her response then turned to look at William.

"Is there anything special I should do?" she asked him.

"After I run in a race and then stretch, I go home and get the prosthesis off. Take a warm shower to keep the muscles limber. Oh," he added smiling. "Take plenty of pain pills."

Giving him a playful shove, she just responded, "Thanks coach." Then sobering a moment, she reached out her hand and placed it on his arm. "No really. Thank you."

He nodded first at her and then gave Matt a chin

lift, receiving one in return before jogging off to his car.

Turning to their friends, she hugged Tony first and then made her way down to all of them. "Guys, this meant so much to me that you would come. I had no idea anyone would even care…" her voice cracked as tears filled her eyes.

As Gabe swung her around he said, "So proud of you girl. BJ had to leave but wanted me to tell you that I'm supposed to give you a hug from him." Hugging her twice, he winked at Matt over her head as Matt rolled his eyes.

"Yeah, yeah, man. You're just trying to get more hugs outta my girl," Matt jokingly accused.

Each of the others hugged her in return before handing her back to Matt, where she was once again tucked into his embrace.

"Let's go babe. I wanna get you home so I can take care of you."

Looking up into his eyes, she said softly, "Honey, you already do."

SITTING ON HER shower chair with the warm water sluicing over her body, Lily leaned back allowing Matt more access. Not letting her do anything, he had lathered her whole body with bath wash and then had her shift around so that he could wash her hair. Feeling completely pampered, she smiled as her hand slid down his naked chest until she grasped his cock. Hearing him groan as she moved her hand up and down his slick shaft, she leaned forward and her lips replaced her hand.

"Oh, baby," he moaned, fighting the urge to fuck her mouth but instead let her take the lead.

As she swirled her tongue around the tip, dipping into his opening, she could feel him surge more. Sucking him deeply, she moved quickly up and down wanting to give him as much pleasure as he always gave her.

Just as she could tell he was swelling, he tried to pull out. Grasping his muscular ass in closer and holding them tightly with her hands, she continued her sucking.

Unable to stop he powered through his orgasm, feeling it rip through him as his hot semen hit the back of her throat. One hand on the shower tile to hold himself up, he placed his other hand on her head, cupping her face. *Jesus, fuck, Jesus. Every fuckin' time is better than the last.*

His ragged breath finally stilled and he looked down at the beautiful woman looking up at him. He immediately put his hands under her arms, pulled her up and backed her up against the shower wall allowing the spray of water to hit his back. Slamming his mouth on to hers he began a ravaging assault. His tongue moved with hers, tangling for dominance. Exploring her sweet mouth, his lips moved over hers.

Lily felt her core rubbing against his dick, noticing it coming back to life again. Desperate for the relief that only he could provide she began moving her hips. She felt him position her over the head of his cock and heard him growl, "Can you take it, baby?"

Clutching his shoulders, she dug her fingers in as her response. In one quick movement, he filled her to the hilt. Throwing her head back against the shower tile, she felt so tiny and weightless compared to the massive man slamming into her.

Thrust after thrust, she could feel the delicious friction building until she thought she would go mad with wanting. Holding on tighter, she could feel her inner walls grabbing his cock.

"Baby, you close?" he growled.

Not having time to answer, she screamed his name as her head reared back hitting the wall as he roared through his orgasm.

Pumping until the last drop entered her waiting body, he looked up suddenly realizing how hard he had been pressing her into the wall. "Oh fuck, baby. Are you all right?" he asked as he gently slid out of her and lowered her back onto her shower chair.

Her smile answered his concerns. Reaching up to grasp his face, she pulled him down for a kiss. Soft. Gentle. Full of promise kiss.

He reached around and turned off the cooling water, then grabbed the towels just outside the shower. He wrapped one around his waist and then another one around her before picking her up again and carrying her to the bedroom.

She began to dry herself but his hands stilled hers.

"No baby, let me."

Her questioning gaze looked into his eyes, only seeing care and concern. "You don't have to, you know?" she said gently.

"Don't have to, but I want to," was the answer.

He dried her off, including her hair, then assisted her in attaching the prosthesis. Kissing her once again before standing, he said, "You gotta get dressed for comfort, LilyBelle. I'm taking you somewhere tonight to celebrate your first race."

"Where are we going?"

"It's someplace special, babe. Just get dressed and I promise you'll have a good time."

AN HOUR LATER they were on the road, driving to a suburb on the outskirts of the city. Matt noticed her eyes kept cutting over to him as she tried to figure out where they were going. Pulling into a long driveway leading up to a modest house, he announced, "We're here."

Before she could form a question, the front door opened and Charlotte ran down the front steps waving, followed by a giant of a man who looked so much like Matt that Lily knew he must be Matt's father.

Eyes wide, she turned her head quickly to chastise Matt for not letting her know where they were going, but he was already out of the truck walking to her side. As he opened her door, she allowed him to lift her out as she gave him her best glare.

Chuckling, he leaned down to gently touch her lips with his saying, "Babe. Your scary look? Not very intimidating."

Before she had a chance to retort she was pulled into a hug from Charlotte, who was exclaiming congratulations over finishing the race. Genuine warmth spread over her as she felt enveloped in acceptance.

"Gonna give an old man a chance, woman?" came the voice from behind.

Matt pulled Lily out of his mom's embrace and turned her gently toward his father. "Dad, I'd like you to meet Lily Swanson. LilyBelle, this is my dad, Max Dixon."

She couldn't help but smile as she looked up into the face that seemed so familiar. Her small hand was taken by his much larger one as he began leading her up to the house.

"It seems as though congratulations are in order, Miss Lily," he said as they walked.

Glancing behind her she saw Matt and Charlotte walking, heads bowed close together, as they followed. Looking up at Mr. Dixon she smiled saying, "Well, I finished the run but I don't know how much congratulations are due."

"My dear, never knock an accomplishment, and finishing your first, or any race for that matter, is an accomplishment," he stated as he opened the front door.

Immediately they were greeted with the sounds of

children as several more adults came forward. Hating being at the center of attention she felt herself shrink back, but Matt's solid form was just behind her, providing security and comfort.

"Baby, this is my sister, Cherry and her husband, Jack. These two little hooligans are their twins, Tim and Joe."

Lily looked at the family, all smiling at her, and felt her insecurity slip away. Stepping forward she embraced Cherry and Jack, then turned her attention to the small boys standing near her.

Charlotte ushered them into the comfortable den where food was laid out on various platters. "Just help yourself everyone." Turning to Lily she explained, "We're real informal here, sweetie, especially when the boys are around."

Settling herself on the couch with a plate of food, she realized how hungry she actually was. Halfway through, she felt eyes on her and turned to see Matt smiling at her.

He leaned over, chuckling as he said, "Babe, I've never seen you eat so much." His eyes softened. "I'm glad, LilyBelle. You need to fuel back up after that exercise."

Lifting her eyebrows in question, she asked, "The race?"

Leaning closer so that his breath was a whisper against her ear, "Yeah, that. And other activities."

Blushing, she couldn't help but grin, until she

looked around and saw the faces of the others in the room. All staring. All smiling.

"Oh, don't be embarrassed darlin'," Max boomed. "Anyone that can put a smile on my boy's face should be preening not blushing."

Laughing, she returned to eating until she noticed the boys sitting on the floor whispering while trying to not be obvious about getting close to her legs.

Leaning down, she asked, "Are you wondering about my legs?"

Joe blurted, "We're not supposed to ask about your fake leg."

Immediately the adults in the room all began to admonish the boys at once as Jack jumped up to take them outside.

"No, no, please," Lily begged. "It's okay. They're just curious." Looking back down into the faces of the chastised boys, she said gently, "Do you want to see it?

Feeling a hand on her shoulder, she heard Matt growl, "Babe, you don't have to do this."

Placing her hand on his legs, she gave a comforting squeeze. Setting her plate on the coffee table, she said, "Come over here, boys."

They scrambled quickly, both elbowing each other for the best view. She pulled her pants legs up, first the complete leg and then the one covering the prosthesis. She slid her shoes off so that they could see her feet.

Joe reached out his hand before snatching it back.

"You can touch it if you want. It looks a lot like my

real foot but it feels different."

The boys spent a few minutes staring and touching, before becoming more adventurous. Tim wanted to see how the joint worked and Joe was fascinated with how it stayed in place. Lily carefully explained how her prosthesis worked and answered their questions.

Tim said, "We read about a pirate who lost his leg in a fight and they called him peg leg."

Jumping in before the adults could try to stifle the boy's natural curiosity, she said, "Well, I am lucky to live in this age or I might have a wooden peg leg too."

Smiling at them, she felt as ease. Accepted. *This is what family should be. Accepting, not judging. Nurturing, not excluding.* Battling back tears, she leaned back in her seat.

The boys ran off to play and she realized the room was very quiet. Looking around she found it hard to interpret the expressions aimed at her.

"W…was that all right?" she asked. "I… um… wanted the boys to be comfortable."

Cherry said, "Oh Lily, thank you. The boys are going to be curious but I would have never wanted to make you feel ill at ease."

Feeling Matt's arm wrap around her shoulders, pulling her in, she smiled. "They're children and curious. I wanted them to see it as a natural part of me and then hopefully they won't feel awkward when I'm around." Becoming flustered, she stammered, "I mean…if I see them again…that is, if I…um…come back."

Matt kissed her head. "Babe, don't think for one minute you're getting away from me," he assured as the other adults in the room clambered to agree.

The afternoon passed easily and before they knew it, they were walking outside to say goodbye. Charlotte and Cherry hugged Lily, both whispering how much they wanted her to come back.

Max took her to the side and as he hugged her, he said, "Girl, just want you to know how grateful we are that you came into our boy's life." Looking down at her questioning gaze, he continued, "He'd been lost to us the past year. First by hooking up with that loser girlfriend, then his accident. Then when his new partner was almost shot, we lost him to the pain pills and the bottle." Pulling her in closer, he said, "Didn't know if we were gonna get our son back. But darlin', you've done it."

Smiling up at the large man with tears in his eyes, she whispered, "He's the only man I've ever been tempted to be with. He lets me be…me."

Finishing their goodbyes, Matt lifted her up into his truck and they started back down the road. After a minute, he pulled to the side of the street and stopped the truck. Twisting to her, he saw her questioning look.

"Just wanted to see if you were all right. I was afraid that you'd be freaked if you knew we were coming to see my family, so I didn't tell you. But babe, you were phenomenal and they loved you. I knew they would, but want to make sure you're okay. I'm realizing that

that was a lot to throw at you."

Lily leaned forward so that her lips were close to his. "I'm tempted to kiss you. Are you good with that?"

Matt recognized his words to her from the first night in his truck. Grinning, he moved forward quickly, one hand cupping the back of her head as he pulled her in for a kiss. Plundering her mouth, he breathed her in as his tongue sought refuge. He controlled the kiss until his dick was painfully straining against his jeans. Pulling back he looked at her kiss swollen lips and lust-filled eyes staring back at him.

"Gonna get you home, LilyBelle. I'm tempted to eat you, fuck you, then hold you all night. You good with that?"

Smiling her response, she settled back into her seat.

He took her home and did just what he was tempted to do.

Chapter 15

THE NIGHT WAS almost pitch-black, the few street lights giving off pitiful illumination. A fog coming from the river slowly crept in, coating the two men. Matt and Shane sat in the dark, crouched behind a dumpster in the alley behind one of the warehouses along the river. Their bulky frames made the wait uncomfortable.

Matt glanced over at his partner, wondering what was going through his mind. Shane had spent several years undercover in a drug gang and coming out had not been an easy process. "You okay, man?"

Shane rubbed his hand over his face saying, "Yeah. Shit memories coming back of a lot of times spent just waitin' and hidin'."

Jeff Robert's description of one of the dealers he had dealt with was identified as a low-life they had been hoping to get their hands on. Finally, one of the detective's snitches had identified this alley as a place that he liked to score.

The air was cool and Matt was glad for the extra jacket. Not knowing how long they would have to stake-out, he shifted to a more comfortable position.

Rubbing his hand across his brow, he felt his scar puckered out against his fingers. *Never think about it much anymore. She never focuses on it.* The thought of Lily slid through his mind, illuminating the dark corners, chasing away unpleasant memories.

The fog was coming in thicker, making the soupy atmosphere even more eerie. Suddenly, movement to their side captured their attention. Making out the figure of a man slipping through the darkness, they followed him with their eyes. The man made his way over to a dumpster and carefully lifted the lid. As they watched, he took out a package and began taping it to the underside of the dumpster lid.

Rushing to action, they pounded up behind the man before he could react.

"Freeze. Keep your hands where we can see them."

The man halted, cursing as he turned around. "Fuck," he bit out.

"Stay right there, Toby," Shane ordered, his gun trained on the suspect.

Matt moved quickly to the dumpster and with gloves on began untaping the package.

"Well, look what we have here," he said, opening the package and finding it filled with pill bottles. Recognizing the names, he read off, "Xanax, Percocet, Vicodin, OxyContin. You've been busy."

A dog barked to the side as it moved through the foggy night, and Toby took the opportunity to try to run.

Matt and Shane took off after him, almost losing him in the dark. Seeing Toby dart around the corner of a building, they split up, encircling him. Shane caught up to him as Matt came barreling around from the other side, tackling Toby and flattening him to the ground.

"You gonna add resisting arrest to your other charges, ass-hole?" he bit out.

"Man, I got rights," Toby cried.

"Uh huh. And we're gonna make sure you know exactly what they are," he said cuffing him.

While Shane read Toby his rights and called for a back-up cruiser to meet them, Matt bagged the evidence. Looking at the bottles, he wasn't surprised to see VanHeusen Pharmaceutical on them.

A couple of hours later, Matt and Shane were still at the station waiting to interrogate Toby. Walking down the hall, Matt confessed, "I want VanHeusen. I just know that dick is behind this somehow."

"You gonna make it hard on Lily if you go after VanHeusen?"

"Her job's almost finished there anyway. And she doesn't work for him. She works for a software company that just has her placed there temporarily." Pausing for a moment he continued, "And I don't give a fuck. I don't want her working there anyway. Got a bad feeling about that place. Someone there knows what's going on and my bet is on Malcolm."

Stalking into the interrogation room they saw Toby sitting at the metal table, a bruise on his face from hitting the pavement when Matt tackled him.

"You see this? I'm suing for police brutality."

"Shut up Toby. You were resisting arrest and I took you down. Got a bruise? Man up and quit your bitchin'."

Toby glowered but got quiet.

Shane sat across from him and Matt placed himself with his back against the door, his massive arms crossed in front of him. Shane pulled out a file and pushed some pictures across the table.

"So, we've got you at the scene of a drop. We've got you identified as supplying drugs at parties. We've got you with drugs in your possession. We've got you on possession, with intent to sell. We've got you on possession of stolen property. We've got you on resisting arrest and assaulting a police officer."

Toby continued to sit quietly but a little of the bravado had left his eyes.

"The way I see it, we got you and you're goin' down. And you're goin' down for a long time."

The silence in the room crept in.

Matt spoke from the side, "So, you gonna make things easier on yourself and tell us what we wanna know or are you gonna be a dumb-shit and sit there not sayin' anything?"

Toby swung his gaze back around. "I talk, I'm a dead man."

"You don't talk, you go to prison, they'll still think you talked and kill you there. Or make your life hell."

Toby stared at the table for a few minutes, fear playing across his face.

"So, what's it gonna be, man? It's late and we both wanna get home to our women. You makin' us stay here for nothin' is just gonna piss us off."

"I don't know nothing," came the reply. "I just get my instructions and go from there."

"Then tell us what you do know."

"My job is to find out where some high school or college parties are at. I go and watch who's using and who's dealing. It's usually some dumb fuck kid who is selling his mom's Valium or dad's pain pills. My job is to isolate those kids and get them interested in doing the same thing, only for more money and they don't have to sneak out grannie's pills."

"So where do you get your supply?"

"I get a text. It tells me where to go to pick up the shit. Then I get another one that tells me where to drop it off. I'm to tell the kid dealer where I'm puttin' it and hang around to make sure they get it."

"I also get the money at that time and take my cut and I get a text telling me where to leave it." Looking up into their faces, he said, "I don't never see nobody. It's all texts and never a number."

Matt left the room and found the officer with Toby's possessions. Pulling out the cell phone, he checked the messages and numbers. Toby was telling the truth. The messages told him where to go and what to do. Handing the phone back to the officer, he ordered, "Get

whatever info you can on where the texts come from."
The officer headed away but Matt already figured that it
would be a dead end. *Probably from a throw-away cell.*

He met Shane as he was coming out of the interrogation room. "Get anything else?"

"Not right now. Let him sit in a jail cell for a couple
of days and he may suddenly develop a memory."

"Damn, they're covering their tracks. This is not
some two-bit operation run by some kids and dumb-ass
dealers buying stolen drugs. It's organized. It's hard to
track. And there's an intelligent person behind this."

Shane, rubbing his tired eyes, looked over at Matt.
"And you're wantin' it to be VanHeusen?

Matt stood silent for a moment. "Yeah. I know it
doesn't make sense 'cause he's rich enough with just the
medical corporation. But something's not right. I know
he's involved. Somehow. Someway."

"Then we keep diggin'."

Looking at his watch, Matt sighed. "Jesus, it's three
a.m. Let's head home."

"You goin' to Lily's?"

"I'm sure as fuck not heading to my apartment. Cassandra is coming in a few days to move the rest of her
shit out and then I'm moving in with Lily permanently."

Shane clapped him on the back as the two men
walked back out into the dark night. This time heading
to a much happier destination for both of them.

ANDREA WALKED INTO Lily's office near the end of the day. "Hate to be the bearer of bad news, but Mr. VanHeusen wants to see you immediately."

Looking up in frustration, she puffed her bangs out of her face. "Why?" she moaned. "I'm trying to get things wrapped up here and am staying late as it is because I needed to see a few more doctors in the building."

"I know, dear, but that was what his secretary told me when she just called." Handing her a cup of coffee she joked, "Here's some liquid fortification."

Giving Andrea a quick hug Lily acknowledged, "God, you're a lifesaver. Are you sure you don't want to leave VanHeusen's when my contract is over and come work for us? You could be my assistant where ever I go."

"Honey, if they leave me down here in the basement of this building much longer, I will definitely be wanting to go with you."

Laughing, Lily walked out and headed to the elevators. Coming out on the top floor, she was surprised to be ushered into Malcolm's office and not the boardroom. *What now?*

Entering she found Malcolm sitting behind his impressive desk, noting its lack of clutter. *How can a man that busy not have a cluttered desk*, she thought as she remembered the clutter she left on her desk in the basement.

The office was softly illuminated, the harsh florescent light was turned off and the gentle lights of several lamps lit the area. The windows showed the dark night with the Richland skyline lit by the lights in other tall buildings.

Malcolm looked up as she entered, his face not as welcoming as the last time she was here. Glancing to the side she saw Allen, Curtis, Penelope, and Carla in the room as well.

Drawing herself up she greeted everyone then turned to Malcolm saying, "Mr. VanHeusen. What can I do for you?"

"I want you to finish your contractual obligation and do it with the least amount of disruption to my staff," he stated firmly.

"Sir, with all respect, that is what I am trying to do. I…"

"I want to know why you keep disturbing the doctors in this building. The records you are asking for are none of your concern."

"Sir, I am trying to run the diagnostics on the programs that I write, which would have been Ellen's job, but with her gone you have given me Carla who," turning to Carla, "I am sorry to say, while she is a very nice woman to work with, she doesn't have the credentials to assist me."

Malcolm's eyes shifted over to Carla's before moving back to hers. "What makes you think she can't handle the job?"

Feeling anger at being forced to publicly embarrass someone, she continued, "Carla doesn't understand the codes I am writing, therefore she has no understanding of how to run any quality control programs to see if there are errors."

Curtis spoke harshly, "You don't need patient information. I've had numerous doctors in the building in the past week complain about the questions you are asking. You need to let Carla handle that and you stick to your job."

Whirling around, she faced him with her hands on her hips. "My job is to make sure that when I leave here you have a working program. What I am finding now are discrepancies between patient names and some of their prescriptions. Something must be wrong with my program and I want to find out what it is."

The silence in the room was deafening. No one spoke. She shifted her gaze among the others, feeling off-balanced but not knowing why. Sucking her lips in for a moment, she waited to see who would break the quiet.

Penelope interjected, "Discrepancies? Would you care to elaborate?"

Curtis interrupted, "There's no need for her to elaborate. Not every system is perfect and not every doctor is perfect either." Turning to Carla he growled, "If you were doing the job you were hired to do, then she wouldn't have to be checking into things that she does not need to know. You have the clearance for patient confidentiality. Not her."

Carla, angry at the faces looking at her retorted, "I was hired to assist. I was hired to gather data. I was not hired to run software diagnostics."

Allen looked over and stated calmly, "Then perhaps you're not the right person for the job. Or perhaps we need to just let Lily finish the programing and then hire another independent company to come in and test it."

Curtis exploded again, "I'm not having anyone snooping in the patient files who shouldn't have access."

Feeling as though the room was closing in on her, Lily quietly walked to an empty chair and sat down. Looking at Malcolm directly and holding his steely gaze, she said, "Sir, I am going to offer my resignation. I will talk to my company tomorrow and see if they want to send another programer in my place. I assure you that they will need the same information that I do, but perhaps you are so dissatisfied with my work that you need a fresh perspective."

Several voices began to clamber all at once. Allen wanted to assure her that no one wanted her to leave while Curtis remained silent, his glare seemed to assure her that he wanted her out. Carla began to defend herself and Penelope was agreeing with Allen.

"Quiet," Malcolm barked. The room once again fell into silence.

Lily noticed the eerie shadows that were across the room as the outside darkness seemed to penetrate inside the office. Turning to Malcolm, she asked, "Sir, what decision have you come to?"

Appearing to study her carefully, he stated, "You will stay. Carla is out. You will do the job of both programer and quality control. You will have access to the doctors, but you report to me and only me. Any discrepancies that you find are to be reported to me and only me."

Penelope and Curtis both sputtered their displeasure at his decision, but were silenced quickly when he shot them a penetrating glare. Allen smiled at her, the only smile in the office. Carla, her face red with anger, stood and stormed out of the room.

Malcolm's gaze came back to the woman in front of him. "Is that acceptable?"

"Yes, sir. It will take me a little bit longer, but I will finish as soon as I can." With that she stood and walked out, seeing Carla get on the elevator. Glad to not be working with her anymore, she was equally glad to not be taking the elevator down with her either.

Andrea had already left by the time she re-entered her office to retrieve her purse and laptop. Looking around the room, the hairs on the back of her neck prickled with the sensation that someone had been there in her absence. Looking around, it appeared that all of the papers were as she left them, strewn across the desk. But then she noticed that some of them were out of order. She was meticulous about keeping her programing papers in strict numerical order. *They are out of order. Someone has been in here looking through my work.*

But why? And who?

Determined to ask Andrea in the morning, she quickly headed out of the door and called for her cab.

(Surveillance)

"SHE'S FINDING OUT things she shouldn't know."

"The boss wants her out of here as soon as possible."

"I'm keeping my eyes on her. Watching her every move. It doesn't seem like she has figured out anything yet."

"Doesn't matter. Just 'cause she hasn't connected any dots yet doesn't mean she won't."

"You need me to do something?"

"Not now. Her house has that cop there and the boss has figured out that it's better with her here. We can keep track of what she is doing."

"You think she's gonna keep poking around until she finds something?"

"Right now it just looks like she's just trying to do her job. She's not looking for anything suspicious, so maybe even if it lands right under her nose she'll ignore it."

"Keep her on edge so that she'll want to leave quickly, but don't scare her. We don't need her suspicious or that cop boyfriend getting any ideas."

"How do you think that she and that boyfriend of hers do it? You think they leave on the fake leg or take it off?"

"Jesus, you're a sick bastard. Just do your fuckin' job and keep your eyes on her."

"Not a problem," was the response, a grin sliding across their face.

Chapter 16

"LILY, I'M GETTIN' ready to leave," Matt called from the front of the house.

She walked from the kitchen, wiping her hands on the dishtowel before tossing it back onto the counter. "Are you coming back here or going into the station for a while?"

He met her in the middle of the room, towering over her as he encircled her with his embrace. "Nah, not going into the station unless something comes up. The movers will be at the apartment within the hour and it shouldn't take them long to get the furniture packed up and moved out."

Looking down and seeing her frown he kissed her forehead, smoothing out the wrinkled brow. "She's not going to be there, babe. Just the movers. I checked."

Huffing, Lily glared up. "How did you know that's what I was wondering?"

"Baby, you're as transparent as glass. No fuckin' pretense with you." Leaning down to capture her lips, he started with a slow kiss. Then it turned hot. And heavy. And deep. Pulling back, he heard her mew from the lack of contact and chuckled.

"I gotta go so I can get back here and –" His cell phone rang, and glancing down at the screen, he cursed. "Shane, what's up?" A few expletives later he hung up.

Lily reached up and placed her small hand on his chest. "Are you needed at the station, honey?"

"Yeah, Shane says a dealer has suddenly gotten chatty after a few nights in jail. Babe I hate to ask, but…"

Lily interrupted, "Of course I'll go. You've already said that Cassandra won't be there so I'll just go over and unlock the doors. Is the furniture marked?"

"Everything that's going is in the front room. The stuff I'm keeping is in the bedroom so just keep that door locked. Are you sure you don't mind? This is your day off."

Pulling him down for a quick kiss, she shooed him out of the door, saying, "Go, do your police thing. I'll take care of the apartment."

A few minutes later, driving to the station, Matt couldn't help but think once again about the difference between the two women he had been involved with. Cassandra would have had a screaming rant about him going to the police station on their day off. Smiling, he thought of Lily. Fuckin' *perfect*.

Walking into the station, he saw Shane. "We gotta get this done, man. Movers coming to get Cassandra's shit out of the apartment and then I'm taking my girl out."

Smiling at his partner, Shane agreed. "Well, then let's get this done."

LILY ARRIVED AT the apartment before the movers and took a few minutes to walk around. The furniture in the living room was modern. Sleek. Impersonal. As she glanced around, she noted the lack of pictures on the walls or personal items. The kitchen was just as bare, as though it could have been a kitchen in any model house that had no real people living there. *Who was he with Cassandra? He certainly wasn't the man that she loved.*

Wandering back into the bedroom, she used the extra key Matt had given her to enter, knowing that he wanted to make sure the movers did not go in there. What a difference. She walked into a room that looked like Matt. Smelled like Matt. His bedcovers were slightly rumpled and she smiled knowing that a perfectly made-up bed was not a priority. His spare change was tossed on the dresser top. Along with…a framed picture.

Lily stopped and stared at the photograph, her heart pounding. She reached up, fingers lightly touching the image staring back at her, tears in her eyes. The picture was of her. At his parents' house. She was looking up at Matt, smiling, and he was staring back at her as though she were the only one in the world. *His mother must have taken that picture.* Seeing an inscription in the bottom corner, she leaned closer. ***LilyBelle All my love.***

She realized that this was the room that he kept all of his personal items in. This was the room that was untouched by Cassandra's things. Taking a deep breath, she slowly let it out, allowing the warmth of the room to soothe over her.

Hearing a commotion at the front door, she quickly left the bedroom carefully locking it behind her and pocketing the key. Throwing open the door, she was surprised to see Cassandra standing there in all her glory, movers behind her.

Cassandra appeared equally as stunned to see Lily. "What are you doing here?"

Stepping back to allow the movers access, she said, "Matt was called away so he asked me to open the apartment and supervise the move."

"The housekeeper?" Cassandra asked as she sailed into the room, expensive perfume following in her wake.

"No actually, I'm his girlfriend," Lily said with a smile. "And you must be Cassandra."

Cassandra's eyes narrowed as she took in Lily before replying, "Wow, he must have really come down in the world."

Refusing to take her bait, Lily turned and told the movers what they were to move.

Pushing by her, Cassandra said, "Excuse me, but I'll direct the movers."

Shrugging as though she were inconsequential, Lily just replied, "Suit yourself," as she hopped up on the kitchen stool to observe.

It did not take long for the movers to take the living and dining room furniture.

Cassandra walked down the hall and tried the bedroom door, finding it locked. Walking back to Lily she asked, "You don't have the key to the bedroom do you?"

Lily beamed her smile on her and replied, "Why yes, I do have it."

Cassandra stood with her palm out. Lily looked at her, a bored look on her face.

The head mover looked over at Lily and asked, "Ma'am, is this all there is?" Lily nodded and they began to leave.

"Well?" Cassandra said, impatience dripping from her words.

"The bedroom stays locked." Looking at Cassandra, Lily continued, "Matt's orders. I'm sure you understand."

"I do not understand. I want that key and I want it now," Cassandra sputtered.

Lily looked at the classic beauty in front of her. It was easy to see how any man would fall for her. Tall, willowy. No hair out of place. Impeccable make-up. But something was missing. Something...*kindness. That's what's missing – kindness. Compassion. Humor.*

As Lily was pondering this she slid off the kitchen stool, when Cassandra came upon her quickly, giving her a push. She toppled backwards.

Cassandra stared down at the woman on the floor with the lower part of her leg exposed as her pant leg rode up.

"Oh my god, you're a cripple. Now I get it. No wonder Matt is with you. He can't get a real woman and you can't get a man who isn't as scarred as you," she exclaimed as one of the movers hustled over to offer his hand to Lily.

He assisted Lily, who looked down in concern as she checked her prosthetic. The mover kept his hands discreetly on her waist to make sure she was steady as she turned her fury on the sneering woman in front of her.

"You had the most amazing man in the world and you tossed him away. You must be insane, but I want to thank you because by doing that you showed him what kind of woman you were really are and that allowed him to eventually find me."

Before she could respond, the front door slammed back with force and "What the fuck?" was roared across the room.

Matt stalked in having heard Cassandra's voice from the hall. Once in, he saw Lily standing awkwardly with her left leg slightly elevated and a man he assumed was a mover with his hands on Lily's waist. And Cassandra. The bitch herself.

He made his way to them faster than Lily had ever seen him move. She put her foot down and winced as she started to approach him. The mover started to grasp her again, but stilled his hands as he saw the look on Matt's face.

Reaching out he scooped Lily up and then turned to Cassandra. "You don't move. You move, you kiss this furniture goodbye." Looking at the mover, he said,

"Thank you for your assistance. You stay too, just in case I have to give you another location to take the furniture."

With that he turned and walked to the bedroom. "Babe, keys."

"Matt, I can…"

"Babe, not in the mood to debate. Keys."

She fished them out of her pants pocket and handed them to him.

Leaning down he quickly unlocked the door and set her gently down on the rumpled bed. Lily was amazed that as angry as he was, he treated her with such care.

Kneeling down in front of her, he lifted her pants leg. "What hurts, babe?"

"My knee twisted a bit when I came down off of the stool. It's straightened now and feels better." Looking into his furious face, she reached out to cup his cheeks. "Honey, I'm fine. Really."

Matt gazed into the eyes of the woman that meant more to him than life. His salvation. His hope. Touching his lips to her forehead he held them there for a moment.

"Babe, I'm taking care of business. I want you to stay here and don't move off that bed."

She started to protest, but quickly snapped her mouth shut. *He needs this. He needs to handle this.*

Nodding he turned and left, closing the bedroom door behind him. Walking back into the living area, he saw Cassandra looking more composed than when he first came into the apartment.

Looking at the mover standing next to the counter, he growled, "What happened?"

"Matt, I was just…" Cassandra began.

"Quiet," he roared. "You don't speak or you'll lose all the furniture."

Opening and closing her mouth rapidly like a fish, she sputtered.

Turning to the mover he nodded again.

"The young woman in the apartment was sitting here quietly when this…lady began to berate her. Then she wanted the key to the bedroom which the other young woman wouldn't give her. When she was coming off the stool to see us out, this…woman gave her a push. I was assisting when you came in."

"I'm the one paying you, you moron. You work for me. How dare you speak about me like that," she screeched.

"Lady, I don't know who you think you are, but you've just lost yourself a mover." Turning to Matt, he continued, "Mr. Dixon, where would you like the furniture delivered?"

"What's it gonna be Cassandra? Your place, or do I tell him to take it to the dump and then I arrest you for assault?"

"I must have been crazy to have been involved with you," she sneered. "Like I told her, you two deserve each other."

Nodding, Matt just replied, "You've got that right.

Now here's how this is gonna go. You walk out of this apartment and out of my life. I don't see you. I don't hear from you. You don't exist to me. You break that, I call Dan here and arrest you for assault. How will that look on your resume?"

With that, she turned and stormed out of the apartment, leaving the men in her wake. The head mover looked over and said, "Mr. Dixon, it's none of my affair, but if you got rid of that," nodding his head at Cassandra's retreating back, "and ended up with her," nodding toward the bedroom, "you're a smart man. And a lucky one."

Matt agreed then tipped the mover as he left. Placing his hand on the back of the closed door, he leaned against it for a moment. His eyes shut, he kept seeing Lily wince as she tried to stand, all the while defending him against Cassandra.

"Matt?" a soft voice came from behind. Turning, he saw her standing in the hall near the kitchen.

She approached him cautiously. "Are you all right?"

He reached her in two long steps and lifted her up in his arms and walked to the bedroom again. Touching his forehead to hers, he claimed, "I hate that you had to go through that. I hate that she said those things to you. And I fuckin' hate that she put her hands on you."

"Honey, its okay. I'm okay."

"You're strong and kind, but baby I'm telling you right now, I'm not fuckin' okay with what just went down."

Lily ran her hands over his face, smoothing the scar on his forehead. "I love you, Matt Dixon."

Matt settled her on her back in his bed, his lips assaulting hers. Drinking her in. Breathing her in. The kiss became wild, tongues clashing and fighting for dominance. Pulling back, he heard her mew at the loss of contact.

Looking up at him, a question in her eyes, she said, "Why did you stop?"

"Baby, it'd be completely selfish of me to give in to my desires right now. You just had a harrowing morning and should rest."

Smiling, she placed her hand on the back of his head, running her fingers through his thick hair. Gently pulling him forward until his lips were just a breath away from hers, she whispered, "Take me now. Please. I want to feel all of you on all of me."

He slid his hands to the bottom of her shirt and pulled it quickly over her head. Her bra quickly found its way to the floor next to her shirt. His shirt joined the pile. Sliding her pants down her legs, he was careful with her prosthesis. Undoing it, he slid it off as well.

Looking down at her beauty, she lay naked on his bed. He stared at her so long that she became self-conscious. Crossing her arms over herself, she heard him growl as he fell onto the bed next to her.

"Oh no, babe, you do not hide that beauty from me." Clasping her nipple in his mouth, he suckled deeply, eliciting a moan from deep within her. "I need you, baby. Can you take it?"

Nodding her response, she felt him slide down between her legs, spreading her nether lips apart with his fingers before running his tongue over her. The warmth that had pooled deep within began to spread outward from her breasts to her pussy. She reached down and grasped his hair, pulling him tighter into herself.

Placing one hand on her stomach, he held her still while his mouth continued its ministrations. Plunging his tongue inside, he reached up to palm her breast while his mouth licked up before nipping her clit.

That was all it took for Lily to go over the edge. Crying out his name, she felt the spasms radiate from her pussy outward until her whole body shook with it. Floating back to consciousness she smiled as he crawled up her body and plunged his rock-hard dick inside.

The friction made her tingle and he was hitting something deep inside that had her digging her fingernails in his shoulders.

Losing control, Matt thrust over and over again, feeling her tight pussy walls squeeze his cock as he continued to plunder her willing body.

Pulling out quickly he flipped her over onto her stomach and then, with a hand under her, he pulled her up until she was on her knees. He quickly slipped several pillows under her stomach to give her support and then plunged in from behind.

This time he was really touching something that had never been touched before and she could tell her second orgasm was close.

"Reach down and finger yourself," he ordered.

She complied. Flipping her clit, she felt her pussy walls begin to contract.

"Hold on, don't come yet," he continued to order.

Whimpering, Lily had no idea how long she could hold off. "Please honey, I feel it. I need…"

Plunging harder and harder Matt said, "Okay, now baby."

She rubbed her swollen nub once again and the orgasm exploded, sending sparks outwards to her whole body. She was lost in her own sensations, but could feel him thrust powerfully.

Pushing through, he felt his balls tighten and then his orgasm had him plunging deeply as he collapsed on top of her before rolling to the side to keep from crushing her.

The two of them lay panting, hearts beating frantically.

"Oh LilyBelle, what you do to me," he said between breaths.

"Me? I just laid here. You did all the work," she joked softly.

Matt pulled her over on top of him, placing her head on his broad chest. Wrapping his arms around her, he slowly moved his hands up and down. Over her ass, up her back to her shoulders and then back down again.

Several minutes passed like that until she finally lifted her head and gazed down into the face of the man she loved.

"You ready to take me home, sailor?" she joked.

"Girl, just lead the way and I'll follow."

THE NEXT DAY, Matt and Lily were up early getting ready for their friends to come over. Deciding that Matt's bed from his apartment was bigger and more comfortable they were moving it to her house along with his chest of drawers. The wood matched well enough for them to use it in the bedroom along with her dresser. The rest of the things were going to be donated to a local charity organization.

"Babe, BJ is on his way here. He's gonna stay here with you while I meet the guys at my old place. We should be back in a couple of hours. Are Annie and Suzanne coming over?"

"Annie is, but Suzanne was going home this weekend to visit with her parents."

Just then the doorbell sounded and Matt opened the door to greet BJ. Shaking hands, Matt stepped back to let him in. Pippi began jumping around and sniffing BJ's pants. "Babe, this dog is going to have to go into the back yard when we start moving the furniture in. Someone's gonna step on this shrimp."

"Hi BJ," Lily said as she walked into the room. "Ready for some work?"

"Always," he laughed.

Matt kissed her and said, "Okay you two, enjoy. I'll

be back soon."

Lily invited BJ to sit at the table and they pulled out their laptops. "It's been a while since I've looked at it, but I'm convinced that Ellen was trying to leave a message. Whether for fun or for work, I have no idea, but we need to crack this."

"I'm on it chief," BJ answered.

For the next two hours, BJ and Lily worked side by side at the table, working the programing language to see what Ellen used. Annie came and worked in the kitchen, fixing some lunch for everyone.

"I think I'm getting somewhere," BJ pronounced. "It appears that she may have used numbers for some type of data she was collecting. Why she hid it in this program doesn't make any sense."

Leaning over to see what he had uncovered, a commotion in the driveway drew their attention.

"They're back," Annie called out.

BJ hit print on some data and said, "I'm printing out what I was finding and you can look it over later."

Placing her hand on his shoulder as she stood, she replied, "You have no idea how much this means to me." Looking down at him speculatively, she noticed the handsome man in front of her. Blond hair with surfer looks. "You know, I have a friend that I think would be perfect for you. I wanted you to meet her today but she's visiting her parents."

"That's okay, Lily. I'm really not interested in meeting someone."

"Hmmm, we'll see," she said smiling.

The men were coming through the front door, Shane and Matt carrying the bedframe. Tony and Gabe followed with the mattress. Vinny and Jobe, more of Tony's security men, followed with the chest of drawers.

"Babe, if you show one of them where to put the chest, we'll get the bed set up."

Annie leaned over and kissed Shane as he passed her in the hall. "Matt," she called out, "I've got lunch for you when you all are ready."

The men made quick work of setting up the bedroom and then headed to the kitchen to grab lunch. Grabbing slices of Annie's homemade pizza and beers they headed to the den to pile up and watch football.

Lily walked out of the kitchen and stood peering into the room at the gathering of friends. Laughing. Sharing. Enjoying. A flashback of the way life was before the accident flooded her mind. Her family watching TV together, her mother bringing in trays of snacks while Rose and Lily sat cross-legged on the floor. Her father laughing at their antics. Her chest squeezed for a moment at the memory as she took a shuddering breath as her eyes burned with unshed tears.

Suddenly, her vision was blocked by Matt's chest as he stood directly in front of her, shielding her from the others. "Baby?" he said softly so as not to embarrass her in front of their friends.

She lifted her eyes and stared into the face she had come to know so well. His look of concern marred his brow and she raised her hand to smooth over the scar. It was so much a part of him that she simply never looked at it. It represented his valor. Honor. Heroism.

"I'm fine, honey," she reassured. "I'm just happy, that's all."

He stared into her face, searching. "Baby?" he prompted again gently.

"I just...took a trip down memory lane, that's all." At his silence, she continued, "Life at home was fun like this. Before..."

Nodding in understanding, he wrapped his arms around her protectively. Holding her, rubbing his hand along her back, he whispered, "LilyBelle, I can't take away the past or what happened to your family. But if you'll let me, I'll give you lots of times like this."

Leaning back so that she could look into his eyes again, she raised her eyebrow in question.

"Lots of times with our friends and lots of time with each other," he explained. "And I've got to tell you, the way I feel about you baby, I wanna house full of family with you."

"What are you saying?"

Glancing behind him, he saw the grinning faces of their friends. Turning back around, he looked down at the woman that had pieced him back together. "LilyBelle, this isn't a conversation I want to have with an audience, but you gotta know. Soon as you agree, I'm gonna put a ring on your finger and we're gonna start making a whole lot of good memories to take away the bad ones."

Smiling, she tucked her face back into his chest and let his warmth seep into her dark corners.

Chapter 17

MATT LOOKED AT Lily sitting in the passenger side of his truck. She sat silent. Stoic. A crease furrowing her brow. Reaching across the space between them, he grasped her small hand. "It'll be all right. They invited us, you know?"

Looking at the strong man holding her hand, she allowed the warmth of his touch to seep into her void. Taking a deep breath she nodded. "Yeah," she answered softly, knowing that this visit could be okay or disastrous. Not great. Never great. But hopefully at least it would be okay.

Pulling into the driveway of a modest two story home in an older neighborhood, they came to a stop. Matt quickly scanned the yard, noticing the perfectly manicured lawn with each bush trimmed to the same shape and size, as well as the precise edging by the walkways.

And the flower beds. All around the yard. Filled with…roses. He heard a soft sigh beside him. "Yeah," she whispered.

Plastering a smile on his face, he leaned over and touched her lips. "I'm right here, babe. Right here."

Hopping out of the truck, he walked over to assist Lily down. Glancing over his shoulder he saw two people come out of the front door and stand on the porch. A petite woman with hair that was at one time blonde but was more white than blonde now, and beside her a taller man with grey hair and a neatly trimmed white beard.

As Lily's feet touched the ground she nervously fluffed out her long broomstick skirt. Flowing and beautiful, it was a recent purchase. Matt had been slowly encouraging her to wear whatever she wanted to wear and not worry about the prosthesis. Being with him and running on the track in shorts had given her the confidence to not worry about people seeing her leg. Looking down now, she knew she had made the wrong choice in clothes for this visit. Feeling her chin being lifted, she gazed into Matt's understanding eyes.

"It's okay babe. Come on," he said taking her hand and linking his fingers through hers as they walked up to the porch.

Lily moved in for hugs as her parents greeted her. Stepping back she introduced Matt. "Matt, these are my parents Daisy and James Swanson. Mom and dad, this is Matt."

Matt noticed that both parents stared at his scar as they shook his hand but said nothing.

"Come in, come in," Daisy exclaimed. "We've got some goodies already for you." She ushered them into the living room where glasses of ice tea were sitting on the coffee table along with cookies.

Quickly taking in the room, Matt noticed the number of framed photographs on the mantle. All of a lovely white-blonde teenager. Rose. Rose in her cheerleading uniform. Rose in what looked like a play. Rose with a date for prom. All Rose. Looking down sharply at Lily to see if she were upset he was stunned to see that she didn't seem to notice. *Or maybe it had always been that way.* The desire to protect flooded to the forefront and as they sat on the sofa, he tucked her safely into his side.

Reaching for her iced tea, Lily's eyes took in the room as well. *Same old, same old. Nothing's changed.*

"Oh, I see you're looking at the pictures. Our Rose was such a beauty. And so talented. When she was cheering, we never missed a game. Or her plays. You would have loved to have seen her in one of her plays." Daisy sat smiling at the others, stuck in memories.

Matt responded diplomatically, "I would have loved to have seen both girls when they were younger."

"Lily was book smart, but just really shy, weren't you dear? But it was Rose that had all the boys after her." Her mother kept looking down at Lily's leg, showing under the skirt. "My dear, I thought you always wore pants. Surly you aren't comfortable with that showing are you?"

Feeling Matt stiffen next to her, Lily quickly intervened. "Mom, I've grown much more comfortable with my prosthesis showing." Squeezing his leg, she smiled up at him. "He's made me see the beauty in myself."

"How did you two meet?" James interrupted. "Lily was her usual vague self when it came to any forthcoming information."

Matt hesitated, not knowing what Lily had said or wanted them to know.

"Dad, I told you that we met at my workplace. There was an…incident, and he was there."

Her father nodded, "Yes, I remember her telling us that you were a policemen. An honorable profession."

Daisy kept looking at his scar so Matt decided to get it out of the way. "I see you are noticing my scar."

Daisy blushed and Lily gasped.

"It's very simple. I was breaking up a fight and I was cut." Straight. Simple. To the point. Smiling, Matt realized it felt good to realize that the scar no longer needed to rule his life.

"Oh, I surely didn't mean to stare," Lily's mom gushed.

James nodded appreciatively as he said, "An injury in the line of duty. Nothing to be ashamed about there."

Matt was stunned. It was one thing to have Lily describe her parents' attitude toward her and the accident. It was another to experience it for himself. Walking the tightrope of wanting to rage against their indifference to the woman he loved and not wanting to make it worse for her, he could feel his anger building silently.

"Mom, dad, please," Lily begged, embarrassed.

An awkward silence descended momentarily before Lily once again tried to maneuver the conversation into safer territory. "Dad, the yard looks really beautiful. You've done a nice job on it."

At this, James preened. "Thank you, Lily. I've been really pleased with it this year as well. Did you see all of the rose bushes? Your mother and I decided to do all of the flower beds in roses and we've had such fun picking out all of the varieties."

"Yes, I noticed," her soft voice came. "They are beautiful."

Her father continued on, looking toward Matt. "We used to have roses, lilies, and daisies. Had those for years, but it was just too much trouble keeping them all up, so we decided to devote our energy to roses. Each year on Rose's birthday we plant a bush. And on each year of her anniversary of being taken from us, we plant another one. They are very difficult to cultivate, you know. It takes pruning at just the right time, special fertilizer, just the right soil."

Lily sighed. Her father's flower beds used to be so full of lilies too. All colors and varieties. She loved them and remembered how Rose used to say that the lilies were her favorite.

"Dad, what did you do with all the lily bulbs you dug out? I could use some in my yard."

"I just tossed them out, daughter. Bulbs can get old and not produce pretty blooms anymore."

The conversation continued in the same vein for the next hour. The Swansons mentioned Rose at every opportunity and Matt saw Lily shrink inside herself.

As they were getting ready to leave, she and Matt walked down the hall toward the guest bathroom. He could feel tension radiating off of her. Slinging his arm around her, he leaned down and whispered in her ear, "You wanna show me your old room and we can go make out for a few minutes?"

Grinning, she turned to face him and grabbed his arm pulling him into a room. He swept her into his arms, tongues tangling, hands roaming over each other's bodies. He finally pulled back and she moaned at the separation.

"You had to stop?" she groaned.

"Well, I realized this was a huge mistake as soon as my dick started trying to press out of my pants," he only half joked.

Glancing down at his bulging crotch, she lifted her eyebrow. "Hmmm, that is a problem in my very conservative parents' house," she giggled.

As Matt looked around the room to try to think of something besides his aching cock, he noticed that the room looked like any guest room. Void of any personality. Void of any memories.

"I thought this was your old room," he queried.

"It was," came the simple answer. "After I was injured, pretty much everything was moved out and all my equipment was moved in. After I left home to go to college, they got rid of everything that reminded them of the accident and just turned it into a guest room."

"And I thought parents always kept their kids' trophies and junk. I guess that's just my mom," he said.

"Oh no," Lily said with sincerity. Walking across the hall, she threw open the door to another bedroom. Matt walked in, the cold reality hitting him.

The room looked untouched in eight years. Pink bedspread with fuzzy pillows that only a teenage girl would love. Boy band posters still on the walls. Cheerleading pom-poms lined the shelves amongst the trophies and pictures. Jewelry and perfume bottles scattered across the dresser. The one thing the room lacked was dust. It was obvious that it was dusted and taken care of. The cold shrine to a lost child. Which would be understandable if it wasn't for the callous treatment of the one that still lived.

Glancing down, he tried to read Lily's face. She simply looked around, neither surprised nor upset. As though complete resignation filled her very soul. She walked over to a picture tucked into the edge of the dresser mirror. The picture was of two teenage girls, both beautiful. Both looking at each other with obvious love.

To My LilyBelle, Love Rose Sisters forever

Matt read the inscription on the photograph. LilyBelle. That was her sister's nickname for her and she allowed him to use it. Warmth slid over him replacing the chill of the somber room.

Turning around in his arms she buried her face in his chest, his arms encircling her. Embracing her.

Protecting her.

"It's really okay, Matt. I know what you're thinking. They just miss her. So do I."

"Baby, I've never lost a child so I can't say what I would or wouldn't do. But to do this and ignore the child they were still blessed to have, that's whacked darlin'."

She shrugged her shoulders in a motion of defeat. "It simply is what it is. It's their way of grieving. My way was moving out, moving forward, and doing what I know Rose would have wanted me to do."

Leaning her head back, she looked up into his blue eyes that were staring back at her. "But do you see why I don't come back very much? Matt, I know they love me. I know they care. But they have not been able to separate me, the accident, and Rose's death. They will always see it as my fault."

"Baby, you gotta know that's not right and it pisses the hell outta me."

Hugging him tighter, she whispered, "All I need is you."

He felt a weight lift. A weight that he carried around and didn't even know that it was there. "I wasted a couple of years of my life LilyBelle. First with the wrong woman, then at the bottom of a bottle of booze and some pills. But you? You take all this and still have so much to give. I'm laying it out, doll…"

Lily looked back up into his intense gaze. "What, honey?"

"You and me are moving forward together. Your parents want to take that trip along with us, they are more than welcome. They can't move passed the past...then I will not let them drag you down. You and me together...babe, we're unstoppable."

At that she reached up to grab his head, pulling him down for another kiss. This one deeper. Hotter. Wetter. And definitely one filled with promise.

Walking out of the room behind her, he grabbed the photograph from the mirror and tucked it carefully into his pocket.

Chapter 18

WALKING DOWN THE long corridor to her office, Lily was counting the days until she was finished with the work at VanHeusen's. The last several days had been exhausting. After their friends left last weekend, Suzanne showed up and had dinner with them. Running late the next morning, Lily had thrown the papers that she and BJ had worked on into her briefcase, hoping to find a moment to work on them this week.

But she felt the walls of work closing in on her. Every day someone was coming in to check on her progress. Allen came by several times to make sure she was all right, but she found it curious that even his visits felt as though she were being monitored. He managed to walk around her office while making small talk, peering over shoulder or picking up papers to absentmindedly flip through them.

Curtis came by with his continuous glower, never even pretending friendship. *Doesn't that man ever smile?* Stalking in, sitting heavily in the chair that had been vacated by Carla he demanded an update. She tried being polite and professional, then snapped.

"Dr. Bennett, I cannot work with these constant

interruptions! My work is precise and constantly having to deal with all of you stalking me is making things slower. Now, you either have something specific you need to ask, in which I would prefer you to email me, or you're just on a fishing expedition. In that case, you are going to come up empty every single time!"

A look of surprise flashed through his eyes as he stood up. Walking to the door, he turned around and said speculatively, "So the mouse can roar," before leaving.

What the hell?

Andrea popped her head in the door, sympathy on her face. "Do you want me to stop them from coming in?"

Rubbing her temples, Lily looked over sighing loudly. "If you can that would be great. But I don't hold any hope that that can happen."

Just then Penelope came to the door. Andrea and Lily sent each other a look before Lily erupted. "No, Dr. Alease. I am not finished. I have not found anything suspicious. No, I am not ready for the doctors to be trained on the new program yet. Anything else I can answer?"

Penelope looked surprised at Lily's outburst. "Um, well I was going to ask you out to lunch, but I see this is a bad time."

"I'm sorry. I really am. It just seems like a parade of people have traipsed through and it's making it so hard to concentrate."

"Well then, it sounds like lunch is just the thing. And after lunch, we'll have Andrea close the door and lock it!"

Smiling, Lily agreed. Over lunch, Penelope brought the conversation around to Ellen.

"I only met her a time or two but I got the feeling that you two were friends."

"We didn't hang out after work if that's what you mean, but we were very friendly co-workers," Lily admitted. Looking up from her salad, she cocked her head to the side asking, "Why?"

Penelope shrugged as she replied, "Oh, I don't know. I just keep thinking back to that last conversation I had with her when I was introduced to you. She walked me out of the room and seemed as though she wanted to tell me something. I always thought that maybe you knew what it was."

Eying her speculatively, Lily said, "I was unaware that Ellen had told you anything. Certainly nothing that she had told me." *Another fishing expedition.* Looking down at her food, she suddenly did not feel hungry anymore. "If you don't mind, I think that I'll head back to work. I have a lot to finish today." Rising, Lily thanked her for lunch before hurrying out of the deli, feeling Penelope's eyes boring into the back of her.

By Thursday, Lily was ready to scream. Entering her office, she greeted Andrea saying, "Want to take bets on who will visit to check up on us today?"

Andrea's eyes grew wide and she nodded her head to

the side. Lily looked over and there was Malcolm. For a second, she didn't know what to say, but suddenly her confidence arose and she looked him in the eyes as she slung her bag onto the chair.

"Well, Mr. VanHeusen. I should have suspected that you'd be next."

She wasn't sure who was more shocked – Malcolm or Andrea or herself. *I've always done my job but taken a back seat to my partners. Always hidden. That seemed safer. Not any more!*

Malcolm quickly overcame his surprise at her comment. "I was merely wanting to ascertain for myself when we might be able to expect to have a working program. I have a board meeting tomorrow and I would like to be able to report."

"Mr. VanHeusen, I am pleased to tell you that I have sent all of my work to the parent company so that they can run the quality controls on it. I plan on being finished with what I need in this building by early next week at the latest. After that you will be working with the technical staff that will put the program in place."

Nodding slowly, his speculative gaze holding hers for a moment, he turned and walked out.

Letting out a long, slow breath she plopped down in the nearest chair looking exhausted.

"Damn girl, that was amazing," Andrea said gleefully. "Lordy, I've been wanting someone to do that since I've been here!"

The two friends laughed as Lily rose from her chair

and made her way back to her office. "Well, I'm working as hard as I can to finish."

Several hours later, Lily walked out and asked, "Are you going out for lunch?"

"Not today. I brought some leftovers."

"Well, I need to walk and stretch so I will run down the street to grab something. I'll be back soon."

Entering a small deli that was tucked back on a side street, Lily ordered and then moved away from the busy counter to wait. Feeling crowded by the mass of people trying to place their orders, she moved a little deeper inside where a few tables were set up. Looking in the corner, she saw Allen sitting at a table with a woman. Starting to call out to him, she saw that they were holding hands. Not wanting to interrupt their possible date, she just moved deeper into the crowd. *Who is he with? She looks like...what?*

As Allen moved back from kissing the woman at his table, she could clearly see that he was with Carla. *Carla? Interesting.* Allen had never even looked at Carla during any of their meetings.

Re-entering the office, she saw Andrea still eating at her desk. "I've got gossip," she announced.

Andrea looked up with a twinkle in her eye. "Oh do tell. I just love gossip."

"I was at the deli and guess who I saw tucked back into a corner? Holding hands? And kissing?"

Andrea cackled, "Lordy, I feel like I'm in junior high school, but I have to admit I can't wait to hear."

"Our dear own Dr. Allen Purser and…Carla!"

Andrea's eyes grew wide and her mouth gaped open. "You're kidding," she exclaimed. "He always made fun of her incompetence and she never acted like she knew him." Then looking doubtful, she asked, "Are you sure?"

Lily grinned, replying, "Oh yeah. They got in a lip-lock that I thought someone would have to pry them apart from. I guess perhaps he found out that even if she wasn't any good at her job she must be good at something…and we can guess what the something is."

Andrea laughed, shaking her head. "I'd have never guessed."

SHANE ANNOUNCED, "LOOKS like Toby is willing to give up a little more. You wanna go with me to interview him again?"

"Jesus, he's pissing me off, draggin' his ass," Matt answered, following Shane down the hall.

"Yeah, well it seems like every week his memory gets a little bit better."

"You think the dumb-ass finally figured out that no one is going to bail him out of jail?"

"If he's smart then he'll finally give us what we need, if he has any hope of getting a shorter sentence."

Walking into the room they once again saw Toby sitting at the familiar grey table, a surly expression on his face.

He looked up as they sat down across from him and he began talking before they asked any questions.

"Look, I don't know nothin' for absolute sure, but I heard talk. Saw things. Figured some things out. But I gotta know that if I tell you stuff, you're gonna talk to the DA."

"Okay, deal," Matt answered. "Don't know what that'll buy you, but it'll count for something."

Toby scrunched his face as he pondered his choices. Finally nodding, he continued, "Like the ones from that big warehouse robbery? Most of the time, the pill bottles were clean, but sometimes I'd see names. My job was to make sure the pills weren't in any bottles with the doc's names on them."

"What name did you see?"

"Van something. VanHowdin or VanHousin or something like that."

Matt raised his eyebrow, looking at Toby. "VanHeusen?"

Toby's face scrunched up as he thought. "VanHeusen? Yeah, that sounds right!" he proclaimed excitedly.

"You dumb-fuck," Shane bit out. "There was a robbery at the VanHeusen drug warehouse, so of course those bottles would be in circulation."

Toby asked, "So you know you got that doctor?"

"VanHeusen isn't a doctor. That is the name of the medical facility and it has a ton of doctors working for it."

Once again, Toby's face showed his wheels turning as he processed.

Matt asked, "You got anything else for us?"

"I thought he was a doctor 'cause I heard about him writing prescriptions when we needed more drugs."

At this, Matt and Shane's attention was once again re-captured.

"What exactly did you hear?" Matt growled.

"That Doctor VanHeusen was making prescriptions out for nobody and we could get our hands on them."

Matt and Shane looked at each other, knowing that Malcolm VanHeusen was not a physician and couldn't write prescriptions, legally or not.

Turning back to the hopeful looking Toby, they continued to question him.

THAT NIGHT OVER dinner, Lily and Matt were talking about their days. "I hate to complain, but Curtis is so foul-tempered."

Matt looked up asking, "Curtis?"

"Dr. Curtis Bennett."

"What's he doing?" Matt asked.

"Snooping around. Coming down to the basement offices and questioning me on everything." Lily paused thoughtfully for a moment. "Well actually, that makes him just like everyone else lately, except he just does it in a much less pleasant way. I get the feeling like they are hawks circling their prey and I'm the prey!"

Matt didn't like hearing about her job described in this way and approached her about the investigation. "Baby, some things have come up and I just wanted your thoughts."

Lily looked across the small table at the man filling her house, her thoughts, and her dreams. Dreams...she realized that she hadn't had her recurring nightmare for weeks. Smiling, she looked into his eyes seeing...questioning? "Uh, did I miss something?"

"LilyBelle, where was your mind just then?"

Blushing, she admitted, "I was thinking about you. And me. I mean us."

Reaching across the table he clasped his hand onto hers, linking his long fingers with her tiny ones. Giving a gentle tug, he said, "Come here, babe."

She rose from her chair and slid onto his lap, feeling his arms wrap around her, engulfing her in their warmth.

"What were you thinking about when you were thinking about us?"

She slid her hand up to cup his jaw, pulling him in for a soft kiss. Barely touching her lips to his. A whisper of a kiss. "I was thinking that I don't have my nightmares anymore since you came along."

"What nightmares were those, babe?"

"Of the night Rose died," she said, a soft smile curving the corners of her mouth. "I used to play it over and over in my mind and then it played over in my dreams. Always very real." She sighed and looked over his shoulder, lost in thought.

"And now, baby?" he prodded.

Her chocolate eyes came back to his and her smile widened. "Now? I just dream of you holding me."

This time he leaned his head forward until his breath washed across her lips. "I'm temped to kiss you, baby. You okay with that?"

"I want that more than anything."

At that he kissed her, leaving no doubt how he felt about her answer.

Several minutes later, pulling back, he reminded her that they needed to talk. Giving a little pout, she stood and they cleared the table before sitting on the sofa.

Twisting in her seat, she looked at him and said, "Okay, fire away."

"I need to bring you up to speed on Ellen's case, but since it's still an open investigation, there are things I can't tell you."

Lily's eyes sought his, seeing the seriousness in his expression. "It definitely wasn't suicide was it?" she asked with a shaky voice.

"The detectives in charge have kept me up on what they're looking at, but it looks very much like homicide."

He hated seeing the flash of fear cross her face as she crossed her arms in front of her tightly, as though to ward off unpleasant news. Giving her a moment to digest the information, he then continued. "Now, you gotta know that you working in a building where there was a homicide of a co-worker of yours is making me crazy."

Nodding, she sighed heavily.

"I need to know if Malcolm himself ever wrote prescriptions that you know of."

Her brow crinkled in confusion. "Malcolm? Honey, he's not a medical doctor. He can't write prescriptions."

"I know, but I just wondered if you had seen anything or heard anything."

Shaking her head she said, "Even if he did try something like that, a pharmacy would never allow it. They would catch it at their level."

Matt sat quietly for a moment, pondering the information. Looking back up quickly he asked, "What if the prescription came through VanHeusen Pharmaceuticals?"

Lily shrugged, saying, "Honey, I don't know how all that works. But I know there are pharmacists there and they would do the same thing that any pharmacist would do."

"Maybe," he said ruefully, deciding to keep his suspicions to himself while vowing to turn the heat up on Malcolm tomorrow.

THE NEXT DAY found Matt and Shane sitting in Curtis' office. As the director over VanHeusen's Pharmaceutical, they were questioning him about the robbery.

Matt noticed that Curtis glowered, just as Lily said

that he did. *What are you hiding behind that pissed-off expression?*

"Detectives, my time is valuable. What do you need?"

"We're still looking at the surveillance tapes," Shane started. "You know we're convinced that this was an inside job."

"The VanHeusen employees are not responsible. Instead of harassing innocent people, you should be doing your job and finding the real culprits," Curtis bit out.

"What makes you so sure that every one of the employees who work there are innocent?"

"What makes you so sure that someone there is guilty?" Curtis shot back as he leaned forward in his seat, eyes narrowed in confrontation.

Matt spoke, "The robbery occurred at the exact time that you have the least number of employees there. They knew exactly where the security door latch button was located, without having to waste any time. Once inside the secure area, they ran down the hall, turning twice to get to a specific room. Didn't stop. Didn't look at any printed directions. Went straight to the room containing the drugs that have the highest value street market right now that are the least able to be tracked."

Curtis listened, his face turning redder by the minute. Leaning heavily back into his chair, he turned to look out of the window in his office. The silence in the room sat like a heavy blanket for a few minutes, the detectives willing to let the quiet penetrate through the doctor.

Finally turning his gaze back to the detectives, he said, "The pharmacists were interviewed and vetted by me personally. It wasn't them." Silence again for a few minutes. "The pharmaceutical technicians were also hired through me. It wasn't one of them either."

Curtis' eyes went back to the window. Shane and Matt shared a look and continued their silence. It was obvious that the doctor was mentally working the problem.

"The receptionist has been there for a number of years, but I confess that the security staff and custodial staff are not employees that I had a hand in hiring."

"Do you contract out those services?"

Curtis' glower continued as he called in his assistant to provide the list of outside service contracts. After a moment, a young woman entered with several files in her hand.

"Dr. Bennett, are these the files that you inquired about?" she asked politely.

Barely looking at them, he nodded sharply at her and barked, "Yes, of course they are."

The young assistant glanced at Matt and Shane, giving an embarrassed smile as she left the room.

Handing the list to the detectives, he looked at them dismissively. "Is that all?"

Standing, Matt and Shane exited his office and walked to the elevator.

"Jesus, is this building filled with pricks?" Shane asked.

Entering the elevator, Matt rubbed his hand over his face sighing loudly. "I don't know who has the bigger stick up their ass – Malcolm or this Curtis guy."

As the elevator stopped on the first floor, Shane noticed that Matt stayed on the elevator. Lifting his eyebrow at his partner he smiled. "Heading to the basement?"

Matt smiled back. "Yeah, let's check on Lily while we're here. I've never seen her office anyway."

Andrea was thrilled to finally meet Matt and equally thrilled to have someone to talk to. Grabbing Shane, she pushed him toward a chair saying, "While they get mushy in there," pointing to the room where Lily was housed, "I'll fill you in on all the characters in this building!"

Rolling his eyes, Shane grinned good-naturedly and sat down ready to listen, giving Matt and Lily a moment of privacy.

Lily drug Matt into her small inner office. "Welcome to my little cave," she joked as she pulled him close.

Not needing any encouragement, Matt wrapped his arms around her body engulfing her in his embrace. Lifting her chin with his fingers he leaned down and kissed her. Simple. Almost chaste at first.

But Lily was having none of that. Not able to rise on her toes, she clasped the back of his head with her hands bringing his face back to hers. Slipping her tongue into his mouth, she turned the kiss into one of heat, passion, want.

Moaning, he angled his head for better access and as their tongues tangled he explored every crevice, drinking her in.

After a moment they pulled back, smiling as they gazed into each other's eyes.

"I love you, LilyBelle," he said, staring into the chocolate eyes that had captured him from the first night.

"I love you too, Matt," she said gently.

Stepping back they both looked down at his crotch, strained with his swollen cock. Lily put her hand over her mouth as she tried to stifle a giggle. He tried to look stern but the look of joy on her face made the pretend irritation impossible.

"Ah woman, what will I do with you?" he asked with genuine affection.

"Keep me?" she queried back.

"Count on it, babe."

After adjusting himself, they walked back into the outer office where Andrea was just winding down with her tales of office gossip to Shane. He shot Matt a look of gratitude as they said goodbye to the women and headed out of the building.

★   ★   ★

(Surveillance)

"YOU SEE THOSE detectives in there?"

"What the fuck are you asking me that for? I'm sittin' here aren't I? Of course I goddamn saw them."

"Hell, what are you so touchy for?"

"I've been given this shit assignment for weeks and I'm sick and tired of watching her sit at her computer and work all day. Jesus fuck, her job is boring. And for what? We've searched the office. She doesn't act suspicious. I don't think that Ellen woman told her shit."

"Well, it's not your job to think, is it? Your job is to keep an eye on her. The boss wants to know as soon as her job is finished."

"Yeah, why?"

"I got a notion that when the job is finished…so is the lady."

Chapter 19

Got a late night, baby.

LILY LOOKED AT the text that came in late that afternoon. Sighing, she couldn't help but feel the dread and worry when she knew he was on a stake-out or an investigation. Rubbing her brow, she looked up when Andrea came in.

"You okay, Lily?"

"Just tired. But…," she smiled as Andrea looked at her closely. "I talked to my parent company and they are ready to send in the IT team to set up the new programs. I figure that by the end of this week, I will be out of here and good riddance."

At that, Andrea's smile slipped just a little.

"Oh, Andrea. I didn't mean you. You are the one thing about this place that I can't stand leaving. In fact," she said as she walked over to her friend, "I talked to my company to see if they would consider taking you on as my assistant."

Andrea's eyes grew wide at this proclamation. "Really? I never thought about leaving VanHeusen's, but I have to admit that I've loved being able to work with you and even Ellen before she died."

"Well, think about it. I'm going to stay here for a little while this evening. Matt is working late and I have something I want to work on."

Andrea gathered up her purse before questioning Lily. "Work? I thought you were basically finished."

"I am, but I had something else I was working on and wanted to try to finish. Something Ellen left me."

Andrea's eyes widened as she turned back to Lily. "Ellen?"

"Yeah. Kind of Ellen's last riddle tribute."

"I know she loved riddles, but what on earth is this?"

"It was one she sent me before she died. A message in a number-problem that I've been working on. I had a friend helping me and I haven't had a chance to work on it lately, but I think my friend was able to decode part of it."

Smiling, Andrea nodded. "She was fun, wasn't she?" she asked wistfully. "Well, if the riddle turns out to be something fun...or sexy, let me know," she said with a wink.

"Absolutely. You're the only one here who really knew her anyway."

"Well, I'll leave you to it," Andrea said. Saying goodbye, she left as Lily settled back into her chair with her laptop.

"Okay, BJ. Let's see what you left for me," she said out loud, pulling out the notebook that he had started for her. The last they had worked on it, he had said that it appeared that Ellen had used a number code that she embedded into an old program. BJ's notes had begun to solve the simple number code.

Popping the thumb drive into her computer, she began to extrapolate the numbers coded within the program, slowly seeing an actual computer program emerging. Smiling to herself, she realized how clever Ellen had been. "Girl, this was definitely your most creative riddle," she whispered to the empty office. Thinking back to Ellen's last riddle, it had been a fun way to come up with a new project of hers – a dating service for computer nerds.

Lily had to laugh out loud at the memory. Ellen had been convinced that the only way a smart, nerdy woman was ever going to get a date was to have their own dating site. *Is this what you were still working on?* Lily couldn't help but remember thinking that even if Ellen's idea had been sound, there was still no chance of the handsome prince coming her way. Then there was Matt. Her prince. Her handsome prince. The one who made her realize that her mother had been wrong all those years ago.

An hour later, most of the extraneous numbers had been removed, leaving the computer program. Looking at her watch, she knew it was getting late. Thinking of heading home, she decided to keep working. *Matt's not home now so I might as well keep going a little bit longer.*

Finally, she had the program scrubbed. She resaved the program to her thumb drive and then ran it. It immediately began loading to her computer under the title **I'm all thumbs when it comes to my data.** *Data? Data?* Recognizing the same line from Ellen's note that she had found under the file drawer, she realized that she had misread Ellen's handwriting. *She wasn't taking about her dates…she was talking about the data on her thumb drives. Data…not dates!*

So what data are you talking about? Looking carefully at the information, documents and spreadsheets downloaded onto her computer, she realized it had nothing to do with a silly dating site. It seemed to be about the project that they had been working on with VanHeusen Medical.

She was amazed at the amount of information displaying on her computer screen. Slowly scrolling through the first few word documents, she realized that Ellen was listing some of the doctors in the VanHeusen's facility and their prescription histories with patients. Then, she included patient numbers with those doctors and their prescription histories. Rubbing her eyes at the lines of data, she wondered what the hell Ellen was doing. *Was this some of the data that you gathered for us to use when developing the programs? Then why hide it from me?*

Determined to understand what it all meant, she settled in to pour over it. She began to see some patient numbers repeated multiple times for drug prescriptions. Not surprised at that information since many patients have to be on medications for years, therefore having multiple prescriptions for the same medicines, she began looking at the dates. Several prescriptions for the same medications to a patient were listed on the same day or within the same week. *That's odd.* Continuing to process what she was looking at, she noticed a trend. Of all the doctors in the building, it seemed to be only three doctors whose names appeared constantly. Doctors who were sending prescriptions to the pharmaceutical building, as though for a patient and yet, they had to have been dummy prescriptions.

Then, the next document showed that there were prescriptions filed with no patient numbers attached. Prescriptions that were billed to insurance companies or Medicare, but for no real patient. *Jesus, this just keeps going.* Eye's wide at the recognition, she realized that Ellen had stumbled on discrepancies and that was what she had tried to hide in the coded program.

Oh my God. She wasn't coding a new riddle. She was trying to get information to me. Information that she didn't want anyone here to know that she had.

Lily's breathing became more labored as her naïve mind began to work the situation just as she carefully worked out a coding problem. *She wasn't just killed because she happened to be in the wrong place at the wrong time. She was murdered because she found out something. Found out too much.*

Glancing up toward the video camera in the corner, she panicked, eyes wide as she stared at the camera. Looking back down, she quickly loaded the program as an attachment in an email and forwarded it to her personal email. *I wish I knew Matt's email address.* Thinking quickly, she added BJ's email address with a quick note and hit **send.**

Grabbing her phone she quickly typed a text to Matt. **Decoded Ellen's msg – found something here – need to see you asap – heading home now. sent BJ copy**

Grabbing her purse and the thumb drives, she pulled on her jacket as she was walking out of the office. Suddenly, as she flipped off the light switch, a body stood in front of her. She screamed as she jumped backwards.

"Lily, what's wrong?" Andrea asked.

"Jesus, Andrea. You scared the shit out of me. Why are you here?"

"I left my cell phone and came back to get it. But the whole way here I was terrified that I would find what you found the night you came back."

Lily grabbed Andrea's arm. "We have to get out of here now. Walk with me…there's safety in numbers."

Andrea's eyes widened. "What? What's wrong?"

"I found out what Ellen had discovered. A ton of prescription fraud. This may be how a lot of the prescription drugs are getting out."

Dragging Andrea along the corridor to the elevator, Lily saw the look of terror on Andrea's face. "Oh my God, Lily, what do we do?"

"We get out of here. That goddamn camera has been on me for weeks and I'm terrified that someone has noticed my behavior tonight."

Entering the elevator, they looked at each other. "Where to?" Andrea asked. "I've got my car in the parking garage. Do you think if someone is watching, we can get out of here?"

"They would be expecting me to go up a floor to the main level and take a cab home. Maybe the garage is safer."

"I can take you home. Or to the police station if that's better," Andrea volunteered.

Lily nodded. "That's the smart play. They won't be expecting that. Jesus, listen to us. For all I know, no one is after us."

The doors to the garage floor opened and the two women walked out cautiously. "My car is over there," Andrea said pointing to a grey sedan. Using her key fob, she clicked the doors and the lights flashed. The two women began to hustle to the car, Andrea's heels clicking on the concrete as Lily's sneakers treaded softly.

Suddenly, from behind Andrea's car stepped a familiar figure. Both women stopped in their tracks.

"Oh Allen, I'm so glad to see you," Andrea said moving forward.

Lily tried unsuccessfully to hold her back. "Andrea, no. He's one of the doctors on Ellen's list," she hissed. "We've got to get away."

Allen sauntered over, his eyes glittering. "Well, well, looks like the little mouse found out what Ellen discovered and now we've got a problem on our hands."

Andrea continued walking right up to Allen and took his kiss as he leaned into her. Lily looked on in stunned silence.

"You? You and…him?" she sputtered. "Andrea, I don't know what he's told you but you've got to believe me. He's one of them. He's one of the doctors that's involved in whatever mess this is."

Andrea turned around, smiling slowly. "You think I'm just his lover? Or that maybe I work for him? You think I'm just some lackey? Honey, who do you think has masterminded this whole operation?"

Before Lily's stunned mind could wrap itself around that proclamation, she was approached from behind by two goons. As she glanced behind her that was the only word that she could think fit them. Just like in the detective shows she watched on TV where the bad guys always had someone who did their dirty work. Goons. And these two fit the description. Large men, mean faces, and dressed in dark suits. One of them grabbed her arms and held them behind her.

"Where do you want her boss?"

Facing Allen, she was stunned once again when Andrea spoke up, "My car."

As the man shoved her over to the silver sedan and was about to open the back door, Andrea sharply said, "No you moron, not in the seat. The trunk." With that she clicked her key fob again and the trunk popped open.

Lily's heart began to pound as she turned her eyes

back to her one-time assistant and pleaded, "Andrea, don't do this. Why are you doing this?"

Jerking her head toward her trunk, Andrea just replied, "Get her in there now and be quick about it. But give me her purse first." Once she had Lily's purse in her hands she quickly rummaged through it. Pulling out the thumb drive and her cell phone she tossed the bag to one of the goons. She pocketed the thumb drive and dropped her cell phone on the concrete before stepping on it. Looking back at Lily's pale face, she just smiled and said, "No trace. We don't want your detective boyfriend to be tempted into finding you through this."

Lily felt her hands tied behind her back before she was picked up and tossed into the trunk. Not gently. One of the goons leaned over, his breath creeping over her as he whispered, "I hope she lets me play with you some, doll. I've been wantin' to for a long time."

Her eyes wide with fear looked up as she saw his leering face just before the trunk lid slammed shut. *Oh Jesus, Jesus help me.*

The pain in her shoulders pierced through her, but she was more concerned about her prosthesis. As long as she still had her two legs, she had a chance to get away. If they took that from her...she was totally at their mercy. But as she lay in the trunk as the car moved away, she knew she was already totally at their mercy.

Chapter 20

THE EVENING WORE on and by the time Matt and Shane had wrapped up their work it was after eleven p.m. Checking his phone messages he read the one by Lily. His blood ran cold as he realized the danger she could be in if she had discovered something that Ellen was working on. Calling her, his panic rose as the call wouldn't go through to voice mail. It didn't even ring.

Looking down the hall, he saw Shane almost leaving the building. Yelling for him to come back, he hustled over to him showing him the email.

"You think she's in danger?"

"I think she's stumbled onto something that must have gotten Ellen killed, so fuck yeah," he responded sharply.

Shane hustled back down the hall, calling out for the few detectives left in the building and having the others called in. Looking over at one of the rookies, he instructed, "Call the chief. And get the homicide crew that was working on Ellen Marsh's murder."

Matt looked up, his phone to his ear. "I'm running home to check on her. She's not answering."

Shane shook his head, "Get Vinny. He lives closer to her. I'll call him. You call Tony to see if they can get a trace on her phone again."

At the word *again,* Matt was reminded of the last time he couldn't find her. That time it was him who had hurt her. This time...*don't think of that.* He dialed Tony.

A few tense minutes later, Shane's phone rang. "Talk. Yeah. You check everything? Yeah. Meet at Tony's. We'll coordinate as soon as we have something."

Matt's blue eyes held his partner's, his heart pounding.

"Vinny checked your house. She's not there. No purse, no coat. Doesn't look like she went home today. Nothing but the yapping dog."

By then several of the detectives and the chief had arrived, being filled in on the suspicions.

Calling Tony again, Matt ordered him to get BJ in. "Get him to check his email and then send whatever information he can to this email address," giving him the contact for one of the detectives at the station. "Have him call me as soon as he looks at it. I wanna know what she found."

The chief looked at the homicide detective, ordering him to get a search warrant for VanHeusen's. "Wake up whatever judge you have to. I want my men in that building tonight."

One of the policemen there walked up and reported. "Matt, I just called the taxi companies that Lily uses and then called the others in the area. No one picked her up at the front of the building today. None of her regulars have seen her."

Matt looked at Shane, their eyes registering the same idea. "We're rolling," Matt called as they hustled down the hall.

The chief looked at several of the policemen around. "Go. Backup."

Arriving at the VanHeusen Medical Building, they moved to the parking garage first. The garage was bathed in florescent light, illuminating the few cars left in the lot. The smashed cell phone close to a parking space was the first thing Matt noticed. Running over he reached down to grab it, but was pulled back by Shane.

"What the fuck, man?" Matt growled, before noticing Shane reaching for the phone with gloves on. Matt scrubbed his face with his hand in frustration.

Shane stood looking at his partner and friend. "Been right where you are. No way you're thinkin' straight now. Keep your wits, but let us handle the investigation. You do not want to fuck this up."

Matt recognized the phone case as Lily's before Shane handed it over to one of the other policemen to bag.

Another detective hustled over. "The security camera out here has been spray painted, but we just got a call from the chief. They're bringing over the search warrant."

Matt looked over at Shane. "You and I need to head

over to Tony's to see what BJ's found." Turning back to the detective, he said, "You all stay here. Let me know what you find." With that, he and Shane ran back over to his truck.

Once at Tony's, they found the situation to be similar to the previous year when Annie was taken and Shane was tearing up the place wanting to find her. They entered the main doors of the innocuous office space and were immediately sent back. Greeted by one of Tony's men, they were ushered to the end of the hall and through the steel security doors. Once inside, a hive of activity buzzed around them. Glancing around they saw Tony's crew had already assembled. Jobe. Gabe. Vinny. All surrounding a computer station, centering their attention on BJ.

Looking up, Tony walked straight over to his friends, clasping Matt by the shoulders. They stared into each other's eyes for just a moment before Tony gave him a head jerk. Walking over to BJ, the others parted slightly, giving them room to look at the screen.

BJ pointed to the board on the wall saying, "Gonna project this up there so you all can see what I am seeing."

The crew turned to see the large screen on the wall, showing various documents. Using his cursor as his pointer, BJ began. "Looks like Ellen discovered fraud and then began investigating herself. Whether to see if it was real or playing detective, no one knows, but my assumption at this point is that she was discovered and someone at VanHeusen's silenced her.

"Looking at these documents you can see where multiple prescriptions were ordered for the same patient on the same day. We can see where the patient picked up their one prescription, but the others were claimed through the pharmaceutical company. It appears to be the same three doctors. Now over here," he continued, "you can see where there are no patient names to go with the patient numbers for these prescriptions. Looks like these are false also. Looks like they are mostly for OxyContin, Oxycodone, Percocet, and Vicodin.

"I haven't had time to look at all her data, but it still seems to come down to these three doctors."

Matt stared at the three names highlighted on the large screen in front of him, rage pouring through his veins. Turning around to face BJ, he spit out, "VanHeusen. He involved?"

BJ looked at him carefully. "I haven't had time to investigate this yet, Matt. I've got no way at this time to tell who else was in on this."

Matt turned to Shane. "I know that fucker's involved."

"Then let's wake him up."

Turning back to Tony, Matt said, "Got no idea who's got her or where they're goin'. We're heading to VanHeusen's place and then over to the jail to pay Toby another visit. Need you to start working on tracking anything you can from those three doctors. Money, friends, bills, loans, places they visit. Hell, I wanna know where they go to crap!"

Tony's men dispersed, heading to their own stations to work, as Matt and Shane headed back out the door. Shane reported to the chief, wanting arrest warrants for the three doctors.

Driving to the VanHeuson's mansion the two men were quiet, each lost to their own thoughts. Shane turned to Matt, seeing his dark visage illuminated by the inside lights of the truck. "What are you thinkin'?"

Sighing loudly, Matt answered, "Trying to work the problem. Trying to figure out where she would be. There's so many goddamn places. We've got detectives scouring Lily's work place, but I just feel like there is no way they would have her there."

Pulling up to the front door once again, they hopped out and Matt began banging on the front door. It took several minutes but a bedraggled butler wearing a distinguished wool robe finally opened the door. Flashing badges they shouldered him back and walked inside.

"Sirs, you cannot be here. Mr. VanHeusen is abed."

"Get him," Matt growled.

The butler stood firm, but soon found that his authority was not going to dissuade. Before Matt could lose it, Shane leaned in and said, "Understand you gotta job to do, so I'm gonna make this easy on you. Get your boss. Get him now. Or we will go find him ourselves, arrest him on suspicion of kidnapping and drug fraud and haul him outta here in cuffs. You got two seconds to decide what you wanna do."

Given that choice, the butler turned and hustled up the stairs. Within minutes, Malcolm came down, a murderous look on his face.

"I'll have you know I have contacted my lawyers. You can expect to hear from them tomorrow."

Before Matt could give in to his anger, Shane spoke up. "That's perfect 'cause you'll need them before the night is over. And just in case you're thinkin' to cover this all up, I'll call my contacts at the newspaper and local television stations."

"You do and I'll sue for libel," Malcolm roared, finally losing his cool.

"Won't be libel. We're searchin' your building right now. With a search warrant. And when the charges of prescription fraud, kidnapping and murder get slapped on you, we'll see how nervous your stockholders get then."

Malcolm reared back, eyes wide. "What…what are you talking about?"

Matt watched Malcolm's face carefully. He could almost believe that Malcolm was truly surprised if he wasn't convinced that Malcolm was at the head of it all.

Malcolm stood in the foyer for a moment, silent and angry. Finally, turning toward the room where they had interviewed him before, he said, "I think you'd better let me know what I'm up against."

Matt and Shane shared a look as they followed him into the opulent study and settled in chairs indicated by

Malcolm. They watched as he walked over to the bar setup and poured whiskey into a tumbler. Taking a sip and then downing the entire drink, he turned back to face the detectives after settling in a chair.

"I'm assuming you have proof of your accusations?"

"We know you have three doctors working in your building who have been involved in prescription fraud, going back several years. We know they have not only been defrauding the insurance companies and Medicare, but the drugs have been hitting the street markets."

Malcolm's face became more concrete as Matt went on.

"We know that Ellen Marsh discovered the discrepancies and was murdered before she had a chance to report it, meaning that someone in your organization ordered her murder. We now know that she secretly sent the information to Lily."

By this time Matt had risen from his seat, stalked over to Malcolm's chair and leaned down to place both hands on the arms of the seat.

"We've got the evidence. A private security agency's got the evidence. The homicide detectives have got the evidence and it has been sent on to the FBI and DEA. But that's all shit to me…"

Malcolm lifted his gaze to the huge man towering over him.

"My Lily's missing from your garage. MY. LILY. Do you get me, man?" His eyes bore straight into Malcolm's face. "You got exactly no fuckin' time to even think about this. You start talking and you start now. No time for lawyering up. No time for stall or any shit roadblocks you are thinkin' about putting up. You talk and you talk now." Leaning in so that their noses were almost touching, Matt added, "Or I swear to God I will tear you apart then take you down."

Malcolm's eyes cut over to Shane, whose passive face registered nothing. Licking his lips, he said, "Okay."

Matt shoved off of Malcolm's chair so hard that it rocked back almost spilling Malcolm. Malcolm pierced them with a glare, but fear was now evident in his eyes.

"I have no idea what you are talking about. I built this company up from nothing over the past twenty years. I poured my blood into it." Sweeping his hand around the room, he continued, "You think this was paid for with illegal drug money. Well, gentlemen, think again. I worked. I sacrificed. Long hours. Hiring the best of the best. Goddamn it," he cursed, rising from his chair.

"And to think that someone was stealing from me and willing to take me down with them." He walked back over to the bar and picked up his whiskey tumbler once again. Then he whirled and threw the glass against the far bookcase wall, shattering the glass.

"Well, if what you say is true, then it's too late to save my company. The feds will be crawling all over it, the stockholders will dump me and I will be crucified in the media."

Matt started for the man, rage on his face. "I just

told you that someone murdered Ellen Marsh and has kidnapped Lily and you are sweating your company? You unbelievable bastard."

Shane stepped in quickly, stopping Matt from advancing any more. Turning toward Malcolm he ordered, "Talk. Now."

Malcolm's face settled into resignation. "What do you need to know?" And then he added, "And I want to know the names of the doctors."

Shane handed him a piece of paper, one that BJ had printed off for him that included a page of the false prescriptions. Malcolm sighed and sat back down in his seat.

"We also know that there was a woman involved. We suspect Dr. Penelope Alease."

Malcolm shook his head. "No, it wasn't Dr. Alease."

Matt and Shane looked at each other before turning their attention back to Malcolm.

"I suspected that Ellen had found something in her research. She was acting strangely around me and my doctors. Then it was reported to me that she had intensified her research when several doctors complained about her questions. My cleaning staff reported that she was staying in the office later and later. I actually hired Dr. Alease to see if she could find out what Ms. Marsh was suspicious of and then hopefully take care of the situation before it became a problem. When Ms. Marsh was killed and it was made initially to look like possible suicide, my concerns were validated, but Dr. Alease had not had the time to find out anything. I kept her on to keep an eye on Ms. Swanson."

"I don't give a shit about any of this right now. A cruiser is on its way here to pick you up so you can save you explanations for them. What I wanna know is where to you think they have taken Lily?" Matt growled.

Malcolm looked into Matt's eyes. Doubt, fear, and even regret passed across Malcolm's face. Sucking in a huge breath, he sighed. "I don't know. I don't have any idea."

"Jesus, Goddamn fuck," Matt cursed.

"What about warehouses? What about storage areas that are mostly empty? Anything by the river?" Shane asked, knowing that was where the drug exchanges had taken place.

Malcolm rubbed his hand over his face. Just then the butler escorted several policemen into the room. "Shall I call your solicitor," he asked his employer.

"Yes." Then turning back to Shane he added, "There are a number of VanHeusen warehouses by the river. Some for medical equipment. None for drugs, but I have diversified into the medical equipment business and own a number of buildings there." Giving the addresses to Shane, he then turned to Matt. "I hope you find her. I never wished her ill."

Growling, "You son of a bitch," as he stalked out, Matt barely made it to the truck before hearing Shane calling the chief and Tony on a conference call.

The chief reported, "We're picking up Malcolm

VanHeusen and Penelope Alease right now and bringing them in for questioning. The FBI and DEA are both working on the data that Ms. Marsh sent to Lily. Why don't you head back here? We're bringing Toby in from the jail for questioning. He's not screaming for a lawyer so maybe we can get more out of him."

Tony responded, "Send us the addresses of the warehouses, Shane. We'll get the floor plans and start working up a search plan."

Stopping at the truck Matt halted and threw his hands forward, leaning them on the hood with his head down. Shane approached and put his hand on his friend's shoulder. "We're workin' it, man. You gotta hang in there."

A sob almost choked Matt as he battled back his fears. "They killed Ellen. They won't stop now. They got nothing to lose."

"Get that outta your mind, bro. You gotta stay strong. You gotta stay focused. You gotta work the problem."

Nodding, Matt silently threw open the truck door and they hurried back to the station as the night cloaked the city.

"HOW'S HE DOING?" the chief asked.

Shane looked up. "How do you think he's doin'? Hangin' on by a thread."

Matt walked back from the men's room where he

splashed water on his face, willing his mind to focus. Wordlessly, he and Shane walked into the interrogation room holding Toby.

"Got no time for pleasantries Toby," Shane started out. "We know who the doctors are. We know they killed Ellen Marsh. We know how they got the drugs and with your help we know how they were distributing them. We know they have kidnapped Lily Swanson. Now what we don't know is where they would have taken her. We suspect the river warehouses, but you're gonna have to keep us from chasin' our tails here and give up everything you know. Or, you face conspiracy for murder and kidnappin' along with anything else I can think of. Ms. Swanson is a particular friend of Matt's and you will not make it in jail alive if you don't start coughin' up some information."

Toby's wide eyes went from Shane to Matt. "I don't know nothin' about no murder or kidnappin'!"

"Talk!" Matt roared.

Toby jumped back in his seat, eyes darting all around. "Okay, okay. Um…I know there's the ware-houses where you got me. There's some down the river from there also. Not too many of them, at least that I know of."

"So far you're not telling me anything I don't know, asshole. How about telling us something we can use before I decide to actually start using you like a punch-ing bag?" Matt spit out.

"You can't do that. I've got rights," Toby sputtered.

"You're right. But I can make a couple of calls and make sure your stay in the city facilities are just filled with friendly visits."

"Shit man. You don't play fair."

"Talk!"

"I've been inside a couple of the warehouses. Mostly large crates that come in. Got labels on them for medical equipment. But they got some underground facilities also, which is kind of weird since they are right on the river."

At this, Matt and Shane leaned forward. "Keep talkin'."

"I had to go take a leak and went inside to find a corner to piss in. Went behind some crates. Didn't even see a door in the wall until it suddenly opened. A couple of guys came out. They didn't see me 'cause I'd jumped back behind a stack. After they left, I was curious, so I opened the door and peeked. Just some stairs heading down."

"What else?"

"Nothin' man. I didn't go down there. It just seemed weird that the warehouse had a basement area."

Stalking out of the interrogation room, they headed down the hall to the conference room filled with detectives, patrolmen, DEA, FBI and others Matt did not even recognize. The chief had them brief the group on the latest information from Toby as the others began reporting from their investigations and contacts.

The group began to argue as to the best tactic to

take. DEA wanted the drugs, but the FBI and detectives argued Lily's safety as a priority. Matt began to sweat, knowing that he was about to lose his cool. Shane, seeing his partner's face, grabbed his arm and pulled him from the room.

Getting right in Matt's face, he said, "Talk to me."

Shaking his head Matt said, "I can't handle this. They're in there talking about the drugs and Lily and all I want to do is rip their goddamn heads off."

"You gotta stay cool. You gotta stay focused. Listen to me, man. The chief is pulling them together. Our FBI friends are focused on Lily. I'm patchin' in Tony's group right now. Chief's getting the S.W.A.T. team briefed. It's comin' together. We're gonna find her."

Matt worked to control his panic. But realized he had never been so scared in his life.

Chapter 21

LILY BOUNCED PAINFULLY in the trunk of the sedan. She worked to loosen the ties on her hands, but to no avail. She then concentrated on keeping her legs as naturally situated as possible to keep the prosthesis from becoming damaged. All while trying not to panic. *No cell phone. No message. No way to let Matt know where I am. Trying* to keep the tears at bay, she wasn't as successful in keeping her heart rate from skyrocketing. *Breathe. In and out. Just like when running. In and out.*

The car came to a lurching stop and she rolled forward hitting her head on the trunk, her shoulders screaming in pain. After a few minutes all she could hear was muffled voices. Then the trunk lid flew open and she was roughly pulled out and placed on her feet. Blinking her eyes to adjust to the light, she had no idea where she was. The room was huge, filled with large wooden crates marked with 'VanHeusen Medical Supplies' stamped on the sides.

Andrea appeared from behind her and continued walking, ordering over her shoulder, "Take her down." Then glancing at Allen she smiled and said, "Come on, baby."

Allen, grinning, fell into step behind her as Lily was pushed along by the other man who held her roughly by the arm.

Walking for several minutes through warehouses the size of football fields, they came to a stop behind a tall stack of the wooden crates. Andrea slipped through, followed by Allen.

"Go," the goon commanded as she stumbled along.

Squeezing through the narrow opening she couldn't help but glance behind her, wondering if the large man pushing her along would make it through. He did, but barely, and had to turn slightly to the side to maneuver the opening.

Lily's mind was rushing, trying to figure out where she was and how she could escape, but to no avail. Clueless, she could feel the panic rising. Behind the crates she saw Andrea and Allen disappear through a hidden door. She stopped at the entrance, peering inside. The only thing visible in the dim lighting was stairs. Going down. She was suddenly pushed from behind and she began to fall forward. With her hands tied behind her back, she was helpless. Screaming, she suddenly felt herself jerked back against the man's body.

"I gotcha doll. Can't have anything happen to you before the boss says so." With that he leaned around, sticking his tongue out and licking her from chin to forehead.

Trying to keep from gagging she heard him laugh as he held onto her arm as she descended the stairs. She began to shiver, but not from the cold.

At the bottom of the stairs, she was forced to make an immediate right into a small room. No windows. A small table and several chairs littered the area. Another metal door was on the far side of the room.

Andrea jerked her head toward a chair and Lily was unceremoniously pushed down onto it. Wincing, she looked around quickly before focusing on the woman in front of her. Allen had grabbed a chair for Andrea, but she shook her head as though she preferred to stand. Shrugging, Allen just took the seat himself.

"Figured it out yet?" Andrea asked.

Licking her lips nervously, Lily just stared dumbly. "I…um…I don't know…"

"Jesus, you really are just book smart, aren't you?"

"Are   you…do   you…um…work   for…Mr. VanHeusen?"

Throwing her head back, Andrea laughed. "Malcolm? Old news, sweetie."

Lily pulled her lips in, the feeling that she was in a play but had no idea who the characters were overwhelmed her. *What do they want from me? They just killed Ellen, so what do they want from me?*

Andrea reached inside her bag and pulled out the thumb drive, waving it back and forth. "Wondering why we didn't just kill you outright?"

Too afraid to answer, Lily just stared.

"Ellen had to die. I made the mistake of thinking that she had left one evening and was searching through her files when she returned. She was smart, I'll give her that. She had already discovered the fraud, but had no idea who was behind it all. She pieced it together almost instantly and attempted to leave. One shot to the head was all it took."

"Oh my God," Lily whispered, the vision of Ellen lying in a pool of her blood in their former office filling her mind. "You. It was you?"

Andrea's smile was her only answer as she smoothed her hair back.

"But...," Lily couldn't find the words to ask the questions swirling around her mind.

"It took a long time for me to figure out how to get Malcolm back, but I finally had the perfect revenge."

Lily could do no more than stare.

"We were once lovers." Seeing the wide-eyed look that Lily gave her, she laughed. "Oh yeah, honey. I was his mistress for years. His wife never knew and I was his assistant at work. It was perfect. I got the sex and she got the laundry to do." Throwing her head back she laughed harder. As she sobered she said, "Then she finds out, threatens to divorce him and take him down."

Pausing for a moment, she then continued. "The bastard moves me from being his assistant to being a secretary that just got passed around the offices. And then I found out that he had moved on to a new lover. Younger. I gave that fuck ten years of my life and then was scraped off."

Leaning down close to Lily's face she said, "But payback is a bitch, sweetie."

Lily leaned back away from Andrea's glare, but her head pressed up against the man standing behind her chair. Jerking forward she grimaced as he pulled her back into his groin again, rubbing his crotch against the back of her head.

"It took a while, but I finally figured out how to start making money off of Malcolm's medical company."

Lily looked at her, shaking her head at the outrageous plan that Andrea had accomplished. "You stole the drugs?"

"Honey, I masterminded the whole operation. Along with Allen here," she said rubbing her hand along his shoulders. "We've made millions off of the drugs. Stolen. On the streets. Fraud. Insurance companies.

"It was perfect until Ellen came along and fucked it all up," Andrea bit out. "But," she said with a slight shrug, "all things have to come to an end. I've got millions and Malcolm's business will be in the toilet."

Seeing Lily's stare, Andrea shook her head again. "My God, I can't believe you don't have all the pieces put together yet. Shooting Ellen at close range wasn't easy, but I made it look like suicide. I knew the police would figure out that it was murder, but that bought me a little time. You? You were easy. Put you in the basement with a camera on you and Barry here," nodding to the man still behind her, "was keeping a close eye on you. And I might add, dying to get something besides his eyes on you."

The man behind her laughed as his hands stayed on her shoulders holding her in place.

"I've been trying to find out what Ellen did with the information she uncovered and was convinced that she would have tried to get it to you. But day after day you just came into work as though nothing was wrong. But you finally found it, didn't you?"

Leaning back down, Andrea moved in close to Lily. "Who did you tell? Who else knows?"

Seeing the questions in Lily's eyes, she said, "Make no mistake, dearie. You're going to die. I just couldn't take a chance of killing you right there at work before finding out what you had told anyone. I need to know if I have some time or if Allen and I need to book a flight to Buenos Aires tonight."

"I um…" Lily began, her mind trying to see how much time lying would buy her. *Anything to give Matt more time to find me alive.*

Waving her finger back and forth, Andrea's smile did not reach her eyes as she said, "No, no dear. No lying. That just makes Barry have to spend more time getting you to tell the truth."

Before Lily could protest Barry slid his hands down the front of her blouse, then quickly ripped it open popping buttons across the floor. He then slipped his beefy hand into her bra squeezing her breast.

Gasping Lily tried to wiggle free but with her hands still tied she was powerless against his assault.

Tears escaping down her cheeks, she cried, "No, please, no."

"He'll stop when I get my answers," Andrea demanded.

"I…sent it to my personal email. I didn't send it anywhere else," she choked out.

Andrea jerked her head toward Barry and he slid his hand out of her shirt. "That makes sense. You wouldn't know anyone else to send it to, would you?"

Lily sucked in air, feeling faint. *Oh Jesus, help me,* she prayed once again.

Andrea leaned down to kiss Allen, purring, "I've got a surprise for you, lover." Lily watched as Allen stood up reaching toward Andrea. Just then there was a commotion at the door. Lily saw the other goon escorting Carla into the room.

Allen's eyes grew wide as Carla immediately headed to him with her arms stretched out.

"Allen, why did they bring me here, honey?"

Allen's eyes darted between Carla and Andrea. Before Carla could reach Allen, Lily saw Andrea pull out a gun from her bag and aim it at Carla.

"No!" Lily screamed, but it was too late. The gun went off as Carla was shot in the back of the head. Blood and tissue splattered out and as her body fell forward it landed at Allen's feet. His look of shock almost rivaled Lily's.

Andrea kept the gun pointed on Allen, her eyes narrowed in anger. "You go behind my back and fuck that stupid cunt?"

"No, no baby. I'd never do that," Allen protested.

Jerking the gun toward Lily, she said, "She saw you. Making out in a restaurant. Are you so fucking stupid that you had to flaunt it?"

Allen, staring at the gun pointed toward his head, continued to protest. "Baby, you know it's only you. I had to lead her on. I had to make her think that she was working for me to keep watching Lily here. That's all. You know I love you."

Just then Lily pitched forward and threw up. Andrea jumped back and looked down with disgust. "Barry. Cut her loose. It's not like she can run off anywhere."

Barry chortled saying, "Just how I want my woman. At my beck and call. Helpless."

As soon as her arms were free, Lily wiped her mouth while trying to work the pins-and-needles out of her shoulders. *Run. They don't think I can run.* She stayed in the chair, pretending to still be sick while hoping to find a way to get out. Refusing to look at Carla's body, she turned so that she could keep an eye on the others.

Allen had weaseled his way back over to Andrea, who had put the gun back in her purse. They kissed as he continued to profess his love. Andrea held his face in her hands as she licked his lips. "I've got the money, you know. I do. You screw around like that again and you can kiss it all goodbye."

Barry interrupted, "Boss, can I have her now? You're gonna kill her anyway so can I play first?" He had moved over to Lily sliding his hand roughly over her breasts again, but with her arms untied she tried to slap him away.

"Oooh, I like 'em when they fight too," he sneered.

"Barry," Andrea barked out. "You do what I tell you to do, when I tell you to do it. Got that?"

Pulling his hands off of Lily he growled, "Yeah, boss."

Lily kept her head down, but the fear almost choked her.

Andrea looked at him with distain. Jerking her head toward Carla she ordered, "Get rid of her first. Through the river door. Then…you can have whatever fun you want with Lily. Just make sure she ends up in the same place as Carla when you are finished."

Lily jerked her head up at Andrea's last comment. *I'm running out of time.*

Andrea and Allen turned to watch Barry as he moved over to Carla's body. Lily swung her head around watching as Barry opened the door on the opposite side. As soon as he opened it she heard water sloshing against the frame. *We are right on the level of the river.*

He hefted up Carla's feet and started to drag her toward the door. Leering at her, he said, "Be right back, girl. We're gonna have some fun."

"Allen," Andrea called in a sing-song voice. "You need to help Barry get rid of her body. It may serve as a good reminder…you know, in case you decide to screw around on me again."

Allen paled at her words, but squatted down to assist. As they stepped through the doorway, Lily saw that they were standing on a low platform right above the water. With their backs to her, Lily jumped up and ran toward the other door. With the adrenaline rush coursing through her body she slammed the door behind her and ran up the stairs. *Go, go, go,* she chanted as she hurried up the stairs as quickly as she could.

Andrea could be heard screaming, "Get her, you morons!" Lily heard the pounding of feet on the stairs as she ran through the next door, slamming it behind her as well.

Going back quickly through the narrow passageway lined with crates, she came out into the warehouse. Large, dark, empty. *I've got to get out.* Deciding to get out of the warehouse as quickly as she could she ran to the nearest stack of crates and scooted around them and continued to run a zig-zag pattern until she could see an outside door.

By this time, Andrea was screeching, "You fucking morons! How could you let a cripple get away? How is she even able to run?"

The muffled sounds of Lily's sneakered feet made it easier to keep her pursuers from knowing which way she was heading. Reaching a metal door, she pulled with all of her strength and it swung open. *Please be an outside door.* Running through it, she immediately felt the blast of chilly air from the river as she continued to run down the dock.

She could hear noises and screaming behind her, but prayed she had a good head-start. *One, two, one, two.* Counting the cadence in her head just like in a race she continued to pound down the dock, desperately hoping to find someone who could help. Looking up ahead, she could see where a parking lot was at the end of one of the warehouses. *Keep going. If I can just get there.*

Suddenly, a figure loomed up ahead, grinning. She stumbled as she came to a stop, heart pounding, breathing ragged. She had forgotten about the other goon – the one that had escorted Carla in. *How did he get here so fast?* Glancing behind her she saw Barry and Allen coming up from behind. And behind them, Andrea stalking up. *I can't let them get me. If they get me, I'm dead.* Turning her head toward the dark, swirling water, she knew what she had to do.

Thinking of nothing but Matt's face, she sucked in a deep breath for courage, then ran toward the edge of the dock and jumped into the black void as it swallowed her completely.

Chapter 22

SHANE CALLED TONY, putting him on speaker. "Pull up blueprints on the VanHeusen warehouses by the river." Giving him the address of the one Toby could remember being in, he said, "Get ready. We're gettin' ready to roll from here. DEA and FBI are with us and Matt needs your crew there too."

Matt looked up with gratitude plastered across his face. The task force with law enforcement might be constrained by regulations. Tony's crew could operate independently if needed.

Matt walked over as the others readied themselves. Shane turned and saw his friend, hand on the wall, head bowed. Alone. Praying. Focused in his mind. Whatever it took to be able to function. Shane remembered last year when Annie was caught in a drug war and was taken. The fear that clawed its way up his throat until he was sure he would choke on it. Walking over, saying nothing, he put his hand on Matt's shoulder.

After a moment he asked quietly, "You ready?"

Matt looked over his shoulder at his friend and partner's concerned expression. Nodding, he pushed himself off the wall and the two men walked over to suit up.

The chief came into the room announcing that the two other doctors had been arrested at home, leaving only Dr. Purser at large. The other two doctors were young, looking for fast money and easily manipulated.

The chief also reminded them that according to the two other doctors, who quickly lawyered up, Allen was not the top of the chain. "And," he added, "It appears that they were working for a woman."

Matt and Shane quickly shared a look. *A woman? Dr. Alease? Carla?* "I fucking hate this," Shane growled. "We go in half blind, not knowing who we're looking for."

"I'm just interested in Lily. Don't give a fuck about anyone else," Matt stated firmly.

The team ready, they headed out of the station. Calling Tony to rendezvous his group with them, they drove toward the river in the dead of night. Making the trip in silence, the darkness only illuminated by the passing streetlights, they headed toward the unknown.

ARRIVING AT THE warehouse that Toby had identified, they parked two blocks away. Matt looked over as he got out of the truck and saw Tony, Gabe, Vinny, and BJ were standing by one of Tony's dark SUVs. The men gathered with silent greetings, circling around with the others in the task force to prepare for their invasion. With duties assigned, the group moved out.

Entering the warehouse, Matt noticed the numerous wooden crates that Toby had identified. "He said the door was on the back side, behind the wall of crates." Spreading out the men stealthily began to search the area. BJ was the first to find the door and Matt hurried over. The task force leader stopped him. "Gotta let S.W.A.T. get in there first. They're trained for this."

Matt didn't care how they did it, he just wanted Lily alive. Nodding, he stepped back allowing the team of four to go through the door and descend. In less than a minute, Matt heard the call over the radio.

"Woman's body found. Shot. Dead."

Matt's knees buckled and he went down on the floor. *No, Jesus fuck, no.*

Shane and BJ grabbed him, assisting him to stand as he kept shaking his head. The next words rocked him further.

"Victim not Lily Swanson. Unidentified."

Slinging his head back with a roar, Matt pounded down the stairs, the others right behind him. Inside the small room he saw the bloodied body of a woman, definitely not Lily. Torn between relief and the realization that he had no idea where Lily was warred inside of him.

One of the S.W.A.T. members had the woman's purse, looking through it. "Carla Montrose," he said with her driver's license in his hands.

Looking beyond the body of Carla, he noticed the lower platform outside near the water. The idea of Lily out there chilled him once again. Turning to Shane, he agonized, "Where is she?"

BJ was looking at something on the floor. "Matt, come over here."

Matt and Shane bent down to see what he was looking at. There in the blood on the floor was a slight footprint. Of a small shoe. The size and shape of a woman's sneaker. BJ looked up and saw a light trail going toward the stairs they just came down. "Matt, maybe she got away. Maybe she's out there running."

They immediately went back up the stairs to continue their search. They quickly lost the trail as her feet had no longer left marks on the floor, but they could see that she had moved in a zig-zag pattern heading toward an outside door. The radios announced that several people had been apprehended on the docks as the men raced through the door.

Matt's attention was immediately focused on the S.W.A.T. team walking toward them with several people in handcuffs. Two of the men he didn't recognize, but he identified Dr. Allen Purser, and...*Andrea? What the fuck?*

Running over to them with Shane and Tony's crew right behind, he plowed into Allen, knocking him down. With one hand on Allen's throat he pounded him with the other, yelling, "Where the fuck is she?"

After three punches, Shane stepped in halting his fist

from flying again. "Come on, man. Let the rest of us have a chance."

Another officer hauled Allen up off of the dock, jerking him to his feet. Allen began screaming about police brutality, when Gabe stepped up and grabbed him by his collar. "You goddamn, mother-fucker. I ain't police. You don't shut the fuck up and tell us where Ms. Lily is, you won't have any teeth left. You'll be sucking your food through a straw while takin' it up the ass bein' someone's bitch in prison."

Allen began to sputter immediately. "I don't know, I don't know where she is." Pointing to Andrea, he immediately turned on her. "It's her. She's the one who did all this. I just went along, but it's her. She's got the money. Ask her."

Andrea's face turned red as she tried to kick out with her feet toward him. "Shut up, you moron. Shut up!" she screamed.

A fierce growl came from deep inside Matt as he grabbed her by her arms, lifting her off the ground. "You goddamn bitch. Where's Lily? Without her, I got nothing to lose lady so you better talk."

Tight-lipped, Andrea fought to get her feet back on the ground. "Gone," she bit out.

Matt shook her yelling, "Where? Gone where bitch?"

Andrea said nothing, but Allen spoke up. "The river. She went in the river."

Andrea unceremoniously crumpled to the ground as

Matt dropped her suddenly. He stalked back over to Allen who was desperately trying to back away from the dark visage approaching. Allen's backward progress came to a halt as he backed into a wall. Of men. Large, angry men who didn't give a shit about regulations. Or procedure. Or the rights of a criminal. Glancing behind him, seeing no aid from the others in the task force, Allen paled.

Matt continued walking until he stood nose to nose. "Not gonna say it again, asshole. What happened with Lily?"

Licking his lips, Allen whimpered. "She was trapped." He hesitated. "She jumped. Into the river. About ten minutes ago."

Matt's heart stopped. Turning, he took two steps away where he stood for a few seconds before whirling back around and hitting Allen in the jaw, dropping him to the dock. Looking up at the S.W.A.T team and DEA, he growled, "Get them the fuck out of here," before turning his eyes back to Shane.

Shane nodded and quickly called in the harbor patrol and coast guard. "Search and rescue needed." The other members of the police force quickly went into action. Tony went over to Shane as Gabe and Vinny went to Matt to offer support.

"Shane, this isn't what we're used to so you gotta tell us what you need."

"Can you get a boat?"

"Yeah. Gabe's got one."

"Get it and take your men. Start searching along the shore. This place will soon be crawling with Coast Guard looking in the water so let's get someone quick over near the shore edge in case she made it over there."

One of the policemen spoke up asking, "Is this going to be a recovery?"

Shane saw Matt's head swivel around, his face contorted in pain. Looking at the young policemen, Shane growled, "No, you fuck. It's search and rescue." Looking back at his longtime friend surrounded by their friends, he repeated, "Search and rescue."

THE NIGHT SKY was soon filled with helicopter search lights shining on the water. The river was filled with boats of all shapes and sizes, also equipped with search lights. Matt stayed on the edge of the dock watching the water swirl lazily by. *They gotta find you babe. You rescued me. I gotta be able to rescue you. I can't do this alone.* The minutes ticked by as several hours passed. The pre-dawn sky began to turn pastel blue as the sun was making an attempt to rise. Matt hated seeing the dawn. While searching in the sunlight would be easier, it also meant that too many hours had passed. He could see Shane arguing with the Captain of the Coast Guard. Turning his head, he didn't want to think of their conversation. *They're gonna want to start dragging the river.* The very idea took him to his knees.

Shane called Annie, wishing he didn't have to tell

her about Lily over the phone, listening to her cry. "Sunshine, you gotta hold it together. Talk to Suzanne, let her know. Matt? He's hanging in, but barely. Babe? I love you."

Shane walked over placing his hand on Matt's shoulder, when his cell phone rang. "It's Tony," he said to Matt. "Whatcha got?" Listening for just a minute, he dug his fingers into Matt who immediately came to his feet. "On our way," he said clicking off his phone.

Chapter 23

THE IMPACT OF the cold water had sent shock waves through Lily. As she sunk in the depth of the dark water, she fought her way to the surface as soon as she could. *Fuck, it's cold!* Knowing that she couldn't survive long in the river, she did not try to fight the slow current. It moved very slowly next to the dock, so she tried to stay near the edge as she allowed the water to carry her along. Focusing her energy on keeping her head above water, her teeth began to chatter. *Jesus help me,* her mind screamed.

Terrified of being swept father out in the river, she was determined to stay with the dock and tried to keep her eyes on the lights that were the only penetration in the darkness. Slamming into a concrete pylon at the edge, her hands flailed out as she grasped the object. The water continued to swirl past her, but she held on with all of her waning strength. *Jesus, let me get back to Matt. He needs me. Please don't let me lose my life just as I am finding my love.*

Glancing around as she hung onto the pylon, she could see that she was near the edge of the dock, which was where she had been trying to run to when she was trapped. Blinking the moisture out of her eyes, she tried to focus on what was beyond the dock. Her lungs hurt with the cold, and while she was grateful for the running exercise she had, she knew that her time was limited. *If I can't get out of the water I'll surely die.*

She thought she could see lights in the distance beyond the dock. Trying to orient herself, she prayed it was toward the shore and not boat lights out in the water. With one last prayer, she pushed off the pylon, back into the swirling river…taking her…away.

Still focusing on keeping her head above the water, she began to try to swim toward the area where she had seen the lights. *Keep moving to the left. Keep moving to the left. One, two, one, two.* Just like with her running, she counted the cadence of her arm strokes and leg kicks. Her prosthesis was not made for water or for swimming and she struggled trying to keep her left leg from not moving. Within a minute, exhaustion and cold was beginning to overtake her. The lights seemed closer, but there was no way she could make it on her own. *Matt, bury me next to my Rose,* was her final thought as she closed her eyes. Giving in. Giving up.

Just as she felt her body going under, her foot drug on something. Her eyes flew open, adrenaline coursing through once again. She kicked out with her right foot and felt nothing but water. *Fuck, what was that?*

Kicking out again, her foot touched something that felt more solid. The darkness of the night blanketed everything so she never saw the tree at the edge of the river until her body slammed into it. Crying out in pain, it took her a moment to realize that she was no longer moving in the water, but that it was moving around her still body. Her hands grasped the branches and she fought her tired muscles to pull herself out of the water.

With her body draped over a tree trunk that had partially fallen into the river, she began to sob. Knowing that would deplete her energy, she couldn't help herself. After several minutes, her sobs subsided and she tried to lift herself enough that she could try to orient herself. The darkness enveloped her, its cloak keeping her from being able to see where she was. *It doesn't matter. I can find my way somewhere. Anywhere. Back to him.*

Using what was left of her arm strength, Lily pulled herself along the tree trunk until she finally could stand on the muddy river bank. With one step, she realized that she had lost the pink sneaker on her prosthetic foot when it caught on a tree limb. Not wanting to lose the other one in the mud, she bent and tried to untie it with her frozen fingers. Unable to accomplish that small feat, she managed to pull off the shoe without untying it.

I can't walk in the sticky mud. It'll put too much strain on my leg. Wiping the cold water from her face, she dropped down. Slowly she crawled up the river bank until she could feel firmer ground. Shivering, she lay for another minute on her side, trying to rest her screaming muscles, but knowing that her body would soon shut down if she could not get warm. As she crawled a few more feet she began to see lights in the distance. Looking back over where she had come from, she could see boats and helicopters swarming over the dock in the distance. *Me? Are they looking for me? They'll never see me from here.*

Realizing she no longer had her lone shoe in her hands, she glanced back down and saw it on the river bank. *Fuck, I can't go back and get it.* Turning away from the river, she began to hobble. Not seeing a road, she just kept staggering forward. *The rescue lights are too far away. They'll never see me. One, two, one, two.*

The cold seeped in until her conscious mind knew nothing else. She saw tall grass growing thickly with clumps of shrubs. Making her way over to the firm ground she lay down, scooting deep in the grass as her body sought warmth. Eyes closing, she drifted off, letting the dark overtake her. To a warmer place. In his arms. Safe. Where she wanted to be.

BY THE TIME Gabe's boat made it to the boat dock, Matt and Shane had just driven up. Jumping out, Matt ran to them yelling, "What is it? What did you see?"

Tony, Gabe, Vinny, and BJ hopped out of the boat, barely taking time to secure it. BJ was the first to get to them. "Couldn't see shit man, it was too dark. Then just as the sun was coming up, I swear it looked like a pink shoe stuck in some limbs hanging over the edge," he gasped, pointing down the river's edge.

"Show me," Matt yelled, as he and Shane jumped

back in their truck. Tony's men piled in his SUV and peeled out of the parking lot. They drove down an access road until they turned off and began driving over the grass toward the river. Coming to a stop, all six men ran down toward the river. Seeing a tree trunk that had fallen into the water's edge, they could see a flash of pink on one of the limbs.

Grabbing binoculars, Matt brought it into focus. "Jesus, fuck. It's hers. It's one of her shoes."

Gabe and Vinny ran down toward the river bank, near the tree. Leaning down, Gabe shouted as he bent over to pick up something. Standing he held her other pink shoe in his hand.

Tony called the rescue crew in so they could begin the search on the land. "Tell them to bring the dogs."

Shane grabbed Matt by the shoulders pulling him in for a hug. "She made it this far, man. She fuckin' made it this far."

Matt felt the sting of tears hit the back of his eyes, but knew he couldn't stop until he held her in his arms once again. Spreading out, the six men began methodically pacing themselves in an area heading from the river bank out, looking for any signs of her. The other rescue workers were just showing up and BJ walked over to them to apprise them of what they had found.

IN THE FAR distance of her dream, Lily could hear her name being called. Over and over again. The voices reached inside her foggy mind until she felt them pull her out of her deep sleep. Blinking at the sunlight, she lay for a minute, trying to decide what was real and what was a dream. Her mind had slowed to a crawl. *In the grass. So cold.* As she awakened a little more, she realized that she couldn't feel her fingers or her toes. Glancing down she saw her hands and then looked at her legs. *Why can't I feel?* She saw that she had a prosthesis but could not get her real toes to wiggle. Her mind continued to clear slowly as she remembered who she was and what had happened.

The desire to close her eyes against the bright sun was strong, but the voices calling her name encroached on the peace. *Lily? My name!*

Forcing her arms to push herself to a sitting position she could see some people walking in a line off to her left, calling her name. Opening her mouth to call out, only the faintest croak emerged. Trying to swallow several times, she rubbed her tongue over her cracked lips. It was to no avail…she couldn't cry out.

Rolling over painfully onto her front, she pushed up onto her knees raising her body above the tall grass, then tried to wave her arms. Every movement sent shards of pain though her, but without a voice she refused to not be found.

As Matt's desperate gaze swept over the field, a movement to his right caught his eyes. A shape was moving. It looked like…*Oh Jesus, fuck. Lily!*

With a roar, he turned and ran toward the pale body

trying to stand. The other men saw Matt rushing to what looked like Lily and they began to run in that direction as well, calling to the rescue squad.

As Lily saw a man running toward her she slumped back down, unable to hold herself up any longer.

Falling down on the ground next to her, Matt grabbed her cold, shivering body, clutching it close. His sobs filled the air as he tried to wrap himself around her. To warm her. Protect her. "I got you, baby. I got you," he chanted over and over, holding her tightly.

He found me, was the only thought that penetrated her foggy mind that was slowly slipping back into unconsciousness.

Gabe and Vinny, both former Army medics, tried to gently check her out while Matt held on tightly.

"Matt, you need to let us see to her," Gabe said softly.

Matt appeared incapable of releasing her body, so Gabe felt for a pulse while she was still cradled. BJ flagged the rescue squads over and soon they were surrounded. Thermal blankets were handed down to wrap around her.

Forcing his arms to lay her on the stretcher, his mind cleared enough to look at her body before she was immediately wrapped. His hands clenched in fists as he shot a look at Shane. *Her shirt was ripped. She had bruises in the shape of fingers on her arms. She had bruises on her breasts. On her fuckin' breasts!*

Shane stepped up to Matt, getting between him and

Lily. "Not now. Focus on her, man. Not now."

Matt shot him deadly look, but Shane just nodded.

"I got you, man. Take care of her now. We'll all take care of the other later."

Matt's attention was diverted as the EMT said, "Sir, are you riding with us?" Nodding to his friends, he watched as they loaded her into the back of the ambulance. Turning one last time to look at the friends who had searched and found her with him, he found he had no words.

They nodded to him as Tony said, "Go, man. We'll see you at the hospital."

With that he turned, jumped into the back of the ambulance and crouched next to her. His Lily.

Chapter 24

"**G**OOD MORNING, BABY. You ready to go home?" Matt asked, walking into Lily's hospital room. Seeing the beautiful woman sitting up smiling at him helped to wipe the memories of the past week away. Well, not quite away. Holding her at night as she woke trying to scream when the nightmares overtook her brought back his rage.

The week had been fraught with scares. At first the doctors were uncertain as to whether she had frostbite in her fingers and toes. The thought of losing more limbs had terrified Lily and she was inconsolable. It was not as serious as the doctors had first anticipated and with treatment she was able to save both.

The investigative detectives had tried to gently question her about the abduction and the time that she was kidnapped, but she shut down. Pulling inside of herself she refused to give any information. As Matt stepped outside of the room, leaving Suzanne in with Lily, he and Shane talked to the other detectives.

"It's okay, Matt. We have them on every charge imaginable and it'll all stick. We won't need her testimony."

Nodding, he watched them walk off. Turning to Shane he confessed, "I'm worried. She seems fine until she goes to sleep, and then the screams start."

"She talk to anyone?"

"The hospital shrink is coming later today. I'm gonna let them talk alone to see if that will make a difference."

Later that afternoon, the hospital counselor spent several hours with Lily, gaining her trust and helping her to talk about some of the events. Her tears broke Matt's heart, but he knew she had to get it all out. The fears. The pain. The terror.

Crawling into her hospital bed he held her all night, afraid to let go. She slept fitfully. He didn't sleep at all. But there were no screams in the night.

Due to the damage to her prosthesis, it was unsalvageable. That brought another round of tears. "It's not that I haven't had others before," she cried to Matt, "But it's like losing my leg all over again. Something was a part of me that's now gone."

Her prosthetist came to visit her in the hospital to discuss her new leg. She knew from past experience that he wouldn't want to take a casting until she had a chance to recuperate a little. "Lily, you know this isn't a good time. We want you healed so that we can get the right measurements for a perfect fit." An older gentlemen with a kind face, he held her hand while they spoke.

Matt stood to the side instantly liking him. Liking

the way he talked to her. The prosthetist soothed her worries and promised that later in the week he would make the impressions.

As he left the room, she looked up at Matt saying softly, "Looks like I'll be on crutches for a while."

Wrapping his arms around her, he pulled her in close, blanketing her in his embrace as he kissed the top of her head. "Baby, you're alive. Alive. That's all that matters."

Sniffling into his shirt she nodded. "You're right." After a few minutes, she looked up at him hesitantly, an uncertain look on her face.

"What is it, Lily?"

Sighing deeply she said, "I think I'm ready."

Not saying anything, Matt just looked at her waiting for her to finish.

"I'll talk to the detectives."

"You sure, babe?"

Nodding, she whispered, "But, only if you're not there. Only Suzanne."

At this he reared back ready to protest, but stopped when he saw her expression.

His jaw tight with frustration, he agreed. "I'll call 'em babe. Whatever you need."

Later that afternoon, a male and female detective came into her room. Shaking hands with Matt, they introduced themselves and he walked out of the room. Suzanne sat on the side of the bed with Lily as they began. After a moment, Lily suddenly said, "No. I can't do this. Not like this."

"What is it, sweetie?" Suzanne asked.

"Call Matt back in."

One of the detectives went to the door to signal for Matt. He walked into the room, concern on his face, as he stalked to her bed and reached for her hand.

Looking up into his face, the one that had saved her in so many ways, she said softly, "I thought I could do this without you. I thought somehow if you didn't hear it from me it would be easier." Looking down at their clasped hands she admitted, "But I need you."

His heart melting once again, he lifted her chin with his fingers. "You got me. All of me. All the time."

Nodding, she turned back to the detectives and told them everything she knew and everything she had experienced. Matt tried not to squeeze her hand when she haltingly spoke of what had been said to her and what Barry had done. Forcing himself to be controlled, he just offered comfort. For now. He would handle Barry later. But Lily would never know.

He did fill her in on the rest of the investigation. As much as he had wanted Malcolm or Curtis to be involved, it appeared that they were not. Curtis admitted to being suspicious of Allen, but could never find anything that pointed to any wrong-doing. Malcolm had begun damage control before the story hit the news. Nervous stockholders, angry patients, and insurance companies lining up for lawsuits was going to keep him busy for years. Andrea's plan of taking him down might still come true. The amount of money that Andrea had made by organizing the sales of prescription drugs on the streets was in the millions.

Lily listened to it all, utterly amazed. *How could I have so misjudged Andrea?* The scope of her illegal activities was beyond Lily's comprehension, but it was the personal attack that she struggled with. *Another thing to talk to the counselor about.*

Tony and BJ had come to visit, saying they had a proposition for her. Intrigued, she listened to their idea. BJ wanted to learn more of the security business than just doing the computer programing for them, so he would need help covering their computer systems. He knew her skills and had told Tony that she would be perfect.

Cutting her eyes over to Matt she glared. "Is this your idea to keep me from getting into trouble by having me work in the middle of a security agency?"

"Babe, I think it sounds great, but this is all on you. This was their idea and it has to be what you want."

Looking up at Tony, she admitted, "It sounds really interesting. Can I come by sometime and see what the job would entail?"

"Absolutely," Tony agreed, leaning down to kiss her goodbye. BJ followed with a hug as he whispered, "Think about it, Lily. You'd be an asset and I know you'd love it."

And now her week stay in the hospital was over and Matt was ready to take her home. She had dressed and was sitting on the side of the bed, holding her crutches. "Did he come?" Matt asked, talking about the prosthetist.

Smiling, she replied, "Yeah. He said he got a good impression and it shouldn't take too long to get a new leg. Shrugging her shoulders she continued, "So until then, I'll have my crutches. I'll be fine."

She slid off the bed and balanced with her crutches. Matt so wanted to pick her up and carry her, but knew she needed to be independent. He grabbed her bag as he waved his arm announcing, "Your chariot awakes, babe."

Epilogue

(Two Months Later)

"I NOW PRONOUNCE you man and wife. You may kiss the bride."

Shane grabbed Annie bending her backwards and kissed her with all the passion he felt. Looking into her smiling eyes he said, "Love you, Sunshine."

Lily, standing in her pale blue bridesmaid gown, smiled over at Matt, looking dapper in his dark suit. He winked at her, knowing that they were both thinking of their wedding that was just a few months away.

As Shane tucked Annie under his arm and they made their way down the aisle, Lily and Matt met and followed them in the recessional. She saw their new friends from the town of Fairfield, Jake and Emma Campbell, and Tom and Carol Rivers, as well as Tony, Gabe, and Vinny. BJ missed the wedding due to a family event but was coming for the reception.

Matt's warm breath washed over her neck as he leaned in to whisper, "Say the word, babe and you and I will grab the minister now."

Giggling, she looked into the eyes of the man who

had tempted her heart away from loneliness. "Somehow, I don't think your mother would appreciate it."

Sighing, Matt reluctantly agreed.

After dinner the fun began, dancing and mingling with all of their friends. Tony joked about Matt making out with his new employee. Lily had taken the job with Alverez Security and was loving it. His agency was small enough that she felt secure without having to be around a lot of strangers, and her skills with computer programing made her the perfect fit.

Lily looked up seeing BJ come into the reception hall. "Matt, I'm going to go see BJ. I've been dying to get him and Suzanne together and they're never in the same place at the same time. Finally, I've got my chance."

Kissing her soundly before she walked off, his eyes then followed her as she made her way over to Suzanne. She was in a jewel-toned blue bridesmaid dress with her long dark hair hanging sleek and straight down her back. Having grown up in Fairfield, she was talking with the Campbells and Rivers. They chatted for a minute before the two women headed over towards the door.

The crowd was dense, but Lily finally pushed her way to BJ. Suzanne turned to wave behind them at some other friends. Giving him a hug Lily said, "I have someone I've wanted you to meet for a long time."

Just then Suzanne turned around and gasped loudly. Lily looked quickly between the two shocked faces.

"Brad?"

"Suzy?"

Lily stood stunned. "You two know each other?"

"I have to get out of here," Suzanne said as she quickly turned around and pushed her way through the crowd.

"BJ? Why did she called you Brad?" Lily wondered out loud.

His face grim, his eyes never leaving Suzanne's retreating back, he replied, "Bradley James Evans. BJ's a college nickname and it just stuck."

Glancing down at Lily's distressed face, he took pity on her. "Honey, it's not your fault she left. It's mine. We've got a history. Goes way back to high school." He dropped his head down to his chest for a moment. Looking up with a determined look on his face, he growled, "Goddammit. I let her walk away once before. Not again." Kissing Lily's head, he turned and stalked back out of the reception hall.

Matt came up to Lily, seeing from across the room that she was upset. She quickly told him what had happened. Pulling her into his embrace, he said, "Babe, nothing you can do about it now. They're not teens anymore. They gotta figure out what they want to do." Tugging her back to the dance floor, he began to twirl her gently.

As the bride and groom left for their honeymoon and the other guests were making their way to the parking lot, Matt gently pulled her away from the crowd. Walking along a path near the church, he glanced down at the sparkly sandals on her feet showing off her painted toenails. She looked down at the same time and wiggled her toes on her right foot.

"Baby…I just…wanted…to tell you…" Not able to think of any words that would describe what he was feeling, he simply placed his hands gently on either side of her face, staring intently into her eyes. Leaning down he said, "I'm tempted to kiss you babe. Are you good with that?" Then he placed a kiss on her lips. Soft. Full of emotion. Full of the promise of love. Life. Family. Growing old together.

Suddenly the words came to him. "I love you with all my heart, Lily. Every breath I take is because of you. Every sunrise is beautiful just because it's another day with you. Every sunset is precious because I got to spend the day with you. You tempted my heart out of its cold shadows and make my life worth living."

With tears streaming down her face, Lily kept her eyes on his and felt him wipe her tears with his thumbs. "I love you too, honey. With everything I have. And everything I will ever have. Forever."

Kissing her once again, he said, "I know our wedding isn't for a couple more months, but baby? As far as I am concerned, the words that were just spoken were our vows."

She nodded replying, "Until death do us part?"

His lips a breath away from hers, he vowed, "Even beyond, baby. Even beyond."

The End

Made in the USA
Middletown, DE
08 November 2016